Going Nuclear

Stephen Hart

This is a work of fiction. Names, characters, businesses, places, events and incidents are either the products of the author's imagination or used in a fictitious manner. Any resemblance to actual persons, living or dead, or actual events is purely coincidental.

Edited by Lynn Cross.

Published by Aventine Press
55 E. Emerson St.
San Diego CA, 91911
www.aventinepress.com

ISBN: 1-59330-688-1

Printed in the United States of America

To Claudia and Jennie.

Chapter One

While the cab weaved through heavy traffic, Arthur Weiss rode quietly in the back, watching out the window as "Blowin' in the Wind" played on the radio in front. He had always liked the song: the moving melody, the questions it raised concerning social injustice, the implication that a better world was possible, if not imminent. It's up to us, the young people, Bob Dylan's nasal-toned anthem seemed to proclaim. But now, its message rang hollow for Arthur. When had the song been written, he wondered, four years ago? Yet the war in Vietnam was raging. The only thing blowing in the wind over there was the likelihood of survival.

Suddenly, the driver jammed his brakes. They squealed, and a nearby horn honked. He then jerked the steering wheel to the right, accelerated, and turned his head to sneer at the driver next to him. Arthur simply settled back in his seat and closed his eyes. Half an hour later, the driver pulled up to the curb. Arthur gave him a twenty and told him to keep the change. He felt a little uneasy about the tip but had too much on his mind to consider it further. Hoisting his young, but stiff, six-foot-three frame from the worn backseat of the cab, Arthur closed the door behind him, a little harder than intended, then made his way up the lush purple-carpeted steps, the steps that led to the massive front doors of the funeral home.

Another breezy day in D.C., he thought, as wisps of cool air blew against his face and trailed through his collar-length blond hair. Pausing on the landing, Arthur took in the spring colors that effloresced around him: the well-manicured lawn, the pristine flowers, the flowering shrubs and stately trees. The whole scene seemed almost too perfect. A Norman Rockwell painting showing the beginning of yet another life cycle. Still, a funeral didn't seem all that incongruous. Even in the warm sunlight and invigorating air, a morbid pall hung heavily, blurring the fragile distinction between life and death. *Nobody stays around long,* he thought. *Just a stupid game. You play, it's over.* But with each step he took, Arthur realized that his immediate concern was seeing his parents. He dreaded seeing them far more than viewing the body of his older brother, his only brother, the brother who had just been shipped back from Vietnam in a body bag. His mother would probably be incapacitated by grief. Arthur didn't want to even think about that. And his father would be insufferably strong, a royal pain in the ass.

At the entrance to the room where his brother lay in state, Arthur observed his father, a square-built man of five-ten, standing erect next to the visitors' log: greeting callers efficiently, competently, all business. Arthur took in his father's dress uniform, the glowing eagles on his shoulders, the crispness of his coat and tie, the perfectly spit-shined shoes. To Arthur, this suggested too much time spent preparing for military etiquette and not enough time contemplating the passing of a slain son, a favorite son. But then, almost immediately, his reaction softened. *Probably just his way of coping,* Arthur concluded. *I suppose the old man's entitled to that much.*

"I want to talk with you," his father snapped as Arthur approached. Arthur took in a deep breath and let it out slowly, trying not to reveal the exasperation he felt with the all-too-familiar tone, a tone that he had managed to avoid for almost four years, having been away at college. His father glanced disapprovingly at Arthur's jeans and hair, then added, "Let's go out to the car." Arthur followed his father silently through the funeral home, back into the fresh air outside, down the steps, around the corner, to the parking lot, to a black Lincoln Continental that shone almost as brightly as his father's shoes. Once seated behind the wheel, his father turned and cleared his throat. "First, I'd like to say I'm glad you came. Your mother will be glad to see you. She's not here right now. She's back at the hotel trying to pull herself together. But your being here will be a big help to her."

"Of course I came," Arthur replied, thinking to himself, *What's he doing? Giving me permission to attend my own brother's funeral?*

"Yes, well, I know things have been a little strained between us lately, but I hope we can put that aside for the time being, for your mother's sake, if nothing else."

"Of course."

"This whole thing seems so odd," His father sighed. "Only a year ago, your brother was graduating with his ROTC commission, in the prime of life. And now, just like that, he's gone." He looked down at the steering wheel and stared at it blankly.

"It really is hard to believe," Arthur agreed, watching his father closely. "Things always seemed to go his way." *Or to put it more honestly,* he thought, *things always seemed to go your way, the Army way.*

"Yes, they did," his father said, nodding, looking up and staring straight ahead. "He must have had some terrible luck over there, just terrible. The whole thing just doesn't seem right."

"How did it happen?"

"His platoon walked into an ambush. Charlie was hiding in front of them and on both sides, like a horseshoe. Once they got to the center, Charlie opened up on them, caught them in a crossfire. It didn't last long. The platoon suffered heavy casualties, and then Charlie was gone. Your brother should have had more jungle training; ROTC wasn't enough."

"It didn't seem like enough to me. It seemed too much like a game. A lot of hoops to go through, but no substance. Maybe that's why I didn't stay in."

"ROTC was your brother's thing, never yours. Of course, you'll be going on to grad school."

Arthur felt another surge of resentment. His father made going to grad school sound like accepting an offer to join the New York City Ballet or some equally androgynous pursuit. Looking out the window, he nodded and took a deep breath. "Yes, grad school," he said.

"That's probably good. I suppose you'll be exempt from the draft, considering what's happened."

"I suppose."

Suddenly, his father grabbed the steering wheel firmly with both hands and turned to look directly into Arthur's face. "I may be crazy," he said, "but I can't believe this is the way things are supposed to end."

"What do you mean?"

"I mean, your brother made the ultimate sacrifice. He died fighting for what he believed in. And there wasn't a better kid on the face of this planet, none. But the job isn't finished, and it won't be finished until North Vietnam is crushed and that goddamned Ho Chi Minh is hung upside down the way Mussolini was after World War II."

"World War II was a long time ago."

"Like hell it was. It was yesterday. The difference is, people had the courage of their convictions back then, that's all. Half of the kids today don't have convictions; don't even know what convictions are." An uncomfortable pause followed. Arthur chose not to respond. "I'm only going to say this once," his father said firmly, breaking the silence, "and I know you don't want to hear it, but I'm going to say it anyway. Nothing can bring your brother back; I'm fully aware of that. But if you took his place, took up where he left off and saw this thing through to victory, I'd feel a lot better about everything—one hell of a lot better than I do now."

"And what if I came back the same way he did?" Arthur asked, his voice raised somewhat. "What then? What will that have proved?"

"Well, for one thing, you probably wouldn't even see combat duty, seeing as how your brother just got killed over there.

But even if you did, and the unthinkable did happen, there is no greater honor than laying down your life for your country. None. And I don't want to hear anything to the contrary either, not today, not with your brother's body lying less than a hundred yards away."

Arthur gave his father an incredulous look. "What are you talking about? Do you think dying for a cause means anything? Ever? It never settles anything. Can't you see that? There's always another cause, always another battle, always another reason to die."

"I guess I should have expected a reaction like this from you," Arthur's father replied deliberately. He tightened his lips and shook his head. "Of course I should have. It takes a degree of maturity to get outside of yourself, to think of the greater good, the big picture."

"Maybe you just don't want to face the reality of the situation," Arthur argued. "Maybe you and your friends at the Pentagon can't admit that the war is a terrible mistake and that Tom and all the others like him are dying for nothing." Arthur was immediately sorry that he had responded so strongly. He sat back quietly as his father stared through the windshield.

"You know," his father replied softly, after a long silence, "I could sit here and talk to you about honor and duty until the cows come home. But if you don't get it, you just don't get it. You're supposed to be so damned bright. Maybe you'll figure it out for yourself someday. In the meantime, I don't want to see any sign of disrespect for your brother today, not from you or anyone else. You've never seen me when I've really lost it, I mean really lost it, but I'm telling you right now, man to man, you could."

"Right," Arthur said, nodding his head slightly.

Arthur's father opened his door, slid out, and slammed it without looking back. Arthur let him go. After a few minutes, Arthur climbed out of the car himself and walked slowly to a park-like area behind the funeral home. Sitting down under a budding tulip tree, he leaned back against the knotted trunk, pulled a joint from his jeans, and lit it, the last of five he had recently purchased. He took a deep drag, a needed drag, a drag that temporarily purged all unpleasantness from his mind.

So why not join up and volunteer for Vietnam? he mused. Take his brother's place, serve his country, make his father proud. His grandfathers had both served in World War I, his father in World War II and Korea, his brother in Vietnam. Wasn't it his turn now? Nobody in his family had actually wanted to go to war, not even his father. But when their time came, they went. So what was so special about his case? Arthur took another drag. The war was considered stupid by most of his friends, the guys he knew in college, but what did that really mean? *Are they just cowards?* he thought. *Am I a coward?* The idea of going into combat clearly gave him pause, no question about that. So, was calling the war stupid just a rationalization to justify avoiding it? Who was he to question government policy? Did he know more about the intricacies of world events than the State Department, CIA, and military establishment combined? *Probably,* he concluded. Most of those bastards were as full of shit as his father.

He took another hit and remembered that he still had to pay his respects to Tom. He released a gust of rich smoke, took another drag, and held it, recalling the days when he and Tom had been kids together. Although Tom had been only a year older than Arthur, he had been obsessed throughout childhood with maintaining his position over Arthur in the family pecking order. It was always Tom who led the way, who told Arthur what was cool and what wasn't—at home, at school, around the neighborhood. And it was always Tom who stepped in when other kids wanted to start something, always Tom who backed his younger brother up. Arthur recalled the one all-out fight that he had gotten into with Tom, when he was thirteen and Tom was fourteen. It had taken place at a park in front of a growing crowd, over some girl they both had wanted to impress. An adult eventually stepped in and stopped it, but to Arthur's surprise, there had been no clear winner. Each boy had managed to inflict several cuts or marks on the other. And following the fight, there had been a period of mutual respect, a period that brought them closer together and made their father's value system, based on physical confrontation, seem like a work of pure logic. Arthur smiled as he let his mind drift back through various childhood conflicts with his brother. But he was always drawn back to the same stark fact: Tom was gone. Any unresolved issues between them would remain unresolved forever.

Back in the funeral parlor, in a room laced with sickeningly sweet floral aromas, Arthur walked up to the casket. He looked down at his brother's face and took in the tranquil expression but didn't feel particularly moved by it. The whole experience seemed too bizarre to support any emotional response. He simply observed that, despite any efforts made by the mortician, his brother did not appear to be sleeping peacefully; he looked dead. *Humans are such weird-looking animals*, he thought. As he turned to leave, Arthur saw his mother approaching, a woman with blonde hair, nearly as tall as his father. His eyes met hers, and Arthur could see that she had been crying. But as she drew nearer, he was relieved to see that she did not appear to be as on edge as he had expected. In fact, her expression seemed almost placid. Arthur waited for her by the casket. Once there, she asked him how he was doing, as if, it seemed to Arthur, it were just another day.

"Fine. How are you doing?"

"Better."

"I can't believe something like this happened."

"Yes, I know." She looked down at the floor.

"Are you sure you're okay?"

"Yes. Your father keeps asking me that. I don't know what he expects me to say."

"Well, the whole thing is such a shock."

"It *was* a shock. I had a lot of trouble dealing with it at first."

"You're doing better now?" Arthur studied her demeanor as she answered.

"Sort of." Their eyes met again.

"Something happened last night that helped."

"What?"

His mother glanced up at the ceiling before answering. "Well, I was looking at your brother here, having trouble believing this is really him, when I reached down to touch his hand. And when I did, I was really surprised at, I don't know, at how inanimate he felt. He didn't feel like a person at all. He felt like a chair or something. It was kind of strange." She glanced at Tom's body and then looked back at Arthur. "And then, all of a sudden, it hit me. If he isn't here anymore, I mean in his body, and he certainly is not, then he must be someplace else, someplace better. And then my faith came back to me full force, and I felt like a weight had been taken off my back. I still feel that way now."

"You think he's in heaven?"

"Yes. Don't you?"

"I don't know. I just know I want to live."

"What does that mean?" his mother asked softly.

"I don't want to go to Vietnam."

"I don't think you have to worry about that. I really don't."

৯

Two days later, at the airport waiting for the plane back to school, Arthur sat reading, for the third or fourth time, the popular novel *The Catcher in the Rye*. After about half an hour, he sat the book face down on his lap and wondered why he found the main character, Holden Caulfield, so easy to identify with. After all, Holden had flunked out of two prep schools, whereas he was graduating from college with honors. And Holden dreamed of running away to a cabin near the woods, whereas he would soon be working on a Ph.D. in physical chemistry. Maybe it had something to do with Holden's candid insights into school life, or his willingness to resist parental authority, or maybe it was his awkwardness with girls. A guilty pleasure at best, Arthur noted with a faint smile.

As he picked up the book to continue reading, a cute, thin girl with long black hair, a prominent nose, and rimless glasses sat down next to him. She appeared to be about his age and wore a short plaid skirt with black boots. Once she had carefully arranged her carry-on bag and purse to her satisfaction in front of her, she turned to Arthur, glanced at his book, and said, "*The Catcher in the Rye.* I read that earlier this year. Is that for class?" She smiled as she asked the question, disconcerting Arthur somewhat.

"No, I'm just killing time. I'm on my way back to school."

"Where do you go?"

"Northwestern. How about you?"

"University of Michigan. I'm a psych major. I'm Mandy, by the way. I had to come back for my sister's wedding. She couldn't wait six weeks for the semester to be *over*, of course. That would have been asking too much, *way* too much. So now, I'm going to have to play catch-up when I get back." She rolled her eyes. "I already have a late paper. I hope my professor understands. How about you? Were you visiting someone?"

"I came back for my brother's funeral. My name's Arthur."

"God, I'm sorry. I didn't know. I wasn't trying to be too personal or anything."

"That's okay. It doesn't bother me to talk about it. These things happen."

"How did he die?"

"He was killed in Vietnam."

"God, you hear about that happening more and more these days, but it still must have been a shock for you."

"More for my family than me, especially my mother."

"I can't even imagine."

"She seemed to find a lot of strength in her religious beliefs. I think she'll get through it okay, eventually."

"I guess religion can be helpful at times." Mandy shrugged her shoulders.

"You don't seem all that convinced." Arthur replied, tilting his head. She crossed her legs, and he found himself glancing at her exposed knee.

"Well, it may be more helpful for some people than for me. I don't know."

"So, you don't believe?"

"Not especially." Mandy frowned slightly as she shook her head.

"Is your *family* religious?" Arthur asked.

"Oh God, yes! They're devout Catholics, especially my father. He thinks young people today don't take religion as seriously as they used to. He thinks that's why things are so out of control these days."

"I think the war has more to do with things being out of control than anything else. But it sounds like your father's views didn't really take with you." Arthur found talking with this girl easier than he would have imagined. He liked the soft resonance in her voice and the way her face lit up when she spoke. *You never know,* he thought. *You never know.*

"Well, I just can't take religion as seriously as my father does," Mandy replied. "I guess to me the whole thing seems to be more about ritual and ceremony than anything else. I mean, there just doesn't seem to be any actual communication with a Supreme Being. I think a lot of the things they teach are good, and I think that following the basic values they try to instill is a good way to live your life. But have you ever tried to pray? For me, it just doesn't work. It seems more like making a wish on your birthday before you blow out the candles."

"I guess I tried to pray when I was younger, mostly in church when I was a kid. Not so much recently."

"What church?"

"Southern Baptist."

"Did it work?" Mandy raised her eyebrows.

"What do you mean?"

"Did you feel like you were getting through to some higher power, or did you feel like you were just more or less talking to yourself?"

"I don't know. I couldn't really tell." Arthur found the directness of her questions interesting.

"But you can tell you're talking to me now, can't you?" she asked, smiling.

"Yes, yes, I can. But I can see you, I can hear you." *To put it mildly*, he thought, looking at her hair and then into her eyes.

"So, close your eyes. I mean, if you did, you would know I'm still here. You would know you're not talking to the air."

"Unless you sneaked away while my eyes were closed," Arthur deadpanned.

"Well, that's always a possibility," Mandy replied, laughing. "But the whole prayer thing just doesn't seem real to me. And if it's not, if it's not real, then the religion itself becomes a house of cards."

"Maybe God gets tired of hearing the same thing over and over again and puts us on hold. Maybe that's why you couldn't get through."

"I knew it. A blasphemer," she laughed, pointing her finger at him. "The fires of hell are waiting for you."

"No, no, no, you misunderstand. I was just trying to explain why prayer doesn't seem to work for you. I was actually trying to help you renew your faith."

"And now you're lying, on top of everything else. I'm going to end up being a saint compared to you."

"That wouldn't take much," he conceded with a smile and shrug.

Her eyes widened. "So, is *your* family religious?"

"Oh, I don't know. We don't talk about it much. My mother's faith seems real enough, but my dad seems to like the idea of religion more than the actual religion itself, if that makes any sense. He seems to like the idea of people conforming to an accepted set of beliefs that makes them part of the same team. I think his world is divided into good guys and bad guys, and belonging to the right religion is one of the things that makes the good guys good."

"And easier to control."

"Probably. He definitely likes to be in charge."

"That's what I see as one of the main driving forces behind religion—people wanting to control other people based on authority pulled out of the air."

"Could be. All organizations seem to have control freaks. I should know about that. My dad's a colonel in the Army."

"So, does your dad control you?"

"He tried to when I was growing up. But since I've been away at college, it hasn't been so easy for him."

"I know what you mean. I've done all kinds of things since I went away to school that I couldn't do at home."

"Like what?"

"Like boys, for instance. Without my dad around, I can do a lot more."

"A lot more?"

"I'm still a virgin, technically, but I've learned a lot."

"Okay…"

"And I've done grass a few times. How about you? Have you done grass?"

"Yeah, more than a few times."

"And I have miniskirts my dad hasn't seen and a bikini he's never going to see."

"So, you've become a wild child."

"Not really. I'm not doing anything the other girls aren't doing. Some of them do a lot more."

"But you're not worried about eternal damnation."

"I got over that a long time ago."

"How did you do that?"

"Well, when I was about ten— "

"Ten?" Arthur interrupted, almost involuntarily.

"I told you it was a long time ago. Anyway, when I was about ten, I was in a religion class. And this one day in the spring, nobody felt like paying attention. We were just kids. We wanted the class to end so we could go outside and play. But the nun could tell that nobody was really interested in what she was teaching, so she got angry with us. She told us to bow our heads and close our eyes. Then she asked if any of us would rather be outside playing than in the house of the Lord. She asked if any of the boys would rather be outside playing baseball than studying God's word. She told us to raise our hands if we would rather be outside, as a way of admitting our guilt and asking for forgiveness." Mandy paused for a moment. "I guess nobody raised their hand, because she got angrier and angrier. She told us to keep our eyes closed and asked if any of us had ever burned our finger on a match or stove or anything. She told us to think about how much that hurt. Then she told us to think about what it would be like if our whole body was burning that way and what it would be like if there was no way to ever stop the burning, throughout eternity. She told us that is exactly what hell is like, and that is what would happen to us if we didn't put God first in our lives."

"That sounds kind of hard-core. What did you think?"

"Even though I was a kid," Mandy answered deliberately, "I thought it was too much. That night in bed, I wondered if she or anyone else really knew what hell is like. I mean, for one thing, death is supposed to be a transition away from the physical world to a spiritual existence. But her description of hell seemed very physical, more like something she would do to us if she were God than anything else. The more I thought about it, the more I became convinced that she was simply trying to scare us, to control us through fear. She didn't know what hell was like; how could she? And then as I grew up in the Church, I saw what seemed to me to be more and more examples of the same thing, control through fear."

"So do you believe in God at all? Is God dead?"

"Oh, like the cover of *Time* magazine? No; I mean, I don't know. But I do think the reality of God and the validity of religion are two different things. To me, there *must* be something out there, but I don't know what. Just look at how complex and sophisticated biochemical processes are, how we could never design or fabricate something as complicated as a living organism. And if evolution is a part of it all, we still don't know why or how any of it got started."

"So, you don't see life as basically a series of chemical reactions that just happen on their own?"

"For me, that view is a stretch. It just doesn't feel right. I look at how vast and strange the universe is: how massive and powerful the stars are, how many there are, how far apart they are. There's a lot going on. And when it comes right down to it, we don't have a clue as to why things are the way they are or how they got that way. And yet, on a more personal level, there does seem to be a spiritual side to humans and other animals as well. It's like there is an essence within each of us that transcends the lives we lead here. I think that's why music seems so powerful at times. It's like music forms a connection between the physical and spiritual side of things." Mandy suddenly turned to look at Arthur, almost as if she were becoming aware of him for the first time. "You know, I don't usually rattle on this much, at least about things like this. My family and friends would be very surprised. They think I'm this very sweet, reserved, conservative girl who pretty much goes along with her conservative upbringing." She raised her eyebrows. "So anyway, why don't you tell me what *you* think?"

"Oh, I think you're right." he answered immediately, imagining knowing her better, imagining a conversation like this with her over dinner after several hours of uninhibited sex in the afternoon. "Human beings don't know much about how or why we got here, and when religions try to fill the gap, the leaders often have their own agenda, with power and money being at the top of the list."

"I guess that makes us both skeptics," she replied, smiling.

"I'm afraid so," he agreed. "We'll probably both end up on the street someday, with a bottle of cheap wine, wishing we had had enough sense to listen to our parents."

They both laughed. "Doomed. We're doomed," Mandy added. "Educated winos bemoaning the plight of human existence." They both laughed again. "Our parents tried, but—" A series of announcements came in over the intercom. Mandy grabbed her purse and bag and looking suddenly stressed, said, "That's my flight."

Arthur found himself leaning forward as he asked, "Do you think you might want to visit Chicago sometime? There are a lot of things to do there."

"That sounds nice, but I have a boyfriend. I'm sorry. I should have told you earlier."

"That's okay. I can't say I'm surprised." He sat back in his chair and looked down at the floor.

"I guess the conversation got a little personal," she said. "I hope you don't mind. Sometimes it's easier to open up about things with someone you don't know. You know, no strings attached. I've enjoyed talking with you."

"Kind of like a one-night stand," Arthur replied, looking past her, nodding his head slowly.

She smiled and said quietly, "Yeah, kind of like that."

Arthur watched silently as she stood, gathered her things, and walked away.

Chapter Two

About three years later, on a sunny spring afternoon in 1969, Arthur stood with several hundred protesters outside the administration building at the University of Illinois. "Hell, no, we won't go," chanted a long-haired young man through a bullhorn. He stood on the steps of the building waving two fingers back and forth in the air as his voice carried over the crowd. A newspaper photographer dropped to one knee and snapped his picture. Soon most of the students were shouting the phrase with the young man, many extending two fingers above their own heads to form their own peace signs. As Arthur observed the enthusiastic demonstrators, the homemade signs, the long hair flowing in the breeze, he was warmed by their apparent solidarity and sense of purpose—young people united against the egotistic insanity of the older generation, young people determined to make a better world.

As he continued to survey the scene, Arthur suddenly spotted an unexpected but familiar face, Joshua Taylor, a wiry young black man who, like Arthur, was working on a PhD in physical chemistry. Arthur wondered what someone like Joshua was doing at the peace rally. Joshua had always impressed Arthur as more or less apolitical, the quintessential lab rat, dedicated to working dutifully on his thesis and not much else.

Suddenly, a contingent of six campus policemen stomped menacingly up the steps to the leader, grabbed the bullhorn from his hand, and ordered the crowd to disperse. The photographer took more pictures. "Leave the area now," one of the policemen ordered mechanically. "Leave the area now."

"Go to hell," Joshua shouted as the crowd began to fall silent.

"Go to hell," more voices echoed, followed by cheers and applause. At that point, one of the policemen, a heavyset young man, pointed his billy club at Joshua, said something to a superior, and then started wading through the demonstrators in Joshua's direction. Arthur also started to work his way toward Joshua, who stood defiantly in place with both arms crossed in front of him.

"You're coming with me!" the policeman cried out as he latched onto one of Joshua's arms.

"Why?" Arthur yelled, arriving at the same time. "He has a right to be here."

"Stay out of this," Joshua snapped at Arthur. He then turned to the policeman, jerked his arm free and shouted, "Fuck you, pig. I'm not going anywhere." The policeman immediately raised his club to crack Joshua's head, but before he could, Arthur, acting on impulse, body checked the policeman, knocking him to the ground. As the two young men stared at the stunned officer, who was still on his back, Joshua yelled urgently, "Let's get out of here" and began pushing his way through the crowd. Arthur followed closely, struggling to get past the maddeningly inert students. Finally able to pick up the pace a bit, Arthur glanced back and saw that the policeman was now scrambling to his feet and would soon be in hot pursuit.

"Let's go," Arthur shouted, pushing at Joshua's back. Once they cleared the crowd completely, they broke into a dead run across campus. Arthur looked back again and saw that the policeman had indeed taken up the chase.

"The chemistry building," Joshua shouted over his shoulder, veering in that direction. To Arthur, this made no sense. He couldn't see running to a place where they could both be easily identified, despite the fact that it was Friday afternoon and the building would be largely vacant. Conceding to the immediacy of the situation, however, Arthur simply followed Joshua's lead, sprinting two more blocks before slowing down to dash up the front steps and into the building. As the main entrance door closed behind them, Arthur looked back once again. The policeman had fallen farther behind but was still after them, gulping for air as he ran. Arthur and Joshua walked hurriedly down the hallway to a set of stairs, then darted up one flight to an office that Joshua shared with two other grad students. Panting heavily, Joshua slipped his key into the office door, gave it a turn, and waved Arthur in. "Leave the lights off," Joshua gasped, closing the door behind them. "Sit down on the floor."

Arthur rested his back against a wall as Joshua locked the door and sat down next to him. "Let's see that pig find us now," Joshua said, grinning. Arthur nodded, grateful for the chance to catch his breath. After several minutes of silence, they heard the policeman's footsteps stalking the hall.

"You have to come out sometime," the policeman yelled, slamming his club against a door several offices down. He passed Joshua's office, then slammed his club on the door of the next office. "You might as well come out. I know you're here."

As the policeman's footsteps faded, Arthur wiped his forehead with his hand, shifted his weigh, and began to speak. But as he did, Joshua raised a finger to his lips. After a bit longer, however, Joshua cocked his head to one side, then whispered, "Okay, I think he's gone."

"Probably is," Arthur replied softly. "I haven't heard anything since he passed by."

"Yeah, but I think we'd better plan on laying low for a while," Joshua said as he fumbled in the pocket of his jeans and pulled out a joint and a book of matches. "Might as well relax a little, though. This is Panama Red, some primo shit by way of San

Francisco." He lit the joint, took a hit, then passed it to Arthur.

Arthur took a long drag. "I think you're right," he said as he released the smoke. "That cop looked pissed. He'll probably be waiting for us at the door all night."

"Yeah," Joshua said, laughing. "Fucking pigs." He took the joint back from Arthur.

"They didn't have any right to interfere with that demonstration," Arthur asserted, shaking his head.

"Where I come from, they don't have the right to pull half the shit they pull, but they do it anyway. Of course, you probably don't have any idea of what I'm talking about. Growing up for you was probably a piece of fucking cake." Joshua took a hit and passed the joint back to Arthur.

"Are you kidding? I would have had it made if the only thing I had to worry about was the police." Arthur took another hit. "I grew up in the military. My old man was a hard-core officer in the Army. Talk about some deep shit." He passed the joint back to Joshua.

"Hell, you don't know what deep shit is. Have you ever been put down on the sidewalk and cuffed and searched just because of the way you look? Have you ever had a friend shot by the police just because he showed a bad attitude?" After a long drag, Joshua passed the joint to Arthur.

"No. But I know something about attitude. When I was a kid, I couldn't disagree with my old man or even look him in the eye wrong without worrying about getting slapped across the face. And he had a razor strap that he liked to use, too. We had to say 'yes sir' and 'no sir' to adults, and we had room inspection every morning: shined shoes, made bed, everything." Arthur took a hit and passed the joint back to Joshua.

"Room inspection and shined shoes. How the hell did you survive?" Joshua laughed and shook his head.

"It may not sound like much, but it was."

"So what were you doing at the demonstration today then, rebelling against your old man?"

"No. I was just watching. I think the war is a big mistake, and I was glad to see people doing something about it. What about you?"

"I needed to be there, needed to participate. It's important to me to do everything I can to obstruct that fucking war."

"Why?"

"Because it's so blatantly racial," Joshua shot back.

"What do you mean?"

"I mean white leaders in Washington, D.C., are ordering young black guys to Vietnam to kill yellow people for no good reason. And a lot of the black guys are getting blown away or permanently injured as a result of this government's stupid-ass policies. That's what I mean." Joshua took a deep drag on the joint and passed it to Arthur.

"It's not just black guys that are being sent over there."

"No, I know there are white guys over there, too. But there are also a hell of a lot of white guys who come down with sudden medical problems, problems that qualify them for a medical deferment. And what about student deferments?" Joshua glared at Arthur.

"What *about* student deferments?"

"How many black guys do you think are in college? How many black guys from the inner city have that as an option? Let me tell you, very few. Student deferments are the most blatantly racist aspect of this whole damned war. It's like the government is saying that white guys are too intelligent to risk losing in battle. Their brains are just too fucking valuable. So we're going to have to protect them and let the lower-intelligent black guys do the fighting and dying. You know, a little natural selection at work."

"White guys are getting killed there, too, educated white guys. My brother was killed there." Arthur took a small hit and passed the joint to Joshua.

"Really?" Joshua's tone softened. "Sorry, man. Some white

guys have gotten killed, sure, but the number of black guys getting killed is disproportionately higher by one hell of a lot. You
have to admit that much. You must know there aren't many
white guys, from good families anyway, actually doing the fighting over there."

"I don't know the exact numbers, but I suppose you could be
right. I would assume there's a much higher percentage of white
guys with student deferments than black guys."

"That would probably be a safe bet." Joshua took a drag on
the joint and passed it to Arthur, holding the smoke for a long
time before exhaling and taking a deep breath. "But no matter
how it breaks down, this bullshit has got to stop. So tell me about
growing up in the Army. You say it was hard."

"Yeah, but I'm not saying it was all bad. It wasn't. In a way it
may have even toughened me up some, but it wasn't easy. That's
all I'm saying."

"What did your father do that toughened you up so much,
besides inspecting your bed and shoes every day, that is?"

"Oh, I don't know, different things. A lot of it was mental
more than anything else. He didn't want us to be too soft or
anything."

"So what did he do?"

"I don't know, lots of things."

"Like what?"

"I don't know." Arthur paused and looked at the floor.
"Okay," he began, looking up. "I remember one thing that sort of
fits. This was when I was about five. It was springtime. We were
living in a house in Oklahoma with a big backyard and trees and
everything, and my mother had just put in a small garden. So
one day I went out back and saw some rabbits hopping around,
little ones and big ones, with cotton tails and everything. And I
thought they were kind of neat, so I went in the house to get a
bowl of water to set out for them. But my dad was there, and he
asked me what I was doing. And when I told him, he immediately got his twenty-two and went out and started killing all the

rabbits he could scare up, even the little ones. And he made me watch. At first when he started shooting, I cried and screamed for him to stop. I was just a kid, of course. But that only made him mad, so he started shooting more, anything that moved, any clump of grass or bush where a rabbit might be hiding. When it was over, he sat me down and told me that he had killed them because they were eating things in my mother's garden. He told me to stop crying and act like a normal boy. He said he wanted me to grow up to be a soldier, not a girl."

"So your father killed some rabbits. I hate to tell you this, but rabbits get killed every day. Are you saying that made you tough?" Joshua took a last hit from the joint.

"I was only five. But there's more. That night I went out to find the rabbits, to see if any of them had lived and needed some help. I found them in a burlap bag, all dead. I tried to put an ear back on one, but it wasn't any use. And then a weird thing happened. I started laughing and couldn't stop. It was like everything was funny: my dad, the rabbits, the ear, everything. And from then on, nothing like that bothered me."

"Nothing like that bothered you? I don't know. Sounds a little strange, more than anything else. But tell me, if watching your father shoot the rabbits made you so thick-skinned, why are you still talking about it now?"

"I was just giving you an example of what it was like growing up," Arthur replied, frowning.

"Okay. Okay," Joshua said, waving an open hand at Arthur." It just sounds to me like your father's view of life is a little different than yours, that's all."

"What do you mean?"

"I mean, the way people see things is usually based on the way they *want* to see things. Your dad wants to see himself as an officer, practical and tough, not overly sensitive, which is not all that different from a lot of black guys I know, by the way. But you don't want to see things that way because you don't have any interest in being in the military, and for you, being sensitive about something that you care about is just an honest emotional reaction."

"I don't know, maybe. So do you think of yourself as tough and practical?"

"Sure, I have to be."

"Why?"

"Look at what I'm up against. Nixon and his crowd play for keeps."

"What do you mean?"

"Take the election last year. Look at how close it was. Then ask yourself, who would have won if Bobby Kennedy hadn't been assassinated."

"You think Nixon had something to do with his assassination?"

"I think it's possible. Very possible. Can't you just hear Nixon telling someone that there is no way in hell he's going to lose to another fucking Kennedy? And Nixon has been in bed with the CIA and the FBI for years, two undercover organizations that hated Bobby Kennedy and Martin Luther King as well."

"I don't know. It's easy to speculate. But nobody's actually after *you*, are they?"

"Not that I know of, but with this government, I wouldn't be surprised."

"Why would you think the government might be after you?"

"Well, for one thing, I'm working with some very serious people now who want to take things to the next level."

"The next level?"

"Yeah. The nonviolent approach just doesn't work, so we're going to have to start playing the game on the government's terms."

"More like the Panthers?"

"No, this is bigger than the Panthers, a lot bigger. But I can't say any more about it. Someone could be listening."

"You think your office might be bugged?"

"Could be. I mean, after all, I am black and politically active."

"You really think race is that much of a factor?"

"Oh, hell yes, man, race is everything, especially with all the white bigots lurking around every corner."

"Yeah . . . Why do you think there *is* so much white racism?

"Because many whites believe deeply that they are superior, and even a suggestion that they may not be drives them crazy. I think it's encoded in their brains, part of some survival instinct. Their brains tell them that they must pass on their superior genes, pure white genes, to the next generation, and anything that might interfere with that passage must be crushed. So yeah, I think the roots of white racism run deep."

"But not all whites are racist."

"More than you think. Do you want to know how I can tell if a white person is racist? And this includes many so-called white liberals."

"How?"

"I walk down the street with a white girl on my arm. It drives them crazy. I know. I've done it."

"How did you know you were getting to them?"

"The looks I got. They wanted to kill me. Not that long ago they *would* have killed me, would have lynched me."

"So you have a white girlfriend?"

"Not exactly. I had a thing going with a white chick for a while, but then my regular girlfriend found out, and I had to cool it. I still see the white girl quite a bit, but it has more to do with trying to stop the war than anything else."

"So she's an activist, too?"

"Yeah."

"Does the idea that you're not supposed to be with a white girl make it more of a turn-on for you?"

"Sometimes. That and her tight little white ass." Joshua laughed.

"So this girl works on demonstrations with you?"

"Yeah, some. But I'm kind of losing my interest in demonstrations."

"Why?" Arthur looked at Joshua closely.

"I don't think demonstrations accomplish that much. They're an opportunity to stir things up a little, maybe vent a little, but that's about all you can say. I mean, take that demonstration today. You don't think anything will come out of that, do you? I mean, the war isn't going to end or anything."

"Probably not."

After a pause, Joshua stood up, opened the office door, and carefully looked down the hall both ways. "I think we can go now," he said.

As they opened the front door of the building, Joshua and Arthur looked to both sides, but the policeman was nowhere in sight. Feeling fairly stoned, Arthur flashed the peace sign at Joshua, who only shrugged.

The two young men then went their separate ways.

Chapter Three

The following week, at the Federal Building in Chicago, Vic Torkis, a balding FBI agent, scooted his chair back and got up from his desk. The time had come to meet with his new supervisor, Frank Bono. *Another day, another test*, he thought as he walked by his desk and glanced at his mug, still half-filled with the coffee that he had not had time to finish. *Fifty years old and still being jerked around by some clown in the corner office.* He paused momentarily and closed his eyes. *My cases start really coming together, and someone new has to step in and fix the situation. Jesus.* The door to Bono's office was open, but Vic knocked before entering.

"Is it nine o'clock already?" Bono asked, looking up from his desk. His voice was irritatingly low and resonant. "Come in. Come in. Have a seat." He stood and extended his hand. "Sorry we haven't met before this, but I'm still learning the lay of the land."

Vic nodded and walked in, noticing with a slight sense of exasperation that Bono appeared to be younger and much thinner than he was. "I guess things are a little different here than in Washington," Vic said as they shook hands.

"Oh, yeah, yeah. Have a seat. So, what do you think about the big change? Covert operations, quite a move. I think you saw the memo yesterday. I know Jim talked to you about it last month, before I got here and everything. So what do you think?" Bono folded his hands on the desk and waited for a response.

"I don't know yet," Vic answered with a frown, his eyes squinting, his brow wrinkled. "But I'm ready to do whatever the Bureau needs."

"Yes, fine, well, I'm sure you are." Bono opened the file that sat on his desk but only glanced at it, apparently already familiar with its contents. He looked back at Vic. "I think you're going to find covert operations a little different from what you *have* been doing up to now. I hope you're ready for it. From what I've read here, you've spent the last ten years or so working on white-collar crimes—embezzlement, things like that."

"That's right."

"Well, that's going to seem pretty tame compared to what you're getting into now."

"How's that?" Vic asked, feeling annoyed by Bono's dismissive attitude toward the work he had been doing.

"Let me start by saying, you are now joining a highly sensitive program, a very secret program, intended, among other things, to negate, if not eliminate, the Black Panther Party."

"Really? I didn't know that covert operations was that focused. I mean, going after the Black Panthers specifically." Vic felt even more put off by the direction the conversation was taking.

"We are. I don't know if you're aware of it or not, but J. Edgar Hoover has identified the Black Panthers as the greatest internal threat to this country. The greatest internal threat. And these days, with all the chaos and revolutionary ideas floating around, that's saying one hell of a lot. In the past year, a group of us have met with Mr. Hoover personally about this several times, several times, and there's no doubt about how he sees this thing. None."

"But do the Panthers really pose that much of a threat, I mean to the government and everything?" Or, Vic thought, is this just an opportunity for J. Edgar to rack up some easy political points? Knock down a straw man while white-collar crimes continue to flourish.

"Absolutely" Bono answered. "The Panthers don't believe in our institutions or way of life or anything else. They're deeply committed to the overthrow of this government."

"But what can they do?"

"They can stir up blacks all across this country, especially the poor blacks in ghettos, and start an armed revolution leading to a real split in the government, with them in charge of the black faction, of course. That's why they have to be stopped now before they get started, before they get a chance to do any significant damage, and before they get a chance to join forces with these campus radicals that are becoming more and more prevalent."

"How do we do that?" Vic asked, feeling the essence of his career slipping away.

"Well, your role in all this will *include* keeping a close eye on any potential interaction between the Panthers and local campus radicals. Regular reports on both groups will be funneled to you, and if the situation calls for it, you will be enlisted to get involved directly."

"What kind of reports will I be seeing?"

"Good question. Good question. We already have a number of operations in place concerning the Panthers. You'll be getting updates on those activities regularly along with updates on student dissidence."

"What kind of operations concerning the Panthers?"

"Well, I don't know if you're familiar with the Blackstone Rangers, for example, but they're a local black gang that's heavily armed and into violence. We believe they could be a serious threat if they ever joined forces with the Panthers. So we're taking steps to prevent this from happening. We're pitting them against each other every chance we get, trying to get them to wipe each other out if we can."

"How are you doing that?"

"We use fake letters and phone calls and newspaper stories to make each side think the other side is looking for trouble. And it seems to be working. There have been several confrontations recently and an actual shooting. We know, because we have informants in both groups."

"What do you mean, fake letters?"

"Oh, we've written open letters to the Panthers in local newspapers, for example, putting down their leaders, accusing them of just being in it for themselves and not really caring about black people, things like that. And then we made it look like the letters came from the Rangers. And vice versa, of course."

"I see." Vic turned away and inhaled through his nose a couple of times, as if he were trying to breathe in some clean air. The activities Bono described seemed creepy to him, unsavory—tactics that he associated more with dirty politics and subversive activities, not the kind of assignment he had envisioned when he joined the Bureau. At this point, it was clear that he would have much preferred continuing with his old assignment, going after slick white-collar criminals who knew full well that what they were doing was illegal but thought they could get away with it because they were a little smarter than the law. This new assignment seemed to be about harassing misguided black kids. True, many of them had contempt for authority, but most could probably straighten out in time on their own if they weren't saddled first with a criminal record. Vic cleared his throat. "This is different from the type of work I have been doing, very different."

"I know it is. But as I said, a big part of your job will be to do everything you can to help undermine and discredit these militant black groups, especially the Panthers. We have to continue going after their leaders, their newspapers, their supporters, everything. I hope you have the stomach for this kind of thing."

"I'm sure I can do what I have to do," Vic replied.

"I hope so. I know these are different times. And some of our older agents have had trouble adapting to the new demands placed on them."

"I'll try to adjust to whatever the situation calls for."

"Good. As I said, of particular concern to us these days is the potential for collaboration between the Panthers and campus radicals. For the most part, these so-called radicals are just college kids blowing off steam. They've had it pretty easy growing up, but now they find themselves in college, facing academic pressure, probably for the first time, with the very real possibility of military service looming in their future."

"Academic pressure?"

"Oh, sure, sure. Most of these college students don't graduate. They find the coursework difficult, and they don't want to put in the effort to succeed. Most of them probably don't even belong in college in the first place. That's one of the fallacies we live with today." Bono tapped his pen on the desk. "Everyone should go to college. So for the ones having trouble, life suddenly seems hard, doesn't seem fair. Life in high school was easy, but now it's not. They want to complain. They want to rebel. And who better to direct their frustration at than what they see as their oppressive government waging an unpopular war? So, we have to make sure these kids don't fall in with the kind of people who could do some real damage, people like the Panthers." An uneasy pause followed. "So tell me," Bono said abruptly, "how did you happen to join the Bureau?"

Here we go again, Vic thought. "Well, I got my law degree in the late thirties while the Depression was still going strong. It was almost impossible to make a living as an inexperienced lawyer in those days, so I took a job in the post office to get by. Then World War II came, and I enlisted in the Army and served in the OSS. After that, a few of us were offered jobs with the CIA, but I didn't want an overseas assignment. So they suggested that I apply for a job with the Bureau instead, which sounded great. Interesting work, security, a sense of accomplishment; all of the things I was looking for."

"Are you happy with your choice?" Bono frowned as he asked the question.

"Sure. Working for the Bureau has done a lot for me. I really appreciate the opportunity I was given." *What is he getting at?* Vic wondered.

"But now the scene has changed," Bono said. "In addition to mobsters and foreign spys, we have college protesters and racial unrest. These are crazy times."

"Yes, but I think a lot of it has to do with the war."

"The war is supported by most Americans. Don't forget that. And our job is to support our government, no matter what our personal opinions are."

"That has never been an issue with me."

"Right. You have a daughter, don't you?"

"Yes, Denise. A good kid, nothing like the young people we've been talking about. She has her head on straight: in her sophomore year down at Champaign-Urbana. She's going to be an English teacher."

Good Lord, Vic thought. It wasn't enough that he had to present a professional, up-to-date image myself. Now his daughter and presumably his wife were going to have to pass muster as well. Vic gazed at the coffee cup on Bono's desk and let his mind drift. His wife. What about his wife these days? For the last few months or so she had become distant, lashing out at him when he tried to talk with her, then retreating into their bedroom to read, preferably alone. Something was definitely wrong, but there was no time to think about that now. He had to sell the image, had to at least make it to retirement. "Yes, we're just the typical American family you never hear about," Vic said. He considered adding, "My wife just makes sure the life insurance policies are paid up," but decided this was no time for bad jokes.

"That's good, very good. You're right, of course. Your daughter is the kind of kid we never hear about in the news. So tell me, have you had a chance to look over the case that was assigned to you yesterday? I asked Jim to pass it on to you with the memo."

"Yes, I did." Vic took a small notebook from his coat, opened it, and began reading: "Subject is Joshua Taylor. Black male, University of Illinois grad student, active in Students for a Democratic Society. Killed two days ago by a bullet wound to the head. No leads, no weapon. Nothing to go on at this point, other than Washington's interest in a white girl that Taylor associated with named Billie Lee." Vic looked up. "So do you think this may have had something to do with the Black Panthers?" he asked.

"We don't know yet, but we are looking for any connection we can find. As you said, this Joshua Taylor was very active in SDS. But he was also black. So he may have had some involvement with the Panthers as well, which could work to our advantage."

"How?"

"Well, if we can show that his murder resulted from differences between the Panthers and student radicals, it could be a big plus."

"You mean, blame it on the Black Panthers?"

"If there's something there; if we can find some sort of connection. We'll just have to see what you can come up with."

"Okay, I'll see what I can learn."

"Fine, fine. You do that."

ॐ

That afternoon, Vic called his wife at work from a pay phone. "Hello, Cathy?"

"Hello, Vic. Is something wrong?"

"No, no emergency or anything. Why do you ask?"

"I don't think you've ever called me at work before."

"Well, I was just wondering if you were going to be late this evening."

"I don't know. It's hard to tell. Things always seem to come up at the last minute. Why, is something going on this evening? Do you have something planned?"

"No. I've just had a bad day, that's all. I wasn't planning anything special. I thought maybe we could talk."

"Oh, I see. What happened?"

"It's just . . . this new guy I have to report to now. And it's my new assignment, too. It's like everything is changing. I don't know if things are going to work out all that well."

"You're not thinking about quitting, are you? You have at least five years until you can retire. You're going to make it, aren't you?"

"I guess. It's just that I feel like I'm getting caught up in something dirty, and this new guy isn't anything like John used to be. I mean, I could talk to John. This new guy is ambitious and sounds like he wants to make a reputation for himself at other people's expense, and—"

"Oh, hold on a second. Bob just handed me a note. Let me read it real quick here. Okay, I *am* going to have to stay late tonight. I'm sorry, but I just got this."

"That's okay. I'm getting used to it."

"Well, it's not like we were going to do anything, and this really is a good job."

"Yeah, okay. I'll see you whenever." Vic pulled down hard on the phone as he hung up.

⚭

That same day, Arthur stopped by the campus newspaper rack on his way out of the chemistry building and picked up a copy of the latest edition. But as he made his way toward the exit, his eye caught the headline on the front page, and he came to an abrupt halt. Splashed across the top was a picture to Joshua with a story reporting that he had been found dead in his apartment. Arthur couldn't believe it. He went outside to the front steps of the building and sat down. What the hell was going on? Did this have anything to do with Joshua's activism in SDS? The recent demonstration? Had the campus police finally gone completely insane? According to the article, the police had no idea who killed Joshua or why. But the whole thing seemed extremely fishy to Arthur, and before he knew it, he found himself at the campus police station demanding to see someone.

"We have a special investigator working on this case," droned the uniformed police officer at the counter, sounding bored. "Mr. Ringham, FBI."

"Why the FBI?"

"I think it has something to do with Joshua Taylor being from another state. The investigation is going to go beyond what we would normally do locally. Mr. Ringham will be here this afternoon. If you want to come back, I'm sure he'll happy to see you. In the meantime, I can take your name and address."

"Fine. I'll be here."

That afternoon, Arthur was ushered into a back office where Mr. Ringham, a thin man with short gray hair and wearing a gray flannel suit sat behind a desk. "Would you like something to drink?" Ringham asked. "We have coffee and water. I think there's a Coke machine."

"No, thanks. I came here because this whole thing sounds suspicious as hell to me. Why would anyone murder a grad student for no reason?"

"Suppose you tell me," Ringham replied patiently. He leaned forward.

"I have no idea. I didn't know Joshua, except for seeing him around the chemistry department. The only thing I can think of is, it may be related somehow to what happened last Friday."

"What happened last Friday?"

"Joshua and I were at an antiwar demonstration in front of the administration building, and the campus police tried to break it up. When they did, Joshua yelled something at them, and then one of the cops came after him and tried to hit him with a club. The cop ended up chasing us across campus."

"So you were participating in the demonstration as well?"

"Yes, I was. It's not against the law, you know."

"I know," Ringham sighed. "And now you think the campus police killed him in retribution because he yelled something at one of them."

"Blacks have been killed for less in this country. Joshua was from a poor background, probably ghetto. He was used to seeing police brutality."

"Right. Of course, we *are* talking about the campus police at the University of Illinois." Ringham let out another small sigh. "I hate to disillusion you, but I think you'll find that the police here have an excellent record when it comes to handling student demonstrations. I think you'll find that police brutality and murder are not exactly problems. Like everyone else these days, the University has had to put their people through rigorous training aimed at handling protesters."

"Of course, you would say that."

"Why?" said Ringham, raising his eyebrows. "You think I'm part of the department here? I'm not. I'm an investigator for the federal government, FBI. And my guess is, we're more interested in finding out what happened to Mr. Taylor than you are. But the campus police are not on our list of suspects."

"So you have a list of suspects?"

"We have some leads. By the way, do you know the whereabouts of a white girl named Billie Lee, blonde, about five-seven?"

"No, but I told you I didn't know Joshua very well, or his friends either, for that matter. Could that have been the problem, though? Him dating a white girl?"

"I don't think so, but I do believe you when you say you didn't know Joshua Taylor very well."

"What do you mean?"

"Just so you know, Mr. Taylor did not come from a ghetto background. His father is a high school principal in St. Louis, and his mother is a history teacher there. Mr. Taylor was a high school track star and an honor student. As an undergraduate, he regularly made the dean's list and participated in student government. He was middle class all the way."

"That doesn't mean he didn't experience police brutality. And he was active in SDS."

"I think your friend was having some fun with you."

"So what happens now?"

"Let's see," Ringham said as he exhaled audibly. "We'll proceed with the investigation, follow all the leads we can, and share the information with headquarters. They seem to have a real interest in this case, although I don't know why."

That night, feeling cold and clammy, Arthur took a long hot shower and smoked a joint before going to bed.

Chapter Four

About four months later, in mid-September of 1969, Arthur sat across the desk from his new supervisor at the University of Notre Dame Radiation Laboratory, Dr. Claude Fischer. Feeling somewhat nervous in the unfamiliar surroundings, he shifted in his weight restively, uncrossing and re-crossing his legs, as Dr. Fischer, a thin, small-boned man, pored over Arthur's graduate school transcript.

"Okay, good, good," Dr. Fischer mumbled, his narrow face diminished further by the large lenses in his wire-rimmed frames. "Looks like you did well in quantum mechanics and kinetics."

"I worked hard," Arthur replied.

"Yes, yes, and your thesis described mechanisms for the initiation of free radical reactions?"

"Right. I think you have a copy of it there."

"Yes, I'm sure I do. I'm sure everything is fine. I know we went over all of this before, but I wanted to refresh my memory. Looks like you have a good background for this area." Dr. Fischer looked up at Arthur.

"Apparently there's still a lot of opportunity in radiation chemistry." Arthur responded eagerly. "A lot of things we don't know yet."

"Yes. That's for sure."

"And I understand the Radiation Lab has been here for quite a while," Arthur added, trying to avoid any awkward pauses. "Of course, this building is fairly new."

Dr. Fischer sat back in his chair and took off his glasses. "Oh, yes, yes, you bet. The building is new, but it all started with the Manhattan Project in the early forties. Dr. Franks told you about that, I believe. We had a 2.5 million electron volt accelerator at the time, which the Army needed. They needed our expertise, too. I think all that work's still classified though, for some reason."

"Dr. Franks did mention something about the Manhattan Project, but I thought the first atomic bomb was developed at the University of Chicago, under the football stadium, by Enrico Fermi and his group."

"It was. But the Radiation Lab here played a significant role as well. All part of the same team. Everyone wanted to do their part. Very patriotic times. Very different from what we have today, if you know what I mean."

"I suppose."

"Now we have a bunch of little know-it-alls running around, protesting the war and everything else they can think of while they write checks off their parents' accounts."

"I guess that is different."

"Let's just say things were much simpler back then." He nodded his head slowly and closed his eyes."

"But don't you think World War II was a lot different than Vietnam? I mean with Hitler and Mussolini being such blatant tyrants."

"No," Dr. Fischer replied. "No, I don't. I think Ho Chi Minh was just as ambitious and reckless as Hitler or any other self-obsessed political dictator. But we let him off the hook. That's the sad thing."

"How is that?"

"We just haven't had the same commitment to winning that we did during World War II. We're not focused enough on victory."

"You don't think we're trying to win?"

"Not enough. Not the way we did before. We went all out during World War II, drafted everyone, then dropped atomic bombs on Hiroshima and Nagasaki. If we hadn't done that, hadn't dropped the bombs, I mean, if we had gone on with conventional warfare in the Pacific, we might very well have gotten bogged down in the Japanese countryside like we are now in the jungles of Vietnam."

"So you think we should nuke North Vietnam? Not that it hasn't been suggested before. That's what Goldwater apparently wanted to do in sixty-four."

"If we could afford to," Dr. Fischer replied, stroking his chin. "If we could afford to, I think that would be an elegant solution, a very elegant solution. The only problem is the Soviet Union. The Russians would very likely launch missiles against us in retaliation. But if we could, I think dropping a couple of nuclear devices on North Vietnam would make a lot more sense than watching our boys get butchered over there, year after year, getting nowhere on the ground. Of course, if the Russians did fire missiles at us, we would fire missiles back at them, and that would be the end of the world as we know it. So, back to square one. But I think a lot of the frustration we feel now about Vietnam comes from knowing that we're fighting with one arm tied behind our back and that Ho Chi Minh took full advantage of the situation."

"We can put a man on the moon, but we can't end the war," Arthur said, repeating a popular epigram. He glanced at Dr. Fischer and wondered if his father's generation would ever get past the World War II paradigm of good versus evil? *Probably not,* he thought. *Just too set in their ways.*

Later that afternoon, his first day on the job completed, Arthur stopped by Dr. Fischer's office to let him know that things were proceeding on course.

"Sounds good," Dr. Fischer said. "The first day's usually kind of hard—a new lab, new equipment. But things will fall into place soon enough. Don't worry about that."

"Thanks. Like I said, I made up the solutions we talked about and worked with the instrumentation a little, so we should be able to start the irradiation and electron spin experiments tomorrow."

"Excellent." Dr. Fischer ran his index finger slowly down the side of his face. "You know, I may have come across a little strong this morning about Vietnam and everything. And God knows, most of the powers that be around here are dead set against the use of nuclear weapons for any reason, even testing purposes. So I—"

"I understand. You were just expressing a personal opinion."

"Right, that's right." Dr. Fischer turned his attention to a report on his desk.

Arthur waited a few seconds longer, then turned and left without saying anything further. As he ambled across the parking lot, Arthur loosened his tie and took off his sports coat. At his car, a white Porsche with a black leather interior, he popped open the door and tossed the coat onto the passenger seat. His first day on the job completed, Arthur decided to take a spin around the campus. He had always been a bit awed by the ambience of Notre Dame: the architecture and statues, the golden dome. As he drove, he recalled his tour through the main building during the job interview process—the ornate wood paneling, the distinguished portraits on the walls, the mosaic-tiled floor, the ever-ascending staircases. Not that the University of Illinois didn't have a traditional college look; it did. But Notre Dame seemed more ideal, somehow. Maybe it had something to do with the students themselves. For the most part, they were more clean-cut, more conventional. A throwback to the early sixties.

As he turned a corner, he recalled the day he'd purchased the Porsche, the same day he'd learned that his PhD thesis was approved. It had been a magical time, an exciting culmination to his college career. He had hoped that owning a hot set of wheels would help jump-start his social life, help him meet the girls in miniskirts who had so far eluded him, but it didn't work out that way. No one's head was turned. No one seemed to care. He thought about his life at the University of Illinois—a Spartan-like existence, late-night hours in the lab and at the library, studying for written examinations and oral presentations, trying diligently to win over his thesis advisor. But his focus on school work didn't fully explain his lack of success with the opposite sex. He'd had opportunities. They just never went anywhere. Maybe it was his lack of ease around girls, the sense that he was out of his element somehow. Maybe he just never learned how to play the game. His only sexual experience had been with his high school sweetheart, beginning the night they both graduated. But that fall, they each left home to attend different colleges, and although they continued to see each other for a while on school breaks, she sent him a letter during his junior year breaking off the relationship, telling him that she was going to marry someone else that spring. He dialed her number several times after that, but always hung up before the call could go through.

After a second lap around the campus, Arthur turned off in the direction of a bar that one of his new co-workers had mentioned, Frankie's, supposedly a good place to meet young women. He pulled into the parking lot, cut the engine, and got out of the car. *So, what kind of girls go to Notre Dame bars?* He wondered. He straightened his tie and put his sport coat back on. Inside the bar, two dozen or so young men, obviously students, were drinking and talking. "Magic Carpet Ride" was playing on the jukebox. And to Arthur's disappointment, there were only two girls in the whole place, both of whom were accompanied by guys. *So much for jumping into the fast lane*, Arthur thought. He climbed onto a stool at the end of the bar, wondering if he would ever feel at home in South Bend.

Five minutes later, as he stared at the half-empty beer glass in front of him, two young women walked in and sat down on two stools next to his.

"I can't believe only five people turned out today," complained the young woman closest to him, a thin red-haired girl in bell-bottom jeans, a tie-dye tee shirt, and sandals. She dropped a handful of fliers down on the bar.

"I know," the second young woman echoed. She had dark hair but wore nearly the same attire as her friend. "The Dow recruiters will be right here on campus in November and nobody cares. I don't know what to say."

Arthur turned to the girls and asked, "Why *would* anyone care?"

The girls looked back at him but said nothing. Arthur suddenly felt very conspicuous. He had no reason to think they would answer his question or even acknowledge him, and his coat and tie certainly didn't help. Feeling that he must look like a freshly minted establishment icon hot off the assembly line, Arthur desperately wanted to tell the girls that his appearance was misleading, that he knew they were talking about protesting the war, that he had protested against the war himself at the University of Illinois, that he simply wanted to join their conversation. He felt his face turning crimson but was afraid to look away, afraid he would lose the girls if he did.

"Who are you?" the brunette asked at last.

"Arthur, Arthur Weiss."

"Are you a professor?" the girl with red hair asked.

"No, I work at the Radiation Lab."

"Are you sure you're not just a student after a job interview?" the brunette gibed, eyeing his tie.

"No, I received my PhD from the University of Illinois last spring. This was my first day on the job. I didn't know what to wear, so I wore a coat and tie. I think I overdressed a little." Arthur cleared his throat. "So why *would* anyone care about recruiters from Dow showing up on campus?"

"Have you been living under a rock?" the brunette asked.

"Dow Chemical makes napalm, in case you didn't know," the redhead added. "It burns and kills everything it comes in contact with, including the people in Vietnam it's dropped on." She scanned Arthur's face for a reaction.

"Of course—I'm well aware of that," Arthur replied. "But what good does demonstrating against Dow do? People have picketed Dow for years. Napalm is still being dropped every day."

"We can't just give up," the redhead insisted, raising her voice somewhat. "Producing napalm is a way for Dow to make easy money, blood money. We want everyone to know what they're doing. We want everyone to boycott their regular products. We're not going to give up until they stop."

"Yes, I know, but—"

A deep male voice interrupted the conversation. "Would you two young ladies like to join my friends and me at that table over there?" A huge young man with a crew cut planted one hand on the bar between Arthur and the redhead. With his back to Arthur, he nearly let his flexed triceps rest against Arthur's chest. Arthur said nothing, despite a strong urge to jump up and shove the young man backwards across the room.

"No," the redhead said firmly. "We're just having a drink, and then we're going to go." His hand still on the bar, the young man turned and sneered at Arthur. After a long second, he skulked back to his table. Arthur wanted to smash the overgrown bastard with a chair or something, but he didn't want any problems with the campus police. And to be honest, the guy looked big and strong enough to easily put Arthur away.

"Those guys are something else," the redhead groaned. "They think they own this town."

"Well, they do, in a sense," the brunette said, smiling.

"Football players?" Arthur asked.

"*Notre Dame* football players," the brunette answered. "They think every girl in South Bend wants them."

"You have to admit they have their share of groupies," the redhead noted. "And they do like to party."

"That's right," laughed the brunette. "Sometimes they get drunk, get up on the tables, drop their pants, and moon everyone."

Arthur looked taken aback.

"Welcome to Notre Dame," the redhead said, grinning at him.

Arthur looked directly at the girls. "You never told me your names,"

"Donna Will," the redhead replied. "And this is Sandy Swenson."

"Glad to meet you."

"So, you moved here to work at the Radiation Lab?" Donna asked.

Arthur noticed that her eyes were taking in everything about him as she talked. "Right. Like I said, this is my first day. I still have unpacking to do."

"Does that mean you're an eccentric scientist or something?" Donna pressed, continuing to smile at him.

"A radiation chemist." Arthur answered with a shrug. "It's an interesting area, at least to me." He looked back into her eyes.

"Where are you from originally?" she asked.

"Everywhere. I grew up in the military. I guess I spent more time in Chevy Chase, Maryland, than anyplace else. That's where I went to high school. My father was assigned to the Pentagon. Still is."

"He probably has a picture of Nixon in his office."

"Probably."

"Did you like growing up in the military?"

"Not really. And I certainly don't want any part of it now. Before I graduated, I had the typical job interviews with major corporations, but they reminded me too much of the Army. All the games, everyone trying to climb the ladder. I came here hoping to do research in an academic environment, without having to deal with all that crap."

"And oblivious to the war."

"No. I've actively opposed it. I can see how ridiculous it is. But it seems like the thing is going to go on forever, no matter what I do."

"We'd better go. Here comes that jock again," Sandy whispered.

"I thought you girls were going to leave," the football player said, standing directly behind the girls with his arms folded. "Did you change your mind or something?"

"They are leaving," Arthur said, standing as he spoke. "With me."

"And who are you supposed to be?" the football player taunted. "The baby Jesus?"

"I'm on the faculty," Arthur replied, in the most authoritative voice he could muster. "And my understanding is that you gentlemen are to treat people with courtesy and respect if you expect to continue representing the University on the football field."

"If you're on the faculty, what the hell are you doing here? This is a student bar."

"I stopped by for a drink with these two young ladies. But if that's a problem for you, perhaps I should take it up with some of my friends in the Athletic Department. They seem to be a little more concerned about image than you apparently are."

"Talk to whoever you want. I could care less." The football player turned back toward his table.

"Right," Arthur said to the back of the young man's head. Turning to Donna and Sandy, he asked, "Are you ready to go?"

In the parking lot, Arthur stopped at his Porsche.

"Is this yours?" Donna asked.

"Yes. Would you like to go for a ride?"

"No. I have to be getting back."

"Well, at least give me your phone number. After all, I saved you from that overgrown Neanderthal in there."

"You're lucky he didn't pulverize you," Donna said, smiling.

"He's lucky I didn't pulverize *him*," Arthur replied.

Donna laughed and wrote her telephone number down on the back of one of the fliers. "You'd better take this before that jock decides to come out here. Oh, too late. There he is."

Arthur's head jerked in the direction of the bar, but he saw no one.

"My mistake," teased Donna, laughing again. She pressed Arthur's forearm briefly between her thumb and index finger. "See you," she said, then turned away and began walking toward her car.

Chapter Five

At his apartment that evening, Arthur decided to retreat into his own space. He lit a joint, plugged his headphones into the stereo, and put on a favorite album. Sitting back in his easy chair, inhaling the sweetly scented smoke, drifting in and out of the seductive riffs of Carlos Santana's guitar, he had just closed his eyes when the phone rang. *Who could that be?* he wondered. It rang again. *Maybe, Donna?* He took off the headphones, placed the joint on the edge of the coffee table, and picked up the phone.

"Hello," he said, sounding uncharacteristically mellow.

"Hello," answered an unfamiliar female voice with a southern accent, clearly not Donna. "Is this Arthur Weiss?"

"Yes," Arthur replied cautiously.

"Well, my name is Billie Lee. You don't know me, but I was a close friend of Joshua Taylor at Illinois. And I was wondering if we could get together and talk a little. I understand you were with Joshua a few days before he was killed."

"Yes. Yes, I was. But I didn't know him very well or anything." *What's going on?* Arthur wondered.

"That doesn't matter. I'm just trying to gather any information I can. According to the authorities, his murder is still unsolved. So I'm doing what I can to get to the bottom of the thing. It would only take a few minutes."

"When do you want to meet?"

"Tonight, if possible. How about Nicola's on Highway 31?"

At the agreed-upon hour, Arthur was sipping hot coffee at a back table when a terrific-looking girl with long blonde hair walked in. She wore boots, tight jeans, and a leather jacket. Hoping that she was Billie Lee, Arthur watched her look around before heading in his direction. She was tan and thin and moved like a cat.

As she approached his table she asked,. "Are you Arthur Weiss? If you are, I've been trying to track you down for weeks."

Arthur stared at her for a moment before answering. "Yes," he stammered, standing as he spoke. "Please, have a seat."

They sat down together, and a waitress appeared. Billie Lee ordered coffee, and Arthur pointed to his cup for a refill. "I'm so glad I found you," Billie Lee sighed. "I've run into so many dead ends lately."

"So why the sudden interest in Joshua? He's been dead for months now, hasn't he?"

"Yes, but before his murder, we were very close." Billie Lee's intense gaze made Arthur's face turn red. "We weren't lovers or anything like that, but we were into political things like SDS, big time. It got pretty heavy toward the end. That's why I think the government killed him."

"You really believe that? I mean—"

"They watched us all the time. They had files on everyone. And Joshua had some pretty extreme ideas. That's why it's important for me to keep going until I've done everything I can to find out what happened."

"And the authorities say they don't know anything?"

"Yeah. The FBI went through the motions, but they claim they came up with nothing, which is not that surprising. So I've been following every lead I can, which brings me to you. Apparently you were with him shortly before he was killed?"

"Yes, I guess so. I knew him a little from the Chemistry Department and from an antiwar demonstration we were both at."

"The antiwar demonstration. The last one before he was shot." Billie Lee nodded, apparently recalling the event. "I would have been there myself, but I had to see some people in Chicago. Was there anything unusual about that demonstration?"

"Not really. Some cops showed up, and Joshua yelled something at them. Before we knew it, we were being chased by one of them. But the cop never got us. And then a few days later, Joshua was dead. So I don't know if his death had anything to do with the chase or not, but it doesn't seem like it now. By the way, how did you happen to get my name?"

"One of the investigators gave me the names of people who had been contacted about the case. I guess he felt sorry for me or something. Anyway, you were on the list. According to the report, you went to the campus police and asked about Joshua." She gently closed her eyes as she took a sip of the coffee that had just been placed in front of her.

"I don't think I can help you. I would if I could, but I have no idea what happened."

"That's okay. Nobody else seems to know anything either. If you do happen to think of something though, please let me know right away. Here's my home number." Billie Lee passed a slip of paper to Arthur. She then sat up straight, took a deep breath, and smiled. "So. You must have moved here recently. I looked for you everywhere in Champaign-Urbana. Then I came across your change of address."

"I got here a few days ago. It's weird not knowing anyone. I guess I still miss being on campus."

"I know what you mean. I graduated over a year ago and moved to Chicago and still can't get used to being on my own. And the bar scene gets old after a while. Did you leave a girlfriend when you came over here?"

"No. I dated around, but I never connected with anyone that way." *Why did she ask that?* Arthur wondered.

"It's probably the times."

"What do you mean?"

"People our age just don't seem to be pairing up as young as they used to."

"Why do you think that is?"

"I think it's because more kids are going to college, and when they've finished, they want to experience more of life before they settle down, especially the girls."

"The girls?"

"Sure. We're becoming more independent than we used to be. Many of us want to participate in political or social movements, and we want to have some fun while we're at it. We don't want it all to stop just because we graduated."

"I can't argue with that. Look, I haven't been here long enough to know a good place to get a drink on Monday night, but if you're not on a tight schedule, you could come over to my place. We could listen to some music, and you could tell me what you and Joshua did in SDS."

"Okay!" Billie Lee replied, beaming. "Do you have any wine, by any chance?"

"We can pick some up on the way."

An hour later, a Simon and Garfunkel album played softly in the background as Arthur and Billie Lee kissed passionately on the couch. As Billie Lee's lips slid down his face and rested against his throat, Arthur asked gently, "Do you want to go into the other room?"

"Maybe," she murmured. She pressed her mouth and body hard against his, pushing him backwards against the couch. When she came up for air a moment later, she purred, "Okay. How do we get there?"

"This way." After disentangling himself from her and knocking over an empty wineglass in the process, he took her hand and led her into the bedroom. Without saying anything, Billie Lee sat down gracefully on the edge of his bed and began pulling off her boots, then her jeans. Arthur started to undress himself but paused to watch her. As she gently tossed her last piece of clothing, her bra, onto a chair, he continued to stare, mesmerized by her tan lines and long legs.

"Come on. You too," she coaxed.

Under the covers, their naked bodies melted together and began to move. Arthur couldn't believe that he was actually having sex with a girl this exciting, this perfect. An hour later, he lay quietly with Billie Lee, recalling every part of her incredible body. Her face rested on his chest. "That wasn't bad," Arthur said to the back of her head. "Not bad."

"Not bad at all," she agreed, leaning up and kissing him on the cheek.

"I hoped something like this would happen when I first saw you, but I didn't believe it really would. It never does."

"Come on. I'll bet you've had your share of girls. It's not that hard these days."

"It's hard to meet someone like you. I didn't realize how lucky Joshua was."

"I told you. Joshua and I never did anything like this." She sounded mildly peeved. "He was very much in love with his girlfriend. She was from his home town and everything. But in a way, you remind me a little of him."

"Really?"

"Not the way you look or anything. It's something else. Probably the way you listen and talk—very analytical. It probably has something to do with being a research chemist." She laughed gently.

"So how did you get to know Joshua?"

"Mostly SDS stuff," Billie Lee replied, snuggling into his chest. "Organizing demonstrations, writing letters to senators and congressmen, things like that. He was very good at that stuff, and he could cut through the bullshit, too. I really miss that."

"What kind of bullshit did he cut through?"

"Well, like SDS itself. He believed we weren't getting anywhere because the government didn't take us seriously. We may have annoyed them from time to time, but it was like they thought we were a sick joke. He said we needed to do something radical, something that would pose a real threat to the security of the country, so the government would *have* to listen to us for a change."

"Like what?" Arthur asked earnestly.

"Different things, different things. Joshua thought we could threaten to put LSD in the drinking water of some major city, or make a nuclear bomb, or threaten to set off forest fires across the country—something that would really get through to them. He believed the only way we could force the Nixon administration to the peace table with us would be through drastic action here at home."

"He did mention something like that to me once, but I couldn't tell what he was getting at. I thought it might have just been talk. Of course, you knew him a lot better than I did."

"Oh, he was radical, but he was quiet about it. And he was smart too, and he had nerve. That's what I liked most about him, his nerve."

"You have to wonder if that's what got him killed."

"I do." Billie Lee nuzzled closer against Arthur. "Of course, an establishment guy like you probably supports the war." She moved one of her thighs up and down against his.

"No," Arthur answered, clearing his throat. "I think the war is stupid like everyone else. Actually, it's probably easier for me to see that than most because my dad works at the Pentagon. He's a colonel in the Army."

"Really? Why would anyone want a job like that?"

"I don't know. It probably has something to do with stability. It makes life a lot simpler for some people."

"How's that?"

"Well, in the Army you don't have to worry about what you're supposed to do or when you're supposed to do it, because the Army tells you. The Army tells you what to wear, what to eat, where to live, and what your status in life is. In fact, they put a symbol of your status right on your uniform for you and everyone else to see."

"So rank is everything."

"Oh, yeah. And people like my dad really get into it."

"Sounds like a bad scene." Billie Lee shook her head.

"It was. My brother and I were always under pressure to get better grades in school and to do better in sports because our dad was an officer in the Army. We could never just be ourselves. It was kind of sick, if you think about it."

"Maybe. But a lot of fathers want their sons to do well."

"Yes, but it was like he couldn't accept us for who we really were. We always had to prove we were winners. Of course, my brother seemed to thrive on that kind of life, the bastard. He was an all-conference linebacker in high school and graduated from college with an electrical engineering degree and a ROTC commission."

"Sounds like you want a different kind of life for yourself."

"I do. I want a life based on individualism, not conformity. I want to do the things that interest me, for me, not to prove I'm better than other people."

"So you don't care about rank or prestige."

"Not rank for the sake of rank."

"You just want to follow your heart."

"Yes, actually. I never thought of it that way, but you're right. I just want to follow my heart."

Some time later, Billie Lee pulled away from Arthur and sat up. She yawned and stretched, then looked at her watch.

"Are you leaving?" Arthur asked, feeling somewhat disappointed. He pulled the sheet up to his chest.

"Yes, I have to go. I have a lot to do tomorrow, but don't worry. I'll call you. We still have a lot to talk about." She smiled at him and added, "I kind of like South Bend."

"Good," he replied, not knowing what she wanted to talk about, but glad that he would probably see her again. She got dressed and kissed Arthur lightly on the mouth. "I know my way out," she said softly. "We'll talk soon." She squeezed his shoulder.

After she had gone, Arthur began mulling over what he had said to her about his father and his brother. Feeling uneasy about being so open with someone he had just met, he walked over to the closet and opened a suitcase that he had yet to unpack. He fished out a letter from his brother, a letter he had kept close at hand since he received it, a letter that had apparently been written shortly before Tom had been killed. He opened it and began reading.

Arthur,

So how's it going? Life here in the real world is as bad as ever, a real shit sandwich. Sometimes I have to wonder about things. We grew up, or at least I did, visualizing war as some kind of noble contest, a clash of ideals. But nothing could be further from the truth. It's land mines planted by people you see every day, sniper attacks, bullshit from the top, bombed-out villages, crawling through the bush in all kinds of weather, and more bullshit from the top. We have to live with refugees created by our destruction, drugs, locals who hate us for good reason, indiscriminate killings to release pent-up frustration, and more bullshit from the top. On a good day we take an enemy position. The next day we give it up. The only thing that changes are the faces in my platoon because some of the guys we had yesterday aren't here today. After a while, you actually get used to the killing and death. That's probably the biggest difference between life here and life in the States. Here, life seems so cheap, is so cheap. The only time it starts seeming important again is when you're getting close to the end of your tour of duty. And on top of everything else, as a platoon leader, I'm expected to inspire these guys, give them a sense of purpose, a will to fight. I tried at first, but I could see that no one was buying my bullshit. So now, all I do is try to help them survive and get back home.

I think about Dad and wonder if fighting the Nazis in North Africa and Europe was a lot different than this. It must have been. No matter how this ends, no one is going to actually be proud of what we've done here. No way. When I played football, Dad used to say it was good preparation for combat. More bullshit. There are no rules here, no clear objectives. It would be like football players using automatic weapons on each other on the field, then running up into the stands to slaughter the fans there, then attacking and raping the cheerleaders on the way back. I'm sure you get the picture. I guess the only thing I can say to you about this mess is, don't make the same mistake I did. Stay out of Vietnam. And please, don't let Mother see this letter or know anything about how it is here. She has enough to worry about. I'll see you when I return to civilization.

Tom

P.S. Have you ever thought about how things aren't the way they seem to be? How things may, in fact, be exactly opposite of the way they seem. I think about dying quite a bit these days, and I have to ask myself, would it really be such a tragedy? It seems to me that dying in Vietnam could actually be a better fate than a lifetime of struggle against "the slings and arrows of outrageous fortune," after which, you wind up in the same place anyway. I mean, what's the point? Why not go out a hero and get it over with? I think we're all playing a game we don't understand.

Arthur folded the letter carefully and eased it back into the envelope. To some people, Tom had in fact died a hero. But what *was* the point?

♋

Later that night, at a pay phone near a motel parking lot, a solitary figure dialed the FBI office in Chicago. "Yeah. Torkis here," he mumbled into the receiver.

"So, Vic, where did you end up?" the penetrating voice on the other end asked. It was the voice of his boss, Frank Bono.

"South Bend, Indiana. Jesus, she's a crazy driver. I followed her down on the interstate this afternoon. She met up with some guy. I believe his name is Arthur Weiss."

"Is he black?"

"No, some white guy. I don't know anything about him yet. I'll put in a request to see what we have on him tomorrow."

"Okay, okay. His name isn't ringing any bells for me, either. I keep hoping she's going to take us to some kind of meeting with the Panthers or something, but it just isn't happening. Is this Arthur Weiss young?"

"Yeah, he looks young. He could be a student, or an SDS activist, or who knows? I have no idea. They met at a restaurant and then went to his apartment. Looks like they did a little partying there."

"That doesn't exactly surprise me."

"Yeah, I hear she gets around, but she must have had some reason for coming over here and meeting this guy. We'll have to see if Washington knows anything."

"Yeah, if this Weiss turns out to be hot, some kind of extremist or something, we could end up bugging his phone and maybe his apartment, too. Is she at his apartment now?"

"No, she left his place and took a room at a motel. That's where I am now, the motel parking lot."

"So, are you planning to come back tonight?"

"No, it's too late. I'm going to spend the night here in South Bend. I saw a Holiday Inn down the road. I'm going to try that."

"That's good. You should probably stay and make some arrangements to keep those two under surveillance in case things heat up."

"Yeah, I was planning to meet with the Special Agent in Charge at the South Bend residence office in the morning and fill him in. If he has enough people to cover the situation, I should be back before noon. Otherwise, I'll just stay on."

"That's good. That's good. I don't know what she's up to. But I know she has to be up to something. Whatever it is, we have to nail it down and get a report off to Washington. We haven't had anything good to report for a while now."

Half an hour later, Vic unlocked the door to the room that he had just rented at the Holiday Inn and dragged himself in. He set his notebook carefully on the desk, took off his jacket, and perched on the edge of the bed. He stared at the phone on the nightstand for about twenty seconds, then picked up the receiver, dialed his home number, and listened. There was no answer. *So where is she this time?* He wondered. *Cheating on me in a motel room like this one?*

His wife was almost ten years younger than he was, trim, still looked good, could easily attract another man. And more significantly, she seemed to have lost all interest in him, including sex. *How long has it been?* he wondered. *Six months, a year?* It was almost like she had given up on their relationship altogether. Maybe it had something to do with his busier work schedule, being on the road more. The past year had been a hectic but productive one, with several breakthroughs on big cases. But had the extra time on the job actually undermined their marriage? No, he didn't think so.

His mind turned to her apparent infatuation with her boss. Was *he* the problem? That seemed like a better bet. But could it really be that simple? Probably not. For years, their marriage had seemed solid, with a kind of mutual empathy between them that made communication easy, no matter what the situation. So how could things have suddenly changed so much? Maybe it was the times. Social change was definitely in the air. Social norms were being challenged at every turn. But were their personal circumstances really that different these days? She definitely seemed preoccupied. But with what? Vic shook his head.

And now that his only daughter was away at college, the house itself seemed almost unfamiliar at times. *Maybe that's it,* he thought. Maybe their life had been too centered around Denise. Maybe they had to find each other again.

He hung up the phone and turned on the television. *The Tonight Show* with Johnny Carson was on. The loner's friend, he mused.

Chapter Six

The following Saturday, Arthur joined a pickup basketball game at the small park near his apartment, three on three. Not that participating had been his idea. He had been shooting baskets by himself at the other end of the court, enjoying a sunny autumn breeze complemented by occasional whiffs of honeysuckle, when he was approached by a smiling young man wearing a gray tee shirt and jean cutoffs. The stranger sported shoulder-length light blond hair, had a matching beard, stood about six-five, was probably twenty pounds heavier than Arthur, and appeared to be in excellent shape. Arthur noted that they were the two tallest players on the court and assumed that the young man and his friends were students.

"You any good?" asked the young man as newly fallen leaves skipped across the court.

"Good enough," Arthur replied with a shrug.

"Ho, ho, we'll see about that," the young man goaded. "Come on down. We need another guy."

"Sure," Arthur responded, forcing himself to go along, reluctant to give up the tranquil seclusion on his end of the court. *I'll probably be paired off against this musclehead too*, he thought as he trudged along to the other end. And he soon was.

"A game to ten," the young man declared, beaming away, looking around at his teammates. "Take the ball behind the line on change of possession."

As the contest got underway, it soon became apparent that the young man was far better at basketball than Arthur. He was

stronger and quicker, could jump higher, and had no problem
sinking fifteen-foot jump shots. In a matter of minutes, the score
was eight to two. Arthur felt both frustrated and humiliated. He
had lost the ball three times trying to score, despite an all-out
effort on his part, despite being the tallest man on his team, and
despite having lettered in high school twice, even though he
never had been a regular starter. With the ball once again in his
hands, this time at the top of the key, Arthur decided to go with
his best move. He would fake a step toward the middle, then
drive to the side for a fade-away jumper from the baseline. True,
he wasn't a great leaper, but his height, along with his ability to
fade back deep before letting the ball go, meant that this shot
had never been blocked, not even in practice. Arthur feigned a
step toward the middle, dribbled to the side, stopped, pivoted,
faded back, and released the ball. The release felt good. Arthur
anticipated the swish of the net, but it didn't happen. His oppo-
nent not only jumped up with him, the son of a bitch swatted the
ball back against his hands, stinging them and knocking Arthur
to the ground.

"Foul!" Arthur yelled as he scrambled to his feet.

"I didn't touch you," the young man argued as he backed
away from Arthur, his shoulders raised, a bewildered look on his
face. "Hey, come on, you know that."

"How did I end up on the ground, then?" Arthur demanded.

"I don't know. I just know it was a clean block."

"Come on. It's supposed to be a non-contact game!"

"I know. I know. And the only contact I made was with the
ball. Look, we're going to have to stop playing if it's going to be
like this. I can't get into an argument with a student."

"I'm not a student," Arthur snapped. "I thought *you* were a
student."

"Hell, no. I'm on the faculty at Notre Dame. I teach in the
Art Department."

"I work at the Radiation Lab," Arthur replied, beginning to
regain his composure. "I'm a researcher."

"No shit." The young man extended his hand. "Jeffrey James, MFA."

"Arthur Weiss, PhD." They gripped hands firmly in the well-established manner of the day.

"*These* guys are the students," Jeffrey said, gesturing toward the other players. "My students, both on and off the court." He gave them a broad grin. "So are you okay now?"

"I guess so. I suppose I got a little carried away. I was just surprised when you blocked the shot."

"So are we ready to start up again?" Jeffrey asked, looking around at the others. "I think it's eight to two."

"No, we've got to be going," one of the students on Arthur's team said, looking around for support. "First exams coming up, you know."

The others nodded, and a second student added, "That's right."

"Sure," Jeffrey said, his eyebrows raised. "You guys want to cut out because you were losing. You *know* you were about to become roadkill." Jeffrey looked back at Arthur and smiled. "Then again, maybe they do have a point. I'm starting to stiffen up. I may be getting a little old for this kind of thing."

"I know what you mean," Arthur agreed, thinking to himself that Jeffrey appeared to be pretty much in peak condition, despite his comment.

"So, why don't we go over to my place and have a beer?" Jeffrey asked Arthur. "I'm only five minutes or so from here. You guys come over, too."

"Thanks, but we really do have to go," one replied.

"Thanks anyway," some of the others echoed.

"Bastards," Jeffrey laughed as the students shuffled off. "See you guys later." He turned to Arthur. "But you come over."

"Sure, Arthur replied." *Nothing better to do,* he thought.

Jeffrey's apartment was in the same complex as Arthur's. But once inside, Arthur could see that the living room had been transformed into a celebration of the new age; oriental rugs adorned two of the walls, and in the middle of the room a water pipe sat on a fairly conventional coffee table, surrounded by cushions. The aroma of incense was prevalent, if not overwhelming, and one of the interior walls had been converted into a mural of brightly painted psychedelic patterns and colors. In contrast, neither the dining room nor the kitchen had undergone a similar metamorphosis. Both rooms were nearly identical in appearance to those in Arthur's apartment.

Here we go, thought Arthur. Here we go.

Pausing in the dining room, Jeffrey said, "So what do you think of UCLA's chances this year? Kareem is gone. But they've got Wicks, and Wooden is a hell of a coach. Still, four in a row is kind of pushing it."

As Arthur began to answer, Jeffrey gestured for him to take a seat at the dining room table and brought over two bottles of ice-cold Heineken's. After more sports talk and another round of beers, Jeffrey pushed his chair back and asked, "Do you mind if I put on some Beach Boys? I know they're not exactly current, but after a couple of beers, I still like listening to them. I prefer the Grateful Dead if I'm doing grass, but with beer, I'm afraid it's still the Beach Boys."

"Fine with me. I've always liked them."

"They remind me of home: Southern California. We used to play them on the beach all the time."

"Everybody used to play them. Beach or no beach. There was something unique about their sound, and their songs were easy to relate to."

"New chord progressions," Jeffrey said. "They didn't settle for the same four doo-wop chords like most of the groups in the late fifties and early sixties. In their day, the Beach Boys took music to a different level. Of course, once drugs came in everything *really* changed." Jeffrey breathed in deeply and exhaled slowly.

"I guess, but everyone likes the music that was popular when they were young. It brings back memories," Arthur said.

"That's probably true. I remember tooling around with my friends on the weekend, trying to score with girls, chugging beer and listening to the Beach Boys. I had a souped-up '57 Chevy. Talk about good times." Jeffrey smiled broadly.

"One of my brother's friends had a car like that. I know what you mean," Arthur said.

"Did you hang out with your brother much?"

"At times. He was a year older than me, so when he first got his license, going out with him and his buddies was a big deal, even if it was in my dad's Oldsmobile station wagon."

"So your brother is only a year older than you. That's cool."

"It seemed cool in the ninth grade. I remember he and his friends were all on the reserve football team. But I didn't play football, just basketball, so they gave me a lot of grief about that. Told me that basketball was for pansies, and things like that."

"Hey, basketball can be pretty rough, especially under the boards."

"Oh, I know, and so did they. They were just giving me shit. We used to camp out, too. Get drunk and talk about what we were going to do when we graduated. Sometimes we would go down to the train yard and climb on top of a car, then jump over to the next car when the train started to move out. That can be pretty exciting."

"Sounds like fun." Jeffrey went over to the refrigerator and stuck his head inside, apparently looking for something to snack on. "Do you see your brother much these days?" he asked.

"No. He was killed in 'Nam, over three years ago, now."

"Oh, I'm sorry. I didn't know."

"That's all right. I didn't tell you or anything. I guess for a minute there, it was as if he were still alive."

Jeffrey returned to the table with some chips and dip. "So what do you think about the war?"

"I think it's stupid. I think my brother died for nothing."

"That must be hard to swallow."

"It is, if I think about it too much."

"Yeah. Of course, a lot of people have similar feelings these days. There's a lot of political activity, especially across campuses. My girlfriend gets into that kind of thing quite a bit, but because she's Native American, her views seem to have more of a racial slant."

"I suppose they would."

"Yes, but she makes a strong case. There has been a lot of white greed and hypocrisy over the years, especially at the expense of other races."

"You mean like slavery?"

"Slavery and Manifest Destiny. Blacks and Native Americans treated like dirt, while white Christians flourished at their expense. You have to wonder what was going on in their heads. Pious believers systematically uprooting thousands of black Africans from their homes to work the fields as slaves in this country, while at the same time slaughtering thousands of Native Americans who refused to turn over their land peacefully."

"Sounds pretty bad when you put it that way."

"Yeah. I think we have a skewed view of history in this country. I think most of us see our wars as well-intentioned noble efforts because of all the press World War II gets. In that war, we actually did oppose real tyrants and atrocities. The effort really was noble. But Vietnam is different. The war in Vietnam is more about controlling their government through military force than anything else. Simple imperialism. But the thing is, there have been many other instances of U.S. imperialism throughout history; we just don't read about them in school."

"What instances?"

"Hawaii, Nicaragua, Honduras, Guatemala, Chile, to name a few."

"Why would the U.S. want to control countries like that?"

"Because we wanted to get at their natural resources and their produce. And at times, these countries provided geographical advantages as well. Over the years, our government has served the interests of both corporations and plantation owners—greedy people looking for a way to make easy money through the exploitation of locals."

"So what do you think the U.S. wants in Vietnam?"

"A military presence, for one thing, like we have in Korea. South Vietnam is a source of rice for much of Southeast Asia, and it is within easy striking distance of China and Russia. Having military bases there gives the United States some real leverage when it comes to negotiating with China and Russia."

"Doesn't sound like much of a reason to die for," Arthur said.

"That's because you're not in line to reap the rewards."

"I suppose. But this is a new age. Most young people want to see an end to the racism and imperialism of previous generations."

"Still, the war goes on. Have you ever protested against it or anything?"

"Not really. I got caught up in a protest last spring, but that didn't amount to much."

"So you're not active in SDS or anything like that?"

"No."

"So do you have a girlfriend or anything?"

"Not at the moment."

"The reason I asked is, I'm having a party tonight with a few friends and students from the department. Why don't you come over?"

"I guess I could." The invitation had caught Arthur off guard. "But like I said, don't know anyone here, at least not anyone that I could bring."

"You don't have to bring a date. Come by yourself. We don't have any rules."

"Okay. Maybe I will, maybe I will."

Back at his apartment, Arthur couldn't help feeling nervous as he dialed Donna Will's number. "Hello?" he said, speaking in an uncharacteristically high register. He cleared his throat.

"Could I speak with Donna Will?"

"This is she."

Arthur exhaled heavily. "This is Arthur Weiss. We met the other day at Frankie's."

"Oh, yes, I remember. The eccentric scientist."

"I hope you don't mind that I called you like this, but I was wondering if you would like to go to a party tonight."

"Tonight? That's pretty short notice."

"I know, but I just got invited myself, and I don't know anyone else. I know it's not the best of circumstances, but I thought I'd give you a call. If you have other plans, I understand."

"You give up pretty easy, don't you?"

"Not really. I just didn't want you to think I made any assumptions or anything."

"What kind of party is it? All PhDs and their dates?"

"No, I don't think so. My neighbor's throwing it. He does teach art at Notre Dame, but I don't think this is a faculty party or anything like that. He's pretty laid back. Actually, I just met him today. So besides him, you would be the only one there that I know. Not that I really know either of you, of course."

"So what time is this party supposed to start?"

"I think it starts about eight. I could pick you up a little before that."

"I don't know. I just met you five days ago, and at a bar at that, and now you're inviting me to a party where you don't know anyone. And you're giving me less than four hours' notice."

"I guess you could put it that way," Arthur said, finding himself amused by her synopsis, despite his nervousness.

A pause followed before Donna answered. "Okay," she said suddenly. " Why not? See you around eight. Do you know where I live?"

"No, I guess I don't."

"I live on campus in Le Mans Hall. You can ask for me in the lobby."

"Okay. That shouldn't be hard to find."

"It's not. See you tonight." She hung up.

Le Mans Hall, Le Mans Hall, he thought. *I'll have to get there early and ask around..*

That evening, Arthur and Donna showed up at Jeffrey's apartment and were ushered into the dark but noisy scene by a girl who appeared to be a student. Soon they became enveloped in a smoky cloud filled with psychedelic music and flashing lights.

"Glad you could make it," a friendly voice called out through the haze. Jeffrey emerged from a group of young people, holding a lit joint in his extended hand. Arthur accepted the joint and took a hit before passing it to Donna. "Hope you don't mind sitting on the floor. That's just the way we do things around here." The strobe light bouncing off Jeffrey's light hair and beard added to his already surrealistic appearance.

"I guess that's okay," Arthur replied, looking at Donna.

Donna shrugged.

"This is Cherrie," Jeffrey said as a tall Native American girl with straight black hair approached. "In the short time I've known her, she's become my muse." After an exchange of greetings, Jeffrey suggested that they take a seat near the stereo next to the lifeless fireplace. "You want to try some magic mushrooms?" Jeffrey asked. He produced a white envelope that contained about ten tiny pills. "Psilocybin pills," he added.

"I don't know," Arthur said. "Do they do much?"

"Enough," Cherrie said. She took one of the pills and swallowed it. "Who else?"

"I dropped a tab earlier," Jeffrey replied.

Cherrie turned to Arthur and Donna. "Come on, you two. This is a great way to see beyond the superficial, to get a glimpse of the reality within."

"What do you think?" Arthur asked Donna.

"Go ahead, but I'm going to pass."

"You're sure it's all right?"

"If you get too messed up, I'll drive," she answered, forcing a smile.

A few minutes later, seated on the carpet in a small circle with the other three, Arthur began to feel euphoric. "This stuff is good," he said as his head bobbed to the music.

"Yes, it is," Jeffrey replied. His voice sounded far away, as if he were in another room. "Have you tripped much?"

"No, not much. I mean, I smoke grass now and then, but I haven't done much more than that."

"I love what it does to colors," Cherrie said. "It's like they come alive."

"The whole art world has been affected by drugs," Jeffrey said, stretching back against the fireplace. "As perceptions change, art changes. These natural drugs bring out what has been repressed in our minds for centuries."

"Except psychedelics, such as peyote, have been used for many years by Indian cultures," Cherrie countered. "To gain spiritual insight, to understand the nature of things."

As he watched her speak about Native American rituals, Arthur found himself enchanted by Cherrie's beauty. He stared at her face as one expression melted into another and felt he could visualize her first as a young girl with shining dark eyes, and then as an old woman with the same eyes.

"Are you stuck?" Donna asked.

"What do you mean?"

As Arthur turned to Donna, he was struck by her soft red hair and her flashing blue eyes. He couldn't believe that someone as terrific looking as she was had agreed to go out with him.

"I mean, you were kind of staring at Cherrie," Donna pressed, looking amused.

"Now he's staring at you," Cherrie said, smiling at Donna.

"It's the psilocybin," Arthur said excitedly. "It makes me want to stop and look at people. It's like I'm seeing them for the first time."

"You just like looking at girls," Donna laughed. "We've got your number."

"Who doesn't? But it's more than that. I'm seeing more."

"Really? What do you see when you look at me?"

"It's your eyes. They're so observant. It's like you see everything that's going on around you, and yet you have no patience for bullshit. It's almost scary how strong that comes through."

"Good answer. And don't forget it." Donna raised her eyebrows at him and grinned.

"If you're into seeing things in people," Cherrie said, "you'll probably want to look at this." She climbed to her feet, stepped away, then returned with an oil painting, a nude figure study. She placed the painting carefully against the wall next to the fireplace.

"Is that you?" Arthur asked.

"Yeah. Jeffrey painted it. What do you think?"

"You look very erotic. Your limbs and everything. It's like they're moving."

"Thank you. I like it, too. I enjoyed posing for it."

"Do you pose often? I mean—"

"Nude? Sometimes. I pose for classes when I need the money. It can be a lot of fun."

"Fun posing nude? I never thought I'd hear a girl actually say that."

"Girls say all kinds of things these days," Jeffrey interjected. "Times are changing."

"Yeah," Cherrie added, "and it really is fun after you get used to it."

"It seems like it would be hard to get used to something like that," Arthur said.

"It depends a lot on how you were brought up and how quickly you can get past your parents' views, if they were uptight about nudity," Cherrie replied. "When I pose, I feel very connected with the students in the class. It's like I'm sharing a personal experience with them in a warm and loving way."

"I guess," Arthur answered softly.

As Arthur took a hit from the joint that was being passed around, Cherrie lit an incense stick and put it in a wooden holder. When she blew out the match, its burnt head fell to the floor, and Arthur suddenly saw about twenty thin black wires jump out of it, wires that seemed to connect the head to the rest of the match. "Quite a trick," he said to Cherrie. "How did you do that?"

"What do you mean?"

"A trick match. I can see the wires. I've been watching."

"The wires?"

"Yes, the wires. I saw them. You know what I'm talking about. They were right there."

"You're probably seeing tracers," Jeffrey said. "There aren't any wires."

"No wires?"

"That's right," Cherrie said. "Watch my hand." She held out one finger and moved it slowly in an arc, leaving what appeared to be a series of fingers deposited in space by the moving finger. Then the finger images evaporated one by one, leaving only the lead finger at rest.

"Wow," Arthur exclaimed. "Tracers."

"Your pupils are dilated," Cherrie said. "Let's play a game." She took the glowing incense stick from the holder and began waving it slowly in the darkened room, making broad figure eights. Arthur was stunned by what he saw. Rich colors emanated from the moving stick, creating an iridescent kaleidoscopic display.

Arthur wondered how she was doing it. "I've never seen anything like this," he murmured, as if in a trance. "The colors . . . wow."

"You're getting colors?" Jeffrey asked. "That's very cool. You know, you may have the makings of an artist after all."

"Where are they coming from?"

"The colors are in your mind," Cherrie said. "Your brain is responding to the light, but the colors are in your mind. You are causing them to happen."

"No way," Arthur insisted. "I couldn't make something like this happen. This is way too spectacular, way too beautiful. I can't even keep up with the colors. They're changing too fast. My brain couldn't be producing this many patterns this fast."

"Just enjoy it," Cherrie suggested. "Don't worry about how it works." She continued waving the stick for several minutes, varying the motion intermittently before bringing the red glow to a rest. "Sorry, but my arm is tired."

"Are you okay?" Donna asked Arthur quietly.

"I think so. This is great. I was always afraid to try psychedelics before. I mean, at Illinois and everything."

"Did you have a girlfriend at the University of Illinois?" Donna asked.

"No," Arthur answered, moving closer to her. "I guess I was too busy. Of course, if *you* had been there . . ."

Two hours later, Arthur and Donna walked slowly back to his apartment. Arthur swayed gently from side to side. "I'm glad the apartment is close," Arthur said. "I couldn't drive anywhere right now."

"I know."

"How are you going to get back to the dorm?" Arthur asked, showing sudden concern.

"I'll have someone pick me up. Don't worry."

He nodded. "Someone will pick you up. Someone will pick you up. I should feel bad about this, but I'm so spaced out right now, I don't have any normal feelings about anything."

"I can tell."

"You have to come in with me," Arthur urged at the door to his apartment. "We can listen to some music, talk some more." Visions of Billie Lee passed through his mind. *Why not again?* he thought.

"I can come in for a while, just to make sure you're okay, but I can't stay long."

"That's fine."

As they sat close together on the couch, he turned and kissed her. She pulled back. "You're incredible," he said as she broke the embrace.

"I like you, too, but I have to be going."

"It's funny how people are attracted to each other. I could sit here and look at your hair and eyes all night."

"I enjoy being with you too, but I don't want you to think of me as some girl you got high with and then took to bed. I want more than that. If not with you, with someone else."

"So you don't want to make love?"

Donna smiled and shook her head. "I can stay here a while longer, but only if you understand that nothing is going to happen."

"Sure. Sure. I never know how these things are going to turn out anyway." Arthur kissed the top of her head. "You really think that Notre Dame jock could have beaten me up?"

"In nothing flat."

Within seconds, Arthur fell into a heavy sleep, his feet on the coffee table and his arm still around Donna.

Chapter Seven

The following morning, at about seven, Donna awoke on the couch in Arthur's apartment. Despite her intention to stay only briefly, she had fallen asleep next to him and inadvertently spent the night.. Feeling awkward, she straightened herself up a bit, then nudged Arthur, who woke up almost immediately.

"Good morning," he said groggily. "I must have drifted off."

"Yes, we both did."

"Are you all right?"

"Yes, fine, I guess."

"So, you decided to stay after all. I must have been more convincing than I thought."

"I guess so." She shook her head and rolled her eyes at him. "You know, I don't usually sleep over on the first date."

"Many girls have said the same thing. Many girls."

"Oh, I'm sure. I'm sure they have." As she spoke, the energy and attraction they had shared the night before suddenly returned, dissipating any embarrassment.

"So, should we get some breakfast, maybe something hot?" Arthur asked.

"That sounds good. How about the Pancake House?"

"Okay, but you'll have to tell me where it is. I'm still unfamiliar with things here."

Feeling almost giddy as they prepared to go, it was clear that neither of them really wanted to see their date end, and getting something to eat at the Pancake House seemed like the next logical step in a refreshingly unnatural progression of events.

"What kind of experiments do scientists like you actually do?" asked Donna brightly as a waitress poured steaming coffee into her cup. She seemed alert, interested, easy to talk to. "You told me it's radiation chemistry, but what does that mean?"

"We look closely at matter after hitting it with radiation. We look for subtle atomic changes, often very brief changes that last only nanoseconds." He sipped at his coffee, liking the way it tasted, liking the way his job sounded, liking Donna, liking life.

"What kind of radiation do you use? Is it dangerous?"

"We use different frequencies of light. Sometimes nothing more than infrared or visible or ultraviolet, which are all fairly safe. At other times we use more energetic forms, which could do some damage, I suppose."

"Energetic radiation?"

"Yes, we have a pressurized Van de Graaff. The radiation it produces is actually a stream of accelerated electrons or protons. We fire these particles into various materials and then analyze what's produced, how much energy is absorbed or given off, what tracks are left. This gives us basic information about atomic structure and reaction mechanisms."

"What is a Van de Graaff?"

"Just a big accelerator. We use it to speed up the electrons or protons."

"Like a big electrode?"

"Yes. Something like that."

"I'm sorry, but I'm picturing the giant electrode in the old Frankenstein movies, the one in the laboratory scenes that brings the monster to life. I know that probably sounds silly to you."

"No, not at all. In some ways, the Van de Graaff is like that. It's forty feet long and twelve feet in diameter and has an electrode and a charging belt, but it's not standing upright. It lies on its side in a cylindrical steel tank filled with pressurized gas."

"You probably think I'm crazy. You're talking about the Radiation Lab at Notre Dame, and I'm talking about Frankenstein movies."

"Are you kidding? I loved those old movies. The mad scientist against the world. The spooky laboratory in the mill. When I was twelve, I used to watch *Shock Theater* every Friday at midnight. I'd sneak into the living room and keep the television on real low so I wouldn't get caught. It was kind of exciting, at least at that age."

"Did your parents not want you watching scary movies?"

"No, it wasn't that. They just didn't want me up past bedtime. They were real control freaks. Still are, especially my dad."

"Did they ever catch you?"

"No. My brother walked in on me once, but he just looked around and went back to bed. I guess he didn't squeal on me."

"What would your parents have done if they had caught you?"

"I don't know. If my father had found out, he might have used the razor strop."

"Razor strop? Do people still do that?"

"Oh, yes. Some people. Sure."

"That's terrible. Kids should never be subjected to something like that."

"I agree."

"It sounds so barbaric."

"Well, you learn to turn your feelings about it off when you're a kid. That's about all you can do."

"That doesn't sound healthy."

"It probably isn't. I guess I wouldn't do anything like that to my kid."

"Good," Donna sighed, touching her head momentarily with two fingers, then taking them away. "Life is hard enough. So anyway, have you worked with this Van de Graaff much?"

"Not yet, but I will. It has kind of an interesting history. During World War II it was used to help the Army develop the atomic bomb."

"How?"

"They blasted a beryllium nucleus with an electron beam to determine how much energy is needed to generate protons. That information was very important, because releasing protons is key to the chain reaction that produces an atomic explosion."

"Have you ever noticed that science always ends up being used for war? I know that says more about politicians than it does scientists, but—"

"Oh, I agree. The work may start out innocently enough, but..." Arthur took another sip of coffee. "Take Einstein's equation: energy equals mass times the speed of light squared. That was derived during peacetime, but the implication was you could make a very explosive bomb if you split an atom."

"Well, no matter what weapons are used, war is stupid and cruel. And I think Nixon should have stopped the killing in Vietnam a long time ago. That's why I joined SDS."

"It's hard to disagree with that. So how long have you been active?" Arthur watched a beam of light reflect off Donna's hair.

"A few of us from St. Mary's joined the Notre Dame chapter last year, but we aren't able to do much."

"Why not?"

"The campus is just too conservative. You saw what it was like the other day. Nobody seems to care about recruiters from Dow or the CIA planning to show up. But SDS has bigger problems than the Notre Dame chapter."

"Like what?"

"Well, last summer at the national convention in Chicago, there were some serious splits in the organization. Some of the leaders and about one third of the members walked out." Donna's face grew serious.

"Why?"

"Mostly politics. Some of the members want the students to unite with workers and make it more of a socialist movement, and others say SDS isn't doing enough to fight racism. And others, like the Weathermen, want to take a more violent approach to opposing the war."

"So what do *you* think?"

"I think we should focus on ending the war peacefully. I agree that we have a lot of other problems in this country, but if we try to change everything all at once, we won't change anything."

"Do many of the local members agree with you?"

"Some do. Actually, I've been invited to a conference next weekend in Chicago with some of the national leaders and students from schools in the Midwest. We want to regroup and reorganize a little after the mess last summer. And we want to put together plans for some of the upcoming peace rallies, like the one in Washington on the fifteenth of November."

"Sounds interesting."

"You could come with me if you want." Donna's eyes locked on his.

"Sure." Arthur found the intensity of her gaze nearly overwhelming, but he began to feel uneasy. He couldn't help wondering if being seen publicly at an SDS function might hurt his career. What would Dr. Fischer and Dr. Franks think? At times, their conservatism seemed almost on par with that of his father. He closed his eyes briefly and decided to postpone thinking about this potential issue until his head cleared a little.

"You don't have to go if you don't want to," Donna said. "You're probably not that interested in politics; most people aren't. I wouldn't be either, except I think Nixon is insane, and he's taking the whole country down the wrong path with him."

"No, no, I want to go. It sounds like a good idea. Let's do it. If nothing else, it will give us something to do together next weekend. Besides, I kind of miss Chicago. I'd like to go back."

"So you do want to see me again?" Donna glanced down at the table, then looked back up at Arthur.

"Sure. Of course. I like being with you a lot. I thought that was obvious."

"Just checking." The lightness had returned to Donna's voice. "I didn't want to pressure you into anything."

"Don't worry about that."

After breakfast, Arthur took Donna back to the dorm. They kissed at the door, and Donna said, "You'd better call me."

"I'll call tonight."

৯৮

The following Monday at the Federal Building in Chicago, Vic met with his boss, Frank Bono. "We got some info back on this Arthur Weiss character," Bono said. He was seated at his desk behind a mug of hot coffee. Vic sat across from him holding his own mug, trying to look awake despite having gotten little sleep the night before.

"What did you find out?"

"Well, it turns out he has a PhD in chemistry, and his dad's a colonel in the Army at the Pentagon. Can you beat that? And he just started working at the Radiation Lab at Notre Dame. You'd think he would know better than to get mixed up with someone like Billie Lee."

"I don't know" Vic replied. "A lot of these kids today are from good families, but they just don't get it. They've had it too easy. Had everything handed to them on a silver platter." Vic gulped down some more coffee.

"That may be, but Washington wants more focus on him. You're going to have to go over there and keep an eye on him for a while. Probably stay for at least a week or two, maybe more. See if he *is* up to anything."

Vic frowned. "I don't know. This isn't a good time."

"Why?"

"I was hoping to spend a little more time at home to work out a few issues."

"Issues at home? Nothing to do with your daughter, I hope."

"No, no. Denise is fine. She's at school right now, doing fine."

"Good. With so many kids going crazy these days, I like to think of your family as the way things should be."

Leave my family out of it, Vic thought. *They don't work for the Bureau.*

"So the issues at home aren't all that significant?" Bono pressed, looking directly at Vic, expecting an answer.

"No," Vic answered with forced composure. "The only issue is that Cathy wants me to spend more time with her. We would like to see each other a little more than we do. She's busy. I'm busy. But she knows that being away at times is part of my job."

"Good, good. A stable personal life is important. I'm not saying we all have to be like Ozzie Nelson, but we have to know who we are and what we stand for. In a sense, we have to be above reproach. If we show any weakness, there's always some-one out there ready to exploit it."

I suppose killing Cathy is out of the question then, Vic thought fleetingly. *That might open up a weakness that could be exploited by enemies of the FBI.* Vic suppressed an inclination to smile. "So I guess the next item on the agenda is Arthur Weiss?"

"Yes, it is. I'm glad we can count on you to take this assignment."

"That's what I'm here for."

That evening, Arthur was roused from a deep sleep by heavy pounding on his apartment door. Quickly pulling on a pair of jeans, he staggered out of his bedroom to answer it and was greeted by Jeffrey.

"Looks like I woke you up. I didn't know you were sleeping."

"That's okay. I was just napping. Come in, come in."

"I can't stay long," Jeffrey said as they sat down in the living room. "It's just that I have an opportunity to score some grass this evening, and I thought you might want in on it."

"How much could I get?"

"As much as you want. For one hundred and eighty dollars, I can get you a kilo. That should last a long time if you don't sell any of it."

"I would certainly hope so. That's one hell of lot of money. Is the stuff any good?"

"Come on. You're talking to a connoisseur. The quality is primo. I get the stuff from one of my former students, who in turn gets it from Peru."

"Don't you worry about drug deals with students? Wouldn't Father Hesburgh shit a brick?"

"Probably, but I do use some discretion. I only deal with people I know I can trust. I have to know they're cool."

"I don't know. An assistant professor getting drugs through a student?"

"A *former* student. Anyway, things are changing. Like I said before, ten years from now, marijuana, and probably a lot of other drugs, will be legal in this country. Instead of spending millions of dollars in a futile effort to stop them, the government will actually tax drugs and come out ahead for a change."

"I don't know. I seriously doubt that people like Father Hesburgh would ever agree to something like that. I hope you're right, but there are still a lot of conservative people out there."

"Of course Hesburgh would never agree. Fortunately for us, he's part of a dying breed."

"Okay," Arthur said, unable to suppress a yawn. " I guess you can count me in for half a kilo. So much for my savings account."

"Good. I should have the stuff next week sometime. I also have a line on some acid, if you're interested in that."

"I haven't really done acid. Of course, that's probably obvious after seeing me do psilocybin."

"Well, here's a tab that's typical of what I can get." Jeffrey stood up and handed Arthur a small pill in a plastic baggie. "Last one. Look, I've got to go now. Let me know what you think."

"Sure." Arthur opened the front door for Jeffrey and watched him go. Wondering if drugs would ever really be accepted by the mainstream, he walked into the living room and turned on the television set. A news program came on, and Arthur sat down on the couch to watch it. He casually placed the acid tab on his tongue, rolled it around, and then swallowed it.

It didn't take long. Within a few minutes, he began to feel the euphoric effects of the drug. And as a newscaster reported the latest on the war, the man's face began to pulsate and change shape. Transfixed by the stream of images, Arthur stared at the screen for about ten minutes, then closed his eyes. When he opened them, he suddenly felt the presence of someone else in the apartment. Without any sense of alarm or danger, however, he got up from the couch and went into to the dining room, where Richard Nixon sat at the table with a dour expression on his face. As Arthur sat down across from him, Nixon, wearing a distinguished blue suit, a bright white shirt, and a maroon checkered tie, began to address Arthur earnestly.

"You know, we can't just pull out of Vietnam. We have to consider world opinion. Do you want our allies, much less our enemies, to think that we are weak? Do you want the power and authority of the United States, precious power that we established through blood and sacrifice during World War II, to evaporate into thin air? Do you want another Korea, another Bay of Pigs? No, Arthur," he said softly. "Not while I'm president."

Arthur was not at all surprised that Nixon had stopped by for a visit. He was content to sit and listen attentively.

"Maybe I should start by telling you that my family was poor during the Great Depression—humble and poor. Life was harsh in those days, but we worked hard, never gave up. And as a young man, I managed to earn a law degree from Duke University, third in my class. Then, World War II came along, and I got a chance to show what I could really do. Those were my salad days, Arthur, good days."

Arthur nodded.

"After the war, I was elected to the House of Representatives, then to the Senate, and then to the vice presidency of the United States, where I served for eight years. Of course, it hasn't all been a bed of roses. I was robbed during the 1960 presidential election by a spoiled brat and his father, and after that, I lost a California gubernatorial election that should have been mine as well. But now I'm back. And I'll tell you one thing, one thing I've learned the hard way. There is no substitute for being a winner. I've been on both sides of the fence, and there's nothing like being on the winning side, nothing like being in. But being a winner means being strong. It can't happen without strength, without power, without God-given power.

"Remember, Arthur, people are no good. Christianity teaches us that over and over again. If you're up, they love you, they genuinely love and admire you. But if you're down, forget it. They have no use for you. This applies to countries as well as individuals, Arthur. Countries must have power to make it, to survive. And conceding to a small backward country like North Vietnam—why, that would mean loss of power, loss of power and prestige that we need to function.

"No, Arthur, we will not concede to North Vietnam—or any other Communist threat, for that matter. And deep in my heart, Arthur, and I say this with all sincerity, I know that by refusing to cave in, I am carrying out God's will. If you don't believe me, read the Old Testament. Whenever an enemy of God threatened His people, God had His people smite that enemy down and destroy him. This happens over and over again in the Old Testament. And I'll tell you something else, Arthur: there is joy to be found in carrying out God's will, in ridding the world of sworn enemies of God. But to do this, you need power. Power is the key. Without it you are nothing, but with it you have everything. The Communists in Vietnam are opposed to God's people, Arthur, and they will pay for their treachery with their lives."

Arthur didn't respond. He just continued listening as if in a trance.

"But why am I the one to carry out this work? Why Nixon, you may ask? Well, Arthur, God doesn't pick just anyone to carry out his plans on this planet. No, God delights in talented people. He wants intelligent people, gifted people. I was picked because of my clear thinking and creative solutions; for my ability to plan, organize, and execute. Take the war. I have a plan, namely, Vietnamization, a phasing in of Vietnamese soldiers and a phasing out of U.S. soldiers. Right now, we have the spectacle of American boys fighting for the freedom of Vietnamese boys while the Vietnamese boys sit on the sidelines. This isn't fair, and everyone knows it. It makes no sense at all. We don't see Russian soldiers or Chinese soldiers fighting for the North Vietnamese or Viet Cong. Only a president like Lyndon Johnson would be stupid enough to let something like this happen. Of course, Johnson is not intelligent, or gifted, or even Godly, for that matter. That's why God wanted me to displace him.

"God has been saving me for this assignment, Arthur. I thought it was all over when I lost the presidential election in 1960, but I forgot that God is very patient and bides His time. He always evens the score. And interestingly enough, Arthur, those people who laughed at me in 1960, those people who made fun of me in school because I was poor—well, their sons will now help me carry out God's will. They may have laughed at me then, but now their sons are under my command. In fact, some of their sons will be called upon to give their lives on my behalf, on God's behalf, carrying out God's will. And as I said before, Arthur, there is deep pleasure to be found in destroying the enemies of God. It's the same kind of pleasure that you get from washing a car that you really love. The filth and grime are washed away, and you are left with something beautiful. But enough about Vietnam, Arthur. I've been cooking dinner for us. Soup is on the stove."

Arthur looked over into the kitchen and saw a huge gray cauldron about three feet high covered with a lid, simmering on a red-hot burner. After Nixon patted the table lightly with open palms, they both stood up and went to the kitchen.

"Let's see how it's doing," Nixon said. "You know, during the Great Depression, we had soup lines. Sometimes, soup was the only thing that stood between poor people and starvation." He lifted the lid slightly. "Smells good."

Arthur thought he saw the beginning of a sinister smile and an evil glint emanating from Nixon's eyes.

"Take a *good* look," Nixon insisted. He lifted the lid off entirely. Arthur looked in and saw what appeared to be a cream-based soup with small cabbage heads floating in it.

He then looked up at Nixon, whose eyes had suddenly become fiery red and wild. "Look again," he roared.

Arthur peered into the pot and was horrified. The soup was boiling gently, but the cabbage heads were no longer cabbage heads. They were small human heads, heads of young decapitated Vietnamese soldiers. Arthur was transfixed.

Nixon began to laugh eerily, but Arthur was afraid to look at him, was afraid to do anything. While Arthur continued starting at the soup, it began to boil with more intensity, slapping the sides of the cauldron. More and more heads bobbed to the surface—some with their eyes open, some with eyes closed, some with peaceful expressions on their faces, some with grotesquely distorted features. Arthur was nauseated and terrified, but afraid to move. The churning continued. More heads bobbed to the surface, and then Arthur saw the one thing he had dreaded the most. The one thing he didn't want to see. The head of an American soldier came to the surface, a head with short blond hair and blue eyes wide open. Arthur darted into the bathroom, slammed the door, and locked it. Feeling deathly afraid of Richard Nixon, he lowered his head over the toilet and heaved vomit into the bowl. When he had finished, he flushed the toilet and looked in the mirror. His face was red and his eyes were wet.

As he began to wash off his mouth, Arthur heard a soft voice coming from the mirror saying, "Do not let Nixon scare you." Arthur looked into the mirror and instantly recognized an image of Jesus Christ wearing a beard, a robe, and a crown of thorns. An aura of white light radiated from the image. "Nixon speaks of My Father," the voice continued, "but he does not know My Father. Nixon's time will pass; I am forever."

Arthur's fear was instantly gone. "What about the war?" he asked. "What does it all mean?"

"Do not concern yourself with worldly events that you cannot control. Love Me above all else, and love everyone that you meet as much as you do yourself. These are the two requirements against which you will be judged."

Arthur looked down at the sink to collect his thoughts, but when he looked back at the mirror, all he saw was his own reflection. Nevertheless, he felt very spiritual, very close to God. He unlocked the door, walked back into the kitchen and looked around. Nixon was gone. The cauldron was gone. The smell of soup was gone. Arthur put his hand on the stove burner where the cauldron had been. It was cold.

Chapter Eight

That same evening, Vic and his wife, Cathy, engaged in a tense exchange at their home in Oak Park. Vic sat stoically in an easy chair while Cathy paced in front of him. "That figures," she said, shaking her head. "Your daughter needs you, so you're leaving town."

"I have to go. I have an assignment. I *did* try to get out of it."

"You know, she's talking about dropping out of school this semester, and she sounds serious. I've tried reasoning with her myself, but I'm getting nowhere. I mean, nowhere. So then I turn to you for help, and you can't manage to find even a little time to talk with her about it. You have more important things to do."

"I'll call her. I'll talk with her now. I don't know how much good it will do, but I'll call her."

"It's going to take more than a lousy phone call. You need to confront her face to face. She has to know that you're serious. She's coming home this weekend. You need to be here for that."

"And why is all of this up to me? Where will you be?"

"What's that supposed to mean? I'll be right here."

"So why can't you talk to her? What's so different about me talking to her?"

"I talk to her all the time, but it doesn't do any good. I just told you that. I think she needs to hear it from someone else." Cathy crossed her arms and glared at Vic.

"So what's the problem — she doesn't respect you anymore?"

"What's that supposed to mean? What the *hell* is that supposed to mean? I'm having an honest disagreement with her, that's all. Nobody said anything about respecting me. My God."

"Maybe it has something to do with your . . . extracurricular activities. Maybe that's why she doesn't listen to you anymore."

"Who the hell says I'm having extracurricular activities? What's wrong with you? Do you have one of your stupid agents spying on me or something?"

"No. I don't have to resort to anything like that. I can see for myself."

"What are you talking about?"

"Well, for one thing, you're constantly late getting home, constantly. And when you do manage to drag yourself in, you're not really here; your mind is someplace else. And when I hear you talking to your boss on the phone, it sounds like a hell of a lot more than business is going on. The other day, you sounded just like a giggling high school girl with a crush on the starting quarterback. It was disgusting."

"God, you're sick, really sick. And what does any of this have to do with Denise?"

"She may have noticed the same thing last summer. In fact, I'd be amazed if she didn't. Plus your little scene last month when you threatened to move out."

"That's bullshit. You're bullshit." Cathy resumed pacing. "I'm busy at work, with work, and that's all. Instead of trying to blame me for this, maybe you should think about how much *you* haven't been around over the years. You weren't ever here the whole time she was growing up. Talk about staying late at the office. I had to do the whole thing by myself. And then the one time I do ask for help, you give me bullshit."

"What does your boss think about the situation? What's his name, Bobbo?"

"Bob doesn't have anything to do with this. God, you just—"

"So why does she want to drop out of college all of a sudden? If you haven't changed, and I haven't changed, then—"

"I think it's her boyfriend, Warren. I told you that the other day."

"She has a boyfriend? I knew she was dating someone, but I—"

"You don't know anything about your daughter, do you? My God, where have you been? She dated Warren all last year."

"I knew she met some guy at school. That wasn't exactly surprising. She's young and cute, but I didn't think anything serious was going on."

"Yes, they met at school, and everything seemed normal enough at the time. But this year he came back looking like some kind of hippie—long hair, a mustache, sandals. And now, he's talking about dropping out of school himself. I don't know what his plans are, or if he even has any, but I think *he's* the problem."

Vic didn't say anything right away. Then, he spoke, softly, "I don't know what's happening these days. These kids have everything, and they can't wait to throw it back in our face. It must have something to do with us. They don't want to be like us, for some reason." He looked at the grandfather clock in the corner, listened to the steady ticking. "Maybe they're right," he added.

"Look, you need to talk to her. Are you going to be here next weekend or not?"

"I'll try to work something out. In the meantime, I'd appreciate it if Mr. Bob didn't call here anymore. If you want to have a fling, at least keep it away from the house."

"I'm not having a fling."

"Sure. Whatever you say."

"God. I can't talk to you about anything." Cathy threw her hands up and began walking out of the room.

Just then, the phone rang. "I wonder if that's the quarterback now," Vic said with a sneer. He picked up the receiver expectantly, but was greeted by Bono.

"Sorry to bother you at night, but there's been a slight change in plans, and I wanted to catch you before you took off for South Bend."

"I was planning to leave at about six thirty or so in the morning."

"That's what I thought. But since the last time we talked, an appointment has been set up for you to meet with Arthur Weiss tomorrow at the Radiation Lab. The cover story is, you're there to interview him as a character reference for his boss, who's up for a security clearance. But what we really want is for you to get a feel for this guy. Is he really some kind of radical, or is he just going along with Billie Lee for the ride?"

"What time is the appointment?"

"It's at nine. Just stop by the secretary's desk there."

"God, I really am going to have to take off early."

"The thing is, though, once you've had your interview with Weiss, you need to come back here. The South Bend office has agreed to keep an eye on Weiss for the time being. But Billie Lee is back in Chicago now, so once you've returned, your focus will be on her."

"Okay, sure," Vic replied.

"I take it that's not Bob," Cathy said loudly. "Are they calling you back to work tonight for some reason?"

"No," Vic hissed, his hand over the mouthpiece. "Stop it."

"Is everything okay there?" Bono asked.

"Yes, yes, everything is fine. Cathy heard us talking and thought I might be taking off for South Bend tonight, but everything is fine now."

"Good. Well, I'll see you when you get back." A sharp click let Vic know that Bono had hung up.

"You know, it's one thing to act like a bitch with me," Vic growled, "but you do need to keep the people I work with out of it. No matter what else, Mr. Bono is my boss."

"That's exactly what I've been telling you about *my* boss."

"Come on. It's not the same thing, and you know it."

"It's more the same than you think."

Vic shook his head but didn't say anything.

"So it sounds like you're still going to South Bend," Cathy said.

"Yes, but I'm coming back earlier than planned. That's why Bono called. I should be back Wednesday."

"So you'll be able to meet with Denise this weekend?"

"Yes, I'll be able to meet with Denise this weekend."

"Good. Maybe you can start dealing with the real problems we do have instead of the imaginary ones we don't have."

The next morning, after several hours of fitful sleep, Arthur managed to wake himself at the normal time. But he was still tripping. The clock radio pulsated as if it were alive and breathing, and when he closed his eyes, a variety of colorful cartoon-like images came into view; including floating stars, revolving planets, and drifting rainbows. *Enough,* he thought, opening his eyes and shaking his head. He had to go to work; that's all there was to it. Forcing himself from the warmth of his bed, he glided into the bathroom as though in a slow-motion dream. There, he struggled through his normal ablutions, then made his way back to the bedroom and got dressed. Still moving slowly, he fumbled his way outside, climbed behind the wheel of the Porsche, and cautiously steered onto the road, arriving at the lab early in spite of his condition. But as he walked unsteadily through the front door, Arthur could tell that his mental faculties were still very much affected. Slowly waving either of his hands produced tracers, and his surroundings, although still relatively new to him, seemed less familiar than before. The walls and floor seemed to not only expand and contract, but also to glimmer with a crisp electrostatic quality, ready to crackle and flash at any moment with released potential energy.

"Good morning, Dr. Weiss," sang out the middle-aged secretary, Mrs. Hill. Normally, Arthur would have simply mumbled,

"Morning" in response. But now he was afraid to look at Mrs. Hill, afraid she would be able to tell that something was wrong. "I couldn't find you last Friday," she continued, as though Arthur had replied, "but a man from the FBI called and said he wanted to talk with you. He said he would come in this morning, if that's all right." She looked up at Arthur with a bright smile and waited for a reply.

"FBI?" he repeated, sounding somewhat dazed. He wondered if he had become caught up in some elaborate drug sting, had been set up by somebody he knew. Perhaps, Jeffrey. What did he really know about Jeffrey? Was Jeffrey an undercover agent of some kind, possibly a narc? Arthur looked at the flowers on Mrs. Hill's desk. "FBI?" he said again. He looked at a picture on the wall behind Mrs. Hill and blinked.

"Oh, yes," Mrs. Hill replied cheerfully. "We see them all the time—so many visiting scientists working here and so much classified information. He probably wants to ask you about one of the other researchers. Everybody gets asked about everybody sooner or later. I even get asked sometimes. If we were all Communists, we could go on forever." Mrs. Hill laughed gently at her own joke. "He said he would be here about nine o'clock, if that's okay."

"That's fine," Arthur answered as he managed a darting glance at Mrs. Hill's eyes and fervently hoped that the FBI agent would be delayed or wouldn't show. "Just let me know when he gets here."

"I'll reserve the conference room."

"The conference room," Arthur repeated.

He turned slowly and retreated cautiously down the hall to his office. Once there, he closed the door behind him and sat down gingerly at his desk, reveling in the cozy seclusion the small room provided. But as he looked up, the coffee mug on his desk began to move, doing a hula dance of sorts, following a rhythm all its own. Arthur wondered if he was about to have another full-blown hallucination—another visit from Richard

Nixon, perhaps, or maybe Albert Einstein this time, or possibly Jane Fonda. If he ever did acid again, he vowed, it would have to be with at least a week's vacation in a completely safe place. He watched the hula dance for a long five minutes, interrupted at last by a knock at his door. He jumped up and opened the door wide. It was Dr. Fischer.

"Good morning, good morning," Dr. Fischer began energetically.

Arthur nodded, trying not to call any undue attention to himself as he sat back down in his chair.

"I have some good news for you. Important stuff." Dr. Fischer remained standing as he spoke. "Dr. Franks wants to meet with us tomorrow morning first thing to review project plans for this year."

"Why?" Arthur asked, unable to see anything good about the news.

"It has to do with funding. I think we're going to be okay, but Dr. Franks has a meeting coming up with the bigwigs, and when they ask, he has to be able to say what we're planning to do and why." Dr. Fischer paused briefly to scratch his neck. "The thing is, this is an opportunity, an important opportunity, for you to present yourself as well as the work we've laid out. All you have to do is list the things we expect to accomplish and be able to justify the approaches that we're using to get there. We went over these things last week, so it shouldn't be hard to do. You know, if you make a good impression, it could help your career more than you realize, and I think you can do it. I really do. Why don't you put together an outline this morning, then bring it to my office this afternoon? That way we can punch it up and smooth out any rough edges before the meeting. This is important; it really is."

"Sounds good," Arthur answered flatly, thinking he was going to have to pull himself together and start functioning again. He closed his eyes and wondered if he could. At least he would be going over familiar ground. He and Dr. Fischer had already assembled detailed project plans for the work to be done. Now, he would have to put together an overview of those plans and try to recall the thinking that had gone into them, thinking that had taken place on better days.

"Great, I'll see you this afternoon, right after lunch." Dr. Fischer narrowed his eyes at Arthur. "Try to get a little more pumped up for this. This is an important opportunity; it really is."

"I will. It's just that I'm not feeling well right now, for some reason, but I'll be okay." After Dr. Fischer had gone, Arthur bridged his forehead with his hand and stared down at his desk. *Got to snap out of it,* he thought. *Come on. Come on.*

An hour later, as he struggled diligently on the outline, Mrs. Hill phoned to let Arthur know that the FBI agent had arrived. Arthur entered the conference room and was greeted by Vic, who, despite his stout, balding appearance, conveyed a menacing air. Vic flashed a set of credentials at Arthur, then extended his hand. "Hi, I'm Victor Torkis, special agent." Arthur found his gravelly voice irritating.

As he shook Vic's hand, Arthur introduced himself, after which they both sat down at the conference table. But Arthur soon found himself distracted by Vic's sports coat. Although Vic's manner was serious, his white shirt cuffs protruded well past the sleeves of his herringbone jacket, which was both too short and too tight for a person Vic's size. Arthur wondered if this Mr. Torkis knew how unprofessional he looked and imagined his father chewing him out as he stood in line for inspection among a platoon of FBI agents.

Then suddenly, Vic's jacket began to expand and contract, blowing up and shrinking as if it were coming to life, as if it would no longer tolerate being worn by a person it didn't fit. Arthur closed his eyes, and when he opened them, he was relieved to see that the jacket had returned to normal.

"So, Dr. Weiss," Vic said, "are you familiar with a Dr. Terry Fischer?"

"He's my boss. I see him every day."

"And how long have you known him?"

"I met him last winter when I first started interviewing for this job." Arthur now felt as if he were floating above the interview and merely observing.

"Last winter. What month would that be?"

"I think it was March."

"Okay, and how often have you had contact with him since then?"

"Well, since I started working here, which was about a week ago, I see him every day. Before that, I saw him several times, mostly last summer."

"Yes, okay, every day for the past week." Vic jotted the information down in his notebook. "As you know, Dr. Fischer has access to a lot of classified information here. That's the reason for the security clearance. Have you ever had any reason to question Dr. Fischer's loyalty to the United States government?"

"No, not at all." Arthur spoke slowly. His eyes were now fixated on the ruby stone in the college ring on Vic's right hand. As Vic entered information into his notebook, with what appeared to be a florid writing style, the stone generated tracers that mesmerized Arthur. *What is light?* Arthur mused. *An oscillating electromagnetic wave. But what does that really mean?*

"Have you ever had any reason to question his integrity or discretion?"

Arthur frowned. "Not really."

"So you've never had reason to question Dr. Fischer's honesty or judgment?"

"No," Arthur replied, finding the question somewhat disingenuous, thinking that everyone lies and shows bad judgment at one time or another.

"Have you ever had any reason to question his morals or character?"

"No."

"Would you recommend Dr. Fischer for a position of trust and responsibility with the U.S. government?"

"Yes, sure, but he's not planning to change jobs, is he?"

"No," Vic answered, leveling a brief but hard stare at Arthur. Arthur's eyes again dropped to Vic's ring. "As I said before, Dr. Fischer has access to classified government information *here* as part of his *current* job."

Arthur lifted his eyes from the ring and looked directly at Vic. He wondered if this Mr. Torkis knew anything about drugs, wondered if he suspected anything, wondered if he realized that Arthur was feeling the effects of acid as they spoke. "Does anyone ever fail one of these security checks?" Arthur asked.

"Not unless they've managed to thoroughly piss someone off," Vic replied with a slight smile. "When that happens, the reference spills his guts with every piece of dirt he can come up with. But we've never had anything like that here at the Radiation Lab, at least not so far. Okay, that's all I need for this part, but there is another matter I'd like to ask you about, if that's okay."

"Sure," Arthur answered, feeling disappointed that the interview wasn't ending.

"When you were at the University of Illinois, I believe you knew a student there named Joshua Taylor. Is that correct?"

"Yes, but I didn't know him well. He was murdered."

"I know. We're still working on the case. Did you know any of his cohorts in SDS? We're particularly interested in his girlfriend. Her name is Billie Lee."

"I didn't know any of the people he hung out with."

You never met her?" Vic looked at Arthur closely.

"No." Arthur felt his face turn red. He sensed that Vic knew that he was lying, but he wasn't going to change his story unless he had to.

"Would you have any idea why Joshua Taylor was murdered?" Vic asked.

"No, not at all. I'm sure you know more about it than I do. Actually, I'm surprised the case is still open."

"I'm afraid we have more questions than answers right now," Vic replied with a shrug. "Okay. Well, if you happen to think of something, or happen to meet up with Billie Lee, please give me a call." Vic handed Arthur a business card. "My home number is on there, too. You can call me at any time."

"Sure."

"That's all I have." Vic scooted his chair back and stood up.

♀

The next day, in an old brick house on the north side of Chicago, Vic, the composed professional, the seasoned warrior, the shrewd observer of human behavior, began undressing in one of the back rooms of what was often referred to as a massage parlor. An attractive girl with flowing brown hair and brown eyes, probably no more than twenty-five, had led him to this scented location. Fittingly enough, she called herself "Susie-Q." After Vic paid her thirty dollars, Susie-Q matter-of-factly told him to take off all his clothes and get under the towel on the massage table. She then left the room. Vic wondered if she would be back to provide the hand relief, as she called it, or whether someone else would show up to actually take care of him. *Maybe she's just the bait*, he fretted. He pictured a pasty-faced, overweight middle-aged woman with a fake smile appearing at the door. But then Susie-Q walked in, looking great. She was barefoot, wore pink short shorts, and had on a small top that showed off her cleavage.

"Just lie back and let me take care of you," she purred knowingly, kneading one of his thighs. As she worked her way up his leg, she pulled away the towel and gently wrapped her fingers around his penis. "Looks like you're ready."

"Yes, you could say that." Vic closed his eyes and turned himself over completely to this girl, responding with abandon to every stroke. Within a couple of minutes, he climaxed fully.

"You were horny," Susie-Q said, cleaning him off with the towel. "If you want to go again, it's only twenty."

"Sure, sounds great." Vic was now feeling better about everything—his probable divorce, his new life, himself. "Give me a minute or two." Susie-Q smiled and gave his penis a slight squeeze. Following the second hand job, Vic lay peacefully with his eyes closed and asked her if she ever fell in love with any of her clients.

"No. I've seen way too much for that."

"What do you mean?" Vic asked dreamily.

"Well, my business is sex, not love. Love is just an illusion anyway, but guys do need sex to be happy, and it's hard for a lot of them to get it."

"Why? I didn't think it was supposed to be that hard these days."

"It's hard for them to get what they want, what they really want."

"Why?"

"Lots of reasons. The girls they want think they're not good-looking enough, or their personality isn't right, or their job isn't good enough. There are a million reasons. It could be anything."

"I guess I never gave it that much thought."

"Don't get me wrong. It's just as bad the other way, if not worse. You wouldn't want me right now if I were twenty pounds heavier. Twenty pounds. It's not that much, but it makes all the difference to guys. I know."

"I don't know if that's true." Vic raised an eyelid. "I really don't."

"Well, I do. Believe me. When it comes to sex, there's a lot of rejection both ways for the most trivial of reasons."

"Why do you think that is?"

"Because nature is cruel, and we're wired the way we are by nature. It probably has something to do with natural selection."

"So sex is cruel."

"Sure, but most people don't like to think about that, so they try to cover it up with sentimentality, which they call love. They're not honest enough to say they want to fuck each other for their looks or power. They'd rather say I want to make love to you because I'm in love with you, and pretend the cruel side doesn't exist."

"So you don't believe in love?"

"I understand how love works too much to actually fall in love myself."

To his surprise, Vic found her insights refreshing, even reassuring. "Sounds like you've thought about this quite a bit."

"I have. It comes with the territory."

Vic smiled. "I suppose this means we're not in love. But I love hearing you tell the truth. I really do."

"The truth costs only thirty dollars."

On the way back to his car, Vic tried to remember if he had ever dated, even once, a girl with that much animal presence, with that much pure sexuality. No one came to mind. And yet she had engaged him so willingly and would again if he simply paid her thirty dollars. And she seemed to enjoy doing it, too. Seemed to enjoy him enjoying her. Man, she was good. And there were no strings attached, either. He got what he wanted. She got what she wanted. Everybody was happy.

And his soon-to-be ex-wife could damn well go to hell. Vic had read the private investigator's report earlier that afternoon before deciding to go to the massage parlor. As he had suspected, his wife was having an affair with her boss, a goddamned divorce attorney at that. And yes, they probably had a lot of fun sneaking around, doing it on the sly; probably made jokes about eluding the FBI. How exciting. But that would get old. It always does. And then where would she be? In another failed relationship? Whereas, at thirty dollars a pop, he could have as many Susie-Qs as he wanted. So who was the loser, and who was the winner? But as he drove away, continuing to reflect on the situation, his euphoria began to fade. *Doesn't there have to be more to life than satisfying the sex drive?* he wondered.

Chapter Nine

That evening, at about nine, Arthur lay across his bed in a deep sleep, still fully dressed. He had arrived home from work several hours earlier, stumbled into the bedroom, plopped down on the bed, and lost consciousness as his head hit the pillow. His presentation that morning had gone well, but the pressure of preparing for it combined with the residual effects of the acid had left him drained.

Suddenly, the phone rang. He fumbled for the receiver in the dark and mumbled a barely coherent "hello" into the mouthpiece.

"So have you been thinking about me?" Billie Lee asked. Her accent was strong and seductive.

"Of course," he answered, as he regained full consciousness. "I think about you all the time. When are you coming back this way?"

"I don't know. Soon, I hope. I was thinking that I—"

"You know, I'm going to be in Chicago this weekend for some technical seminars. I should have told you. I don't know why I didn't. I'm not going to be there long, but I could probably break away and meet you somewhere, if you want."

"You'd better make some time to see me. And I don't want any excuses, either. Let me know your schedule as soon as you can."

"I will, I will. I just have to work out a few details." Arthur thought fleetingly about the awkward situation he was putting himself in, trying to juggle time between Donna's SDS meeting and Billie Lee, but he was too excited by the sound of Billie Lee's voice to back away. "Funny you should call, though. Someone was asking about you yesterday, an FBI agent."

"Really? What did he want?"

"He wanted to know if I knew you or any of Joshua's friends. Apparently they're still investigating Joshua's murder, but the agent mentioned you by name."

"That's very interesting. They must be getting nervous. I must be getting close to something they don't want me to know about."

"I told the agent I'd never met you. That may have been a mistake, but I didn't want to say anything without knowing what he was up to."

"I appreciate that; I really do. I want to keep those guys in the dark as much as possible, at least until I know something. I don't want to make it too easy for them to cover their tracks."

"Right."

Billie Lee paused for a few seconds, then said, "So tell me, are you seeing any other girls these days?"

"I don't know. Once in a while, I guess. Why?"

"I want you to be thinking about me when I see you. Just me, you know?"

"No problem."

Later that evening, Jeffrey stopped by Arthur's apartment with a sample of the marijuana, or "quality weed," that Arthur had agreed to buy. As they sat in the living room on the floor, Jeffrey lit up a joint, took a hit, then passed it to Arthur. "I thought we should see how good this stuff really is," Jeffrey gasped through his exhale. "Kind of like wine tasting before you accept the bottle. Speaking of which, I brought a bottle with me. Do you have a couple of glasses?"

"Okay, but I can't get too high tonight. I'm just coming off that acid you gave me, and I have to work tomorrow." He retrieved two glasses from the kitchen, and Jeffrey poured a little Mateus into each one.

"By the way, how *was* that acid?" Jeffrey asked. "It was supposed to be good."

"Strong. At first, I felt really high. Then I had a hallucination that seemed completely real. It was like I was talking to Richard Nixon in person. And then there were all kinds of visual distortions. It was definitely a . . . departure."

"I didn't mean to cut out on you like I did, right after I gave it to you and everything, but I had already agreed to see some of my students about the projects they're working on. Still, I should have asked you to hang on to that tab for a while, maybe drop it tonight or something. At least that way you wouldn't have been tripping on acid for the first time by yourself. That can be a bad scene."

"It just took me a long time to come down. I didn't allow enough time for that. And then, while I was still struggling to get it together, at work no less, an FBI agent stopped by and wanted to interview me. Can you believe it? The FBI. Talk about timing. I was still seeing tracers. Things were still shrinking and expanding."

Jeffrey looked directly at Arthur. "What did he want to see you about? It wasn't about drugs or anything, was it? You seem so straight."

"No, not about drugs. At first he asked me questions about my supervisor. He wanted to interview me as a character reference because my supervisor is up for a security clearance. Of course, I had nothing but good things to say about my supervisor. I don't know him that well, anyway. But then this agent asked me about a guy I knew in college."

"Who was that?"

"Joshua Taylor, a black guy. He was big into SDS and ended up getting killed. But I didn't know Joshua very well, so I couldn't tell the agent very much about him. Then he asked me about a girl that Joshua knew in school, a white girl named Billie Lee." Arthur began to feel slightly queasy. He hadn't meant to mention Billie Lee to anyone, at least not until he knew more about her, but he suddenly felt a deep trust in Jeffrey, an uncharacteristic willingness to open up about everything. He wondered if it had something to do with the wine.

"Billie Lee? Did you know her at the University of Illinois as well?"

"No, I met her only recently. I didn't know her in school at all. But Joshua knew her real well. He was an antiwar activist, and so was she. She thinks the government killed him, by the way."

"So how did *you* meet her?"

"She called me about a week ago and said she wanted to get together and talk with me about Joshua. She said something seemed fishy to her about his murder, and she was investigating it on her own."

"This Joshua was actually murdered?"

"Yeah, that's what the paper said."

"And his murder is still unsolved?"

"Apparently. Billie Lee came over from Chicago to see me about it, to see if I knew anything. I didn't, of course, but we talked about it some. She thought his murder may have had something to do with his political activities. That's when she said she thought the government may have been behind it. But the thing is, she was the one the FBI agent really seemed to be interested in. It seemed to me like all the rest was just preliminary bullshit to get to what I knew about her."

"Why do you think the FBI is so interested in her?"

"I don't know, but I didn't tell the FBI guy about meeting with her or anything. I just said I didn't know anything about her."

"But you really don't know much about her, do you? I mean, you only talked with her that one time, right?"

"We did a little more than talk," Arthur said. He took in a deep breath and let it out.

"Like what?"

"Well, she was really hot, blonde, real good-looking, easy to talk to. We hit it off right away and ended up in bed together at my place. It was so easy; it seemed so natural."

"That may be, but I liked that girl you brought to the party the other night. What was her name? Donna?"

"Yeah, I haven't known her very long either, but we really seemed to click. I guess she's kind of conservative about sex, but that doesn't seem to bother me, for some reason. I guess whatever happens, happens."

"I know what you mean. I haven't known Cherrie all that long either, but we seem to have a pretty good thing going."

"Donna and I are planning to go to some SDS meeting in Chicago this weekend. She's pretty much into that kind of thing. I just hope nobody at the Radiation Lab gets wind of it."

"I don't think you have to worry about that, unless you plan to be on television."

"I'm not planning to be on television, but I do have my own clandestine operation in the works." Arthur raised his eyebrows.

"Like what? I thought you liked to be upfront about things."

"I do, but this is an exception. I'm planning to slip away and meet with Billie Lee while I'm in Chicago."

"I take it that Donna doesn't know anything about Billie Lee or your plans to get together with her."

"I certainly hope not. I figure I'll break away from the SDS thing for just an hour or two, then get back before any damage is done."

"You're playing a sort of risky game, don't you think?"

"Yeah, but I'm not really married to either one of them. And besides, I think I can pull it off."

"Well, good luck. I have to wonder, though, why that FBI agent was so interested in this Billie Lee."

"I don't really know. He didn't reveal too much."

"You said Billie Lee was an activist. Has she tried to get you involved in anything like that?"

"No. I think she was active at one time, but I don't know if she is now or not. Our thing is physical, though. We have a very good physical thing, very good. But this situation brings up a kind of interesting point."

"What do you mean?"

"Well, I'm really attracted to Billie Lee; anyone would be. And I really like her. I enjoy talking with her and being around her. But it's not really the same thing as falling for her. You know what I mean?"

"I think so. I think you're saying she's not the kind of girl you'd want to settle down with."

"I think that's right. But I don't really understand it. I mean, if a girl is really cute and personable and intelligent and sexy, like Billie Lee is, doesn't all that add up to the kind of girl you'd want a long-term relationship with?"

Jeffrey shrugged his shoulders.

"For some reason, the answer for me is no, I don't think so. But with a girl like Donna, the answer is, could be. I could easily see myself in a long-term relationship with her. She has many of the same characteristics as Billie Lee, and I like them both a lot, but for some reason, the feeling for Donna is a little different. I guess I don't really understand."

"I don't think anyone does." Jeffrey shook his head.

"Of course, things may not work out with Donna; I just met her."

"I guess you have to stay flexible, especially with the juggling act you're trying to pull off. I know Cherrie and I are in a good place right now, but tomorrow — who knows?"

"Yeah, who knows about anything?" Arthur suddenly felt very tired.

༄

The following Friday afternoon, amid cool but sunny breezes, Arthur and Donna left South Bend for the SDS conference in Chicago. Proceeding slowly through the city, Arthur enjoyed the passing montage of autumn colors as the Porsche engine hummed softly in the background. Recalling the presentation he had made earlier in the week, Arthur couldn't help feeling that he had arrived. His research was off to a good start, and Dr. Franks had suggested that some of his work would likely be published. Still, now that he was behind the wheel, Arthur was glad to be getting away from the lab for the weekend. As he took the entrance ramp onto the toll road, the Byrds' version of *Mr. Tambourine Man* began playing on the radio. Feeling generally optimistic and excited about being with Donna, Arthur glanced over at her and caught the wind flowing through her hair. "It's hard to think about politics on a day like this," he said. "Vietnam seems far away."

"I know, but it's not. It never is."

"Yes, but the way things are going, SDS could start playing less of a role soon."

Donna shot a quick glance at him. "Really? What do you mean? We had some problems last summer, but we still have a lot to do. The war is a long way from over."

"Oh, I just thought, with all the recent changes, that the peace talks might open up a little, maybe help the war wind down."

"That's what the administration keeps saying, but they've been saying that for a long time."

"I know, but Ho Chi Minh is dead now, which means new leadership for North Vietnam. And Nixon is withdrawing some of the troops. The signs are there."

"Maybe, but I think we still have a basic problem. Nixon is looking for a compromise that will allow the United States to save face, and I don't think North Vietnam wants to let us off the hook that easily. They've already paid too high a price. I think they want nothing less than our unilateral withdrawal, preferably waving a white flag as we go."

"You really believe that?" Arthur asked, sounding a bit disappointed.

"Yes. Yes, I do. I'm not saying it should be hard to end the war. I'm just saying politicians have a way of making simple things difficult."

"So now it's up to SDS to step in and save the day."

"We need to do anything we can do to help. Of course, we can't do it alone, but we can have an effect. We just have to stay with it."

"Do you ever wonder if you're being watched by the government, like the FBI or somebody like that? Supposedly, they have dossiers on everyone involved with the Movement."

"I don't worry about things like that."

"Well, I don't want them getting anything on me. It could put my security clearance in jeopardy. It could mean my job."

"You're not going to lose your job. You're not doing anything subversive or illegal. You're simply going to an SDS planning session. The members are going to decide what demonstrations we want to have and what the speeches should emphasize, things like that. These days SDS has become almost passé."

"I don't know," Arthur replied, leaning back in his seat. He pushed his hands against the steering wheel and straightened his arms before returning to a more relaxed position. "You have to admit that SDS has been pretty far out there at times. They've held massive demonstrations across the country at hundreds of colleges, and some of them have gotten pretty violent, like seizing the buildings at Columbia last year."

"It's just the times. Once in a while things do get out of hand, I admit that, but through it all, SDS is still committed to non-violence. You have to put things into perspective. You have to remember we've had police riots at the Democratic Convention in Chicago, black riots in Watts and Detroit, the assassinations of Robert Kennedy and Martin Luther King, demonstrations overseas. The list goes on and on and on. In a lot of ways, these are insane times. All SDS is trying to do, at least the members I work with, is show that large numbers of thoughtful people are opposed to the war and will not support it. That's the main—if not the only—point."

"These are insane times, no doubt about that."

"So, what would your family say if they knew you were going to an SDS meeting?" Donna asked.

"I can't even fathom that. My dad thinks I should be in Vietnam right now upholding the family honor. He sees any antiwar group as a bunch of traitors."

"Really? I thought by now everyone knows that the war is a mistake, even hawks like your father."

"My father's views will never change. So what's your family like? You've never said much about them."

Donna hesitated before answering. "I don't like to talk about them," she said quietly. "That's what I like about college. It's a chance to get away from the past and live your own life."

"They can't be that bad. They weren't mean to you when you were growing up or anything, were they?"

"No. No. It's just that . . . they're very wealthy." She turned to watch Arthur closely as she spoke. "That's the main thing. I grew up on Manhasset, an only child, spoiled rotten, if you listen to my mother. My father calls himself an investor, but he mostly inherited his money. He's about twenty years older than my mother."

"That doesn't sound so bad. What's your mother like?"

"She keeps trying to fix me up with guys from 'good' families, which means very rich families. But I don't like the way she thinks. To her, things are too black and white—you're either rich or you're poor."

"What was growing up rich like? There must have been some good things about it."

"I don't know. I remember going to the ocean a lot when I was really young—boarding schools, skiing in Europe on winter holidays, sailing in the summer."

"And now you're a student activist, living on your own in South Bend. Isn't that a pretty big change?"

"No, not as big as it might seem. But it is nice to do something that counts, for a change. The war has created a lot of horrible suffering and tragedy. And the same establishment figures who represent the uneven distribution of wealth in this country are largely responsible for the mess in Vietnam."

"People like your father?"

"In a way, but my father doesn't really support the war, or much of anything, really. Politics bore him. He just complains about the stock market and how much the war costs and then lets his broker make tons of money for him. I guess he's apolitical more than anything."

"I can't imagine my father *ever* being apolitical. He sees life in terms of winning and losing, good guys against the bad guys. My brother getting killed in Vietnam didn't even slow him down. He still thinks we should be over there fighting as hard as we can."

"So he's opposed to the troop withdrawals?"

"Oh, yeah. He thinks Nixon has sold out. He doesn't believe in backing down. Ever."

"You're the only one in South Bend who knows anything about my family background," Donna said, looking at him intently. "Everyone else thinks I'm middle class, or even working class."

"That's kind of odd, isn't it?"

"No, it feels good. When I graduate, I'm going to pay my father back for everything—tuition, room and board, books— everything."

"I see."

An hour later, Arthur pulled off the freeway to get some gas. Donna pointed at a nearby diner and suggested getting something to eat. "Let's just try it. I missed lunch. I just want a sandwich. It won't kill you."

"I don't know," Arthur grumbled. "It looks like a dive to me." A few minutes later, they were seated at the counter. As Arthur studied the menu, he couldn't help overhearing a nearby conversation.

"You should'a seen what was at the store this morning," a heavyset man in a flannel shirt blurted out in a high pitched voice. He was seated a few places down from Arthur and appeared to be in his early thirties. His comments were directed at two companions seated on the other side of him. "I guess they was hippies. I think that's what you call them. All I could tell for sure was there was two of them, a boy and a girl. But I couldn't tell for sure which was which." The men all laughed. "They both had long hair that looked like some kind of rat's nest, and the one, the boy, at least I think it was a boy, wore beads around his neck. And get this. I'm not making this up now. He had these sandals on with little bells on them. I'm not kidding—little bells. I thought I was going to shit right then and there."

"That stuff makes me sick," said the man farthest down. Arthur shot a glance at him. He was fairly tall and thin, almost rangy, and wore cowboy boots. He dangled a cigarette between two fingers.

"You keep seeing that stuff more and more," said the heavyset man. "I was just getting some beer for our fishing trip, and there they was in all their glory."

"I'd like to take a pair of scissors to some a them hippies," the third man said. He appeared to be at least twenty years older than the other two. "Take their hair right down to nothing and let 'em start over again, maybe get it right this time."

"I'd like to get a hunting license for hippies," the thin man declared. He took a hard drag on his cigarette. "Put the sons of bitches out of their fucking misery and be done with it."

Feeling a surge of anger, Arthur responded strongly. "Don't you guys have anything better to do than sit here blowing off about young people? Maybe they dress the way they do because they don't want to be mistaken for losers like you."

"Well, well," the heavyset man said, swiveling his seat toward Arthur. "What have we got here? Looks like a little college boy with his little college girlfriend. If you don't like what I'm saying, why don't you come over here and shut me up?"

"Let him go, Dwayne," the older man put in. "He looks like he might cry if you hit him one."

"There are many kinds of people in the world," Arthur said, trying to regain his composure. "You don't have to be afraid of someone just because he looks a little different than you do."

"I'm not afraid of nothin'," the heavyset man said. "Especially you."

Arthur rose to his feet. "Maybe you should be."

"No!" Donna cried out. "Don't."

Suddenly, a small middle-aged man wearing a short-sleeve shirt and a tie appeared. "What's going on here? I'm the manager, and I don't want any problems. I can have the state police here in two minutes." He stepped in between Arthur and the heavyset man, who was still seated.

"Talk to him," the older man said, pointing at Arthur. "We was just sitting here, minding our own business, getting ready to go fishing, and he starts yelling at us, telling us to shut up or he's going to make us."

Arthur looked down at the floor in exasperation.

"Maybe you'd better leave," the manager suggested, giving Arthur a worried look.

"Yes," Donna agreed. "Let's go."

Arthur looked up at the manager, then over at Donna. "All right. No problem. I didn't want to eat at a place like this anyway."

As Arthur and Donna started toward the door, the man in cowboy boots stood up and blocked Arthur's path. "Any time, pretty boy," he taunted, glaring at Arthur. "Just let me know."

"Right," Arthur replied, pushing by him.

Chapter Ten

Back on the road, Arthur and Donna remained silent as they drove by rural towns and cornfields, through the stench of Gary–East Chicago–Hammond steel mills, and finally onto a maze of busy Chicago toll roads.

Slowing down for the heavy traffic, feeling the approach of the city, Arthur found dealing with the weaving cars and intimidating semis draining. But he didn't complain. He simply clenched the wheel tighter and hit the brakes now and then to avoid collisions.

"Why did you get so angry back there?" Donna asked, finally breaking the silence. "Why would you care what those guys in the diner thought?"

"They were playing games. Especially the guy in the flannel shirt."

"Really? I thought they were just talking among themselves. I wasn't even paying attention to them."

"The fat one was talking loud enough for us to hear him on purpose. He was trying to provoke us. I get so tired of stuff like that—people who want to ridicule anyone who looks the slightest bit different or anyone who looks like he may have gone to college recently."

"You can't fight everyone who acts like a jerk."

"I know. I know. Now that it's over, I'm glad nothing happened."

"The people we're going to meet in Chicago are a lot different. They're not petty about the small things, and they're open minded to other points of view."

"I hope you're right."

"No, really. One of the things I like most about the Movement is the people I've met."

"If you say so, but sometimes I think the problem is that people are people."

Finally arriving at the Palmer House, Arthur felt numb. He slid the Porsche into a parking space, climbed out slowly, and stretched hard before helping Donna gather their luggage. As they entered the hotel, Arthur still felt tired, but Donna was obviously excited. In the lobby, she took the conference itinerary from her purse and studied it, sharing with Arthur the various committee meetings that were scheduled on site in several conference rooms over the next two days. She then scanned the check-in area for any familiar faces, but saw no one.

Fifteen minutes later, as they unpacked in their room, Donna reminded Arthur that she would be meeting with some of the other attendees that evening. "You're invited too, of course," she said. "It should be fun."

"It's your call. I just hope I'm not too straight to fit in."

"Don't worry. You're fine. We're supposed to meet in Sandy Zimmerman's room. She's from the University of Wisconsin."

"Sounds good."

"I'm glad you took Monday off," Donna added softly. She draped both of her arms around Arthur's neck as he stood in front of the open closet, about to arrange the items that he had just placed inside. "That way we can see a few things before we go back. Relax a little."

"Dr. Fischer didn't seem to mind," Arthur replied, encircling her back with his arms. "I guess the timing was good." He kissed her, then drew back. Her arms were still around his neck. "So what happens . . . tonight?" he asked awkwardly. "I mean, after the party."

"I'm not sure." Donna pulled her arms down and stepped back. "Technically, we've slept together before."

"I suppose you could say that. We have fallen asleep together on the same couch, but we've never really *slept* together."

"Still, that's more than I've done with anyone else." Donna forced a smile. "We'll just have to see."

"Okay, fine. I was just wondering."

Donna stepped closer to him, placed her hand on his arm and kissed him on the cheek. "Let's just let things happen naturally. We don't want to lose the magic."

"I may get a little frustrated at times," Arthur said, his eyes locked on hers, "but you don't have to worry about losing the magic."

A few minutes later, Donna and Arthur knocked at the door where the party was being held. "I haven't seen Sandy since last spring," she said excitedly.

"Sounds like a lot of people in there." Arthur said.

"Come in, come in," a bubbly girl with long brown hair cried as the door swung open. "Donna, it's been ages." She gave Donna a big hug.

"I missed you, too," Donna replied loudly, backing up as she spoke. "Sandy, this is Arthur. Arthur, Sandy."

Twenty to thirty young people were already in the suite, wearing jeans and sweaters, talking and drinking and smoking grass in small groups. Arthur turned to Donna, but she was suddenly swept away by several young women with whom she was obviously familiar.

Now by himself, Arthur stepped back and listened to the conversations taking place around him. Several young women were talking about Woodstock. Apparently, one of them had actually been there. A group of guys were talking about the possibility of a draft lottery and how fair or unfair it might be. Several others were speculating about the upcoming moratorium demonstrations scheduled across the country. Arthur looked around the room again for Donna, but his attention was diverted by a young man with a red beard who was sitting cross-legged on the floor toward the middle of the room.

The young man leaned forward and squinted at Arthur. "I don't recognize you," he said. He held a lit joint in one hand and looked a bit stoned. "I'm David Payton, University of Chicago." He extended his free hand up to Arthur, who stepped forward, reached down, and shook it.

"Arthur Weiss. I work at the University of Notre Dame."

"Work at the University of Notre Dame. So you're not a student there?"

"No, I work at the Radiation Lab."

"The Radiation Lab. That's interesting. Would you care for a hit?"

"Sure." Arthur reached down and took the joint.

"So you're not a member of SDS?" David leaned back and stretched his arms out behind him.

"No, but I have a friend who is, Donna Will."

"Oh, yes. She's pretty active. The women are starting to get more involved these days. Probably a good thing."

Arthur passed the joint back to David, who took a hit, then sat it next to him in an ashtray on the floor.

"So tell me, what kind of educational background do you have? What kind of background do you have to have to work at the Radiation Lab at Notre Dame?"

"I have a PhD in physical chemistry from the University of Illinois."

"That's impressive. I'm in medical school myself." Arthur sensed that David was waiting for him to react. "My father's a neurosurgeon at the Mayo Clinic. I hope to join him there some day. Have a seat."

Arthur sat down across from David on the floor.

"I'm sort of responsible for this little conclave," David continued. "I'm hoping to help organize our efforts over the next day or so to better address the challenges ahead."

To Arthur, David's voice seemed to be taking on a slight nasal quality, connoting a sort of grating pretentiousness. "I see," Arthur replied. Several others sat down on the floor next to Arthur and David, forming a loose circle. Then, Donna also appeared and took a seat next to Arthur.

"The first thing we need to do is regain our focus," David said, seemingly addressing no one in particular as the size of the group around them continued to increase.

A cute girl with long brown hair, wearing a very short yellow miniskirt, sat down in a chair behind David. She crossed her legs, and Arthur glanced at her, feeling mildly exhilarated by his crotch-level view. *The times are a-changin'*, he thought. *The times they are a-changin'.*

"I've given this matter a lot of thought," David continued, "and it seems to me that we need to redirect our efforts."

"What are you proposing?" the girl in the miniskirt asked with wide, innocent eyes. Arthur took the opportunity to gaze at her legs, maintaining a deceptively blasé expression on his face.

David frowned. "I think we have been going at this thing from the wrong direction," he said. "We've focused our attention on the establishment leaders, on the people in positions of power and influence, on the ones we've seen as most responsible for this mess. But the plain truth is, they're not going to change. They simply are not, no matter what we do. They don't care what we think. They don't care what anyone thinks. So we need to focus our efforts on the other end. We need to direct our attention to the ordinary people who make continuation of this war possible."

"Like who?" Arthur asked. "Dow Chemical? They've been the target of—"

"I was thinking more in terms of the military," David interrupted, looking directly at Arthur. "Specifically, the soldiers, the guys our age doing the actual fighting over there. The ones directly responsible for inflicting the horrors of war."

"What horrors are you talking about?" Arthur replied, beginning to feel anger well up within himself. "Most of those guys are just trying to survive. For most of them, the whole thing is a living hell."

"Lieutenant Calley comes to mind," David snapped back. "Burning villages, decapitations, napalm, throwing prisoners who won't talk out of helicopters. We've managed to put some real psychopaths over there."

"Most of our troops don't engage in that kind of shit. Come on," Arthur countered.

"Maybe not, but even the more routine day-to-day killing is bad enough. I mean, what the hell are they doing there?"

"I'm sure many of them wonder the same thing. Don't you think our soldiers are as much victims of this thing as the Vietnamese?"

"No, I don't," David replied. "Not everyone who receives a draft notice ends up committing atrocities in Vietnam."

"But what choice do they have?" Arthur persisted. "The government is forcing them to go, forcing them to fight in order to survive. Now you're trying to say they're responsible for what's going down there?"

"They can become conscientious objectors. They can go to Canada. They can go underground. If they're already in the military, they can find sanctuary in Sweden."

"In other words, they can face a stiff prison sentence, along with loss of contact with their family and friends, loss of their whole way of life, loss of their identity as a person."

"Yes, if they think that's a *better* alternative to slaughtering innocent people while risking their own lives at the same time."

"That kind of puts them in a bind, don't you think? I mean, that leaves them with no good answers."

"Sometimes decisions are hard, but that doesn't mean you can walk away from them."

"You don't seem to be facing any hard decisions," Arthur said. "Life doesn't seem to be particularly difficult for you."

"I have a student deferment. If I lost it, I'd be in the same boat they're in."

"Something tells me you have enough pull to beat the draft, no matter what circumstances you find yourself in."

"Look, I agree that you may be right in some cases. Some of these guys probably are hapless victims who got caught up in a system they didn't understand and found themselves participating in a war before they knew what hit them. But there are a lot of other guys over there who actually know what they're doing. Think about the officers, the guys who went through ROTC or OCS. They're educated. They had four years to think about what they were going to do. And still, there they are, leading the killing and mayhem."

"I don't think it's quite that simple," Arthur responded softly, trying to suppress the rage he felt building up. "I still think the ones responsible for this thing are the old farts on top, not the young guys on the bottom who are being pressured to carry it out."

"Just following orders is no excuse," David said, shaking his head. "Do you think the men who ran the Nazi concentration camps, I mean the ones who carried out the day-to-day atrocities, were completely innocent? Are the troops in Vietnam who pump napalm through tunnels and bullets into civilian bystanders that different?"

"I think it's pretty easy to judge other people who find themselves in an extremely tough situation, especially when you're carrying out that judgment from a lofty perch, insulated from any of the blood and guts yourself."

"But—"

"No matter what their motivation," Arthur said, his voice rising, "no matter how much false bravado they mustered up to cover their fears, no matter how misguided the objectives given to them were, no matter how much they may have disagreed with those objectives, they did what they perceived as their duty. And they carried out their duty while risking their own lives and limbs." Arthur took in a deep breath, then blew it out strongly. "Can you imagine going out on jungle patrols for an entire year, watching out for snipers, trying to avoid stepping on land mines? Can you imagine the disillusionment? I don't think so. I think harassing the veterans who come back from Vietnam is unfair and mean spirited. They're part of us. They've been through a lot. Many of them have been messed up by the experience. They need our support. They need our appreciation. They sure as hell don't need our condemnation."

"So we're supposed to celebrate the baby killers," David sneered. A final surge of anger started to bring Arthur to his feet, but Donna placed her hand on his forearm.

"Arthur's brother was killed in Vietnam," she interjected. "They were close."

"I see," David answered slowly, stroking his beard. "But that doesn't change *anything*. In fact, *that's* the point. A lot of brothers are being killed over there, and a lot of sisters and parents and children, as well. Both Vietnamese and American."

"This is going nowhere," Arthur said, rising slowly to his feet. He glanced at Donna to more or less assure her that he was under control. "I think our troops, who for the most part are serving honorably, are being taken advantage of by our leaders. And I think our leaders are the ones who should be held accountable. I think trying to scapegoat our soldiers and veterans shows a real lack of leadership on your part. And I mean you alone." Arthur leveled a hard stare at David, then turned and walked toward the door.

"There are none so blind as those who will not see," David called to him.

"I couldn't agree more," Arthur muttered, slamming the door.

Back in their room, Arthur sat on the edge of one of the beds, staring at the floor as Donna entered quietly. "I'm sorry," he said.

"The last thing I intended to do here was get into a debate with one of your so-called leaders, but I couldn't just sit there and listen to his condescending bullshit . . . I don't know."

"I know," Donna replied quietly, taking a seat at the end of the bed. "David has some good ideas, but he has trouble dealing with what he sees as criticism. I think he's just trying to find a way help to stop the war."

"Yeah, but to blame the vets and the guys being drafted?" Arthur closed his eyes and shook his head.

"He's desperate. Nothing is working."

"Maybe *he* doesn't think anything is working, but there *is* promise in the air."

"Like what?"

"Well, like I said earlier, Nixon is bringing some of the troops home. That's at least something."

"But the war is still going strong," Donna sighed. "North Vietnam is sending fresh troops in every day, and Nixon is going to probably resume the bombing. He's not going to give up. He just likes playing mind games."

"Maybe," Arthur replied, "but this mess might be too big for a group of college students to deal with." Donna shot a look at him, causing him to pull his head back sharply. "Not that the effort isn't worthwhile. But the whole thing may just be too much for any group to influence, no matter how solid the effort is."

"That may be part of the problem," Donna replied wistfully.

"What do you mean?"

"I don't think we are getting a solid effort these days. I think our top leadership is coming unglued. I have to agree with you that harassing the vets as they come back from Vietnam is misguided and wrong, but it doesn't stop there."

"You think the SDS leadership is coming unglued?"

"Yes, take the Democratic Convention last year in Chicago." Donna shook her head. "Tom Hayden, one of our most prominent leaders, got caught letting the air out of a delegate's tires. My God, that made us look like a bunch of silly pranksters instead of a serious political movement. And then there's the trial of the Chicago Seven—Hayden and Jerry Rubin showing up in court like it's a big joke, blowing kisses to the jury, firing insults at the judge. It was like they were turning our entire effort into some kind of media circus."

"The media does seem to be playing more of a role."

"What are you saying?" Donna asked with a sigh.

"Well, maybe there is too much playing to the media. As you say, Hayden and Jerry Rubin seem to enjoy playing to it. And on the other side, Spiro Agnew is making a career out of playing to it. And Nixon certainly seems to enjoy being in front of the cameras these days. Maybe if some of these guys spent more time working on solutions and less time working on their television image, they could bring this stupid-ass war to an end."

"Maybe. But I think the problem goes a little deeper than that."

"What do you mean?"

"I think people hate making tough decisions. I think they're always looking for the easy way out."

"What people?" Arthur asked.

"The American people."

"I don't follow you."

"Well, in 1964, Barry Goldwater took the position that the United States should do whatever it takes to win in Vietnam. He based his position on the idea that it doesn't make sense to get into a war you're not committed to winning. Lyndon Johnson took the position that we could have it both ways. We didn't have to give up, but at the same time, we could wind the war down. He lied, of course, and ended up escalating the war himself. But he managed to paint Goldwater as an extremist, and he won the election in a landslide. Then, in 1968, Eugene McCarthy came along and said we should simply get out of Vietnam. Again, don't fight a war that you're not committed to winning. But he too was painted as an extremist and couldn't even get the Democratic nomination. Instead, the American people elected

Richard Nixon, who once again told them they could have it both ways: an honorable end to the war without conceding to North Vietnam. But obviously, he lied as well. To me, the lesson is that the American people will go for the comforting lie every time."

"You sound discouraged," Arthur said.

"I am. I can just imagine my father seeing Tom Hayden on television and then telling me he can't believe I'm part of an organization being led by someone like that. I mean, Hayden has his good moments, but—"

"How about your mother?"

"She would be even worse. But the thing is, I can't give up. No matter how ridiculous the politics in this country are, the killing and suffering in Vietnam are real."

"So are you going to work with this David Payton tomorrow? If so, I hope I didn't screw things up for you too much tonight. I really mean that."

"I don't know. I'll do what I can. He's not the only one here."

"Yeah, I suppose. Who was that girl sitting behind him in the chair?"

"Oh, you mean Karen, the girl with the thigh-high miniskirt?" Donna raised her eyebrows.

"Oh, was she wearing a miniskirt?" Arthur asked, with exaggerated innocence. "I didn't really notice." He smiled at Donna.

"I can see I'm going to have to keep a close eye on you," she replied. They rolled into a close embrace on the bed.

"So. Is the time right now?" he asked, raising his head a bit.

"Yes," she answered, holding him tightly. "Yes it is."

The next day, Donna left early, and Arthur spent most of the morning sleeping in. When he finally did get up, he made some coffee and began reading the morning newspaper, which had been left outside their door. But as he scanned the sports page, it suddenly occurred to him that he could call Billie Lee. *Why not?* he thought. Despite the intimacy that he had shared with Donna the night before, Billie Lee was Billie Lee. To help prevent any feelings of guilt from dampening his building excitement, he focused on the task at hand. Let's see, he reasoned, Donna will be preoccupied with meetings the rest of the day, so the question is, is Billie Lee available? Arthur winced as he realized that he hadn't called her as he said he would. But he could certainly try now. What did he have to lose? Feeling nervous, he picked up the receiver and dialed Billie Lee's number. She answered on the second ring.

"So where are you staying?" Billie Lee asked.

"The Palmer House."

"That's great. That's not far from my place at all. Why don't I come over and meet you for a drink?"

"That sounds good. Or maybe I could come over to your place? The thing is, I'm sharing a room with a couple of guys, and I never know when they're going to barge in on me."

"Okay, let me tell you how to get here. Just don't keep me waiting too long."

Early that afternoon, Arthur knocked at Billie Lee's door. She answered wearing nothing but a tailored silk shirt. Arthur was dumbfounded. Her blonde hair cascaded freely down in front, and her tan legs contrasted vividly with the white fabric that barely covered her bottom.

"Come in," she said brightly. "I couldn't see any reason to get dressed up."

"No. No reason to do something like that. You look very hot, by the way."

"You really think so, do you?" Billie Lee pulled at the buttons on his shirt.

About an hour and a half later, Arthur awoke from a sound sleep. Billie Lee lay next to him with her eyes open, her naked hip pressed against his. "Are you awake?" she asked, rolling over to face him, propping herself up on one elbow.

"Yeah. What time is it?"

"You didn't sleep long. Just half an hour or so."

"I really dropped off. That was great."

"Thanks," Billie Lee replied, smiling. "You were great, too."

"I have to be getting back," Arthur said. "Nothing but meetings from here on out. But we have to do this again; I mean, we have to get together again. Maybe I could come over next weekend."

"Sure. Give me a call. We'll plan something." Billie Lee pulled Arthur's pillow toward her and cradled it in her arms. "Do you really have to go back to South Bend this evening?"

Yes," Arthur answered, climbing out of the bed and pulling on his pants. "I'd rather stay here with you, but I can't."

"I guess some SDS students are holding meetings today, over at the hotel where you're staying," Billie Lee said, looking at him with wide eyes.

"Really? Are you going to take part?"

"No. I'll leave that for the kids still in college."

"I guess you've outgrown SDS, in a way," Arthur said. With his shirt now on, he sat down on the side of the bed to put on his socks and shoes.

"More than you know. Even at the time Joshua was killed, I was becoming involved with a project that went way beyond the scope of regular SDS."

"Like what?"

"You don't want to know about it. You really don't."

"Sure I do," Arthur insisted congenially. "Go ahead."

"Well, at the time, a small group of us were ready to take things to the next level. But I shouldn't really get into it."

"That's okay. You can tell me. I'm not going to say anything to anyone."

"Okay. I guess I can tell you a little about it, because you're not going to believe me anyway."

"Try me."

"Okay. This very select group I was in thought SDS was getting nowhere in stopping the war. We tried a lot of things, but nothing worked. So after a lot of thought—are you ready for this—we decided to build a small nuclear bomb."

"A nuclear bomb?" Arthur gave her an incredulous look. His shoe fell to the floor. "Why?"

"I told you, you wouldn't believe me."

"What were you going to do with this *bomb*?"

"We were going to place it near a government installation of some kind and then notify the authorities right away. We weren't going to detonate it or anything."

"Why?"

"Because we wanted the government to recognize us as a serious nuclear threat, like it does other countries in the world. We figured that was the only way we could get through to them. It makes sense, if you think about it. Even though we weren't going to do anything destructive, we did want to scare the living hell out of them and let them know they weren't dealing with a bunch of naïve college kids. We believed this was our only hope of getting them to negotiate an end to the war with us."

"And Joshua was into this plan?"

"Oh, yes, he was a big part of it. He was going to convert uranium into plutonium for us."

"How was he going to do that?"

"I can't give you any specifics, but if you're ever interested in joining a project like that, let me know. I could introduce you to some people who could make it happen."

"You're still planning to go through with this thing?"

"I've already said way too much. I may have even put you in jeopardy. Just think about it. If you're interested, let me know."

"Sure," Arthur replied.

Early that evening, at about five thirty, Arthur met up with Donna in their room and was genuinely glad to see her. She was busy looking for something in her suitcase and simply glanced up at him and said hello.

He returned her greeting and feeling energized from his tryst with Billie Lee, imagined that he now appreciated Donna even more. "I hope things went okay today," Arthur said. "I slept in. I guess I was tired, but I feel better now."

"That's good. I mean, that you feel better." She closed the suitcase. "This has been a long day."

"Do you want to get something to eat? Go out to a nice restaurant? Get away from the hotel for a while?"

"No, I just want to stay here with you tonight. Let's order something from room service and spend the evening in—see an old movie or something." She sat down next to Arthur and inched closer to him.

He moved toward her and put his arm around her. "If you say so." He briefly pressed his head against hers. "This doesn't have anything to do with last night, does it? I mean, with me getting upset and arguing with Prince David?"

"No, no. Don't worry about it. Nothing came of that."

"Don't you have any meetings or parties to go to tonight?"

"Nothing I want to go to." Donna pulled away and backed up on the bed. "You know, you would think these guys would be a little more enlightened."

"What do you mean?"

"I mean, they're supposed to be part of a new social awareness, but they don't really care what the women have to say about anything. It's like we're not even there."

"What happened?" Arthur put his hand on her arm.

"You don't want to hear the sordid details."

"Of course I do. What happened?"

"Well, Sandy and I put together this idea for one of the meetings that we thought was pretty good. We called it campus cluster support, or CCS for short. We figured that schools that are close together geographically could form groups, or clusters, and that the members of each cluster would be expected to support the demonstrations of fellow members. We pictured a network of these clusters all over the country with activities coordinated so that turnout on small or conservative campuses like Notre Dame would be improved right away."

"The guys didn't like the idea?"

"The guys didn't even *listen* to the idea. Every time Sandy or I tried to say something, one of our so-called leaders would jump up and start talking in vague generalities—the big picture, conceptual thinking. The only problem was, they never said anything new or practical. It was like they were off in their own world. And in the end, all they wanted from us, the submissive females, was coffee or someone to make copies for them. I didn't even go to some of the sessions this afternoon. I was too pissed off."

"Staying in the room all night sounds fine to me. Like you said, we could catch an old movie, maybe a horror flick."

"*You're* not like that, are you? You don't expect women to wait on you and never express their opinions?"

"I've never asked you for coffee or copies. I hope you've noticed that." Arthur smiled.

"No, really, do you think women can be intelligent?"

"Just so you know, one of the things that most attracts me to a girl is her intelligence. And as for you, I think you're brilliant."

"You're hopeless," Donna said, while running her fingers through his hair.

෴

The next day, in a small Italian restaurant in Oak Park, Vic and his daughter ordered fettuccine Alfredo. "So, I understand you're thinking about dropping out of school next semester," Vic said.

"That's right. I just don't see the point."

"You don't see the point?" Vic rolled his eyes. "What about being a teacher? What about working with kids? I thought that's what you wanted. I thought that was a big deal to you. Just last year, you—"

"It was. It may be again someday, but not now."

"So what happened? Your mother tells me you've been seeing some hippie lately. Is that what's behind all of this?"

"It doesn't have anything to do with Warren, if that's what you mean. Believe it or not, I can think for myself."

"I know you can think for yourself. I'm well aware of that, but why would you throw away the chance for a teaching career? It seemed so important, then all of a sudden . . . I don't get it. Can you see why I'm confused?"

"I suppose. It's just that I've learned to see things more clearly. I have a different perspective now."

"A different perspective? Concerning what?"

"Concerning everything—school, the establishment, exploitation of people. I don't want to be a part of the system anymore."

"And you got this wondrous perspective since last summer?"

"If you're going to patronize me, I can just—"

"No, no. I'm sorry. I am. I'm just trying to understand. So what do you mean when you say 'exploitation of people'? Who does this?"

"The system—schools, corporations, the military. Most people are used by these organizations, then thrown away. Only a few actually benefit."

"You really believe that?"

"Sure. Take colleges and universities, for example. Most kids believe in the beginning that they can earn a degree and get a good job after they graduate. But a large majority of them don't make it. The schools take their money, and these kids get nothing in return except low grades and a sense of failure."

"Not all kids fail. You're still doing okay, aren't you? Your mother said—"

"This isn't about my grades."

"What about this Warren character?"

"He's doing okay, too. And he's majoring in aeronautical engineering, which isn't that easy. And he's got a lot going on. But that's not the point."

"Okay, what *is* the point?"

"What bothers me is, I'm actually training to become *part* of the system. If I become a teacher, I'll be giving grades to kids myself. I'll be saying that some kids are college material, some kids are borderline, and some kids are only qualified to learn a trade or do general labor. It's like the selection process at college, only at a lower level. Why should a high school English teacher have that kind of influence? It doesn't make sense."

"You don't see a need for reading and writing skills in the professions?"

"Yes, but the system is so inflexible, and grades are so permanent. Maybe you're at a point in your life when you're having serious personal problems, like poverty or a bad home environment. These things are very common today. Or maybe you're just not motivated, because you're immature or feel out of place—whatever. That doesn't mean it's going to be that way forever. But the grades that you earn during that time in your life do follow you around forever like a black cloud, and I would be expected to assign those grades."

"You don't think there should be consequences for what you do or don't do in life?"

"I think the consequences of a bad academic record are too severe. I don't think you should be labeled at an early age with failure that you could reverse at a later time if you had the chance. I think everyone should get as many chances as they need. And I don't think the opportunity to get ahead should be left up to the teachers in some school system, who many times aren't that competent or fair in the first place."

"The world is a competitive place. There's no way to avoid that."

"Competition can be very destructive."

"Don't you think the world would be kind of dull without competition?"

"If people want to compete for some award in the arts, or some championship trophy in sports, or some political office, that's fine. That's not what I'm talking about. But things like food and shelter and education and health care should be available to everyone, at least at some basic level, no matter what. Otherwise, people who don't play the game well, or don't have a fair chance to play because of background or race, get caught up in a cycle of ignorance and poverty. And worse yet, their kids do, too."

"So you're talking about some kind of utopian Marxist scheme—from each according to their ability, to each according to their need. I know that kind of thing is popular on campuses these days."

"No. It's not quite that simple."

"Well, you must be aware that this country has been going in a Marxist direction for quite a while now. There are all kinds of government programs in place like welfare, the Job Corps, Social Security."

"And yet there's poverty and prejudice everywhere you look. What I'm talking about is changing individual perceptions about life: incorporating love and empathy into the mix for a change, seeing each other as we are and caring for each other anyway. Recognizing that just going through human existence is enough of a trial. We don't need to make it harder than it already is."

"So you're saying, love thy neighbor."

"That's better than beat thy neighbor's brains out."

"But you can't get away from competition. It's part of who we are. Any time two people want the same thing, you have competition. And it doesn't matter if they're in a capitalist country, a Communist country, or a peasant village in Vietnam. People will compete for things they want. At least capitalist countries are upfront about competition, which usually makes things fairer."

"Do you *really* think things are fair in this country?"

"More so than in other countries. Between our free press and open capitalist system, there's less chance of backroom shenanigans than what you see in other places around the world."

"I don't know about that. Almost everybody cheats if they get the chance. Take the FBI. It doesn't go out of its way to deal fairly with political enemies. It uses every trick it can."

"That's different. The Bureau deals with criminals and foreign agents who have no respect for our laws or way of life.

Sometimes, the only way to defend yourself against people like that is through deception followed by brute force."

"Maybe, but the definition of who's a criminal seems to be getting wider all the time."

"Look, for all of its faults, the system that we have right now in this country works about as well as any system can. We're just human beings. We're never going to reach the kind of heaven on earth that you seem to be searching for."

"But we could make a start. And, in a way, you touch on a good point. When ministers talk about heaven, how great it's supposed to be and all after we die, they never say anything about the wonderful competitive environment that exists there. That must say something about the nature of competition."

"Look, all I want to see you do is take care of the business that's in front of you today. If you do that, I can tell you from experience that heaven and all the other things that come tomorrow will take care of themselves."

"And I'm just saying life doesn't have to be so harsh and unfeeling."

"Sometimes, I'm afraid it does," Vic concluded.

৯

That evening, having dropped Donna off at the dorm earlier, Arthur was unpacking his suitcase when Jeffrey called. "So, did you pull it off?" Jeffrey asked.

"You mean seeing Billie Lee when I was in Chicago? Yeah, I guess you could say I pulled it off."

"And you managed to do it without getting caught?"

"Yeah, things worked out okay." Arthur felt awkward talking with Jeffrey about Billie Lee and wondered why he had ever mentioned anything about her to him in the first place.

"So, is she still looking into the death of that black student who was murdered? What was his name?"

"Joshua Taylor. She didn't say anything about his murder this time, but she did tell me something about him."

"What?"

"Well, I'm not supposed to say anything about it to anyone, so I would appreciate it if you keep anything I tell you confidential."

"Sure."

"Apparently, before he was killed, they were working together on a secret plan to force an end to the war."

"That sounds ambitious enough. What were they going to do?"

"They were going to make a small nuclear bomb. Then they were going to plant it in some public place but let the government know immediately where it was. The idea was to prove they had nuclear capability so the government would have to listen to what they had to say. Then, they were going to demand that the United States pull out of Vietnam, or else."

"Or else what?"

"The next bomb this group planted would be detonated, I guess. But I don't think they expected things to go that far."

"I have to tell you, that plan sounds really crazy. I know you have a thing going with this girl, but do you really want to get mixed up with someone like that? That's probably why the FBI is interested in her."

"I know. The whole thing does sound crazy, but she seems very serious about it. And sooner or later, somebody *is* going to have to do something about that stupid war. She's right about that part."

"I don't know," Jeffrey mumbled.

"I guess the plan was for Joshua to convert some low-grade uranium into weapons-grade material for the bomb. She even suggested that I could take his place on the project, if I wanted. I backed away from her offer, of course, but I have to admit, I do get the feeling I may be getting in over my head."

"Do you think that's what the easy sex is about, her trying to bring you into the plan? Not that you're not a stud, of course."

"I don't know. I guess we'll just have to see how things go from here."

"You know, this whole thing sounds pretty heavy to me. I'm glad you let me know about it."

"Yeah, I guess."

"Well, this way you don't have to feel like the Lone Ranger or anything. I'm glad you clued me in."

"I suppose. I guess I don't know how real any of this business about a bomb actually is. The only thing I know for sure is real is the sex."

Chapter Eleven

Several weeks later, Donna and Arthur stood at the kitchen counter in his apartment looking over an array of culinary items that included bowls, pans, spoons, measuring cups, flour, and sugar. "You may have lived a sheltered life up until now," Arthur said, affecting an aloof air, "but the time has come for you to learn the art of baking from a true master. I don't want to brag, but back in Paris I was the toast of the town."

Outside a cold, unrelenting rain pelted the roof.

"I see," Donna replied. "Apparently you've managed to become quite the domestic. Maybe my father should hire you as a master chef. We could have a torrid love affair behind his back."

"We're already having a torrid love affair behind his back. Besides, he probably couldn't afford me. Talent doesn't come cheap, you know."

"So what would your family think about our torrid love affair? Would they be shocked, or would they think this a step in the right direction?"

"I don't know," Arthur answered, speaking normally. He glanced out the window as lightening flashed and a peal of thunder sounded. "My father doesn't seem to like anything I do, but my mother would probably be okay with it. Of course, she'd want us to get married right away and start producing grandchildren for her."

"I can't imagine being married, at least not yet."

"Me either. There's plenty of time for that."

Arthur started mixing some of the ingredients with a wooden spoon. "I hope these brownies work. Anything to stop inhaling. It's been reaming my lungs out like crazy lately."

"Your body is trying to tell you something," Donna said.

"I guess." Arthur set the spoon on the counter. "You know, when Jeffrey turned me on to this recipe, he told me that the high you get from *eating* grass is actually better than the high you get from smoking it. So I don't know why more people aren't finding a way to eat it."

"At least you're not doing psychedelics anymore. I can't imagine what that would be like."

"Like being awake during a crazy dream. I've had enough of that forever. Life is strange enough. I don't need anything to intensify the experience."

"So you just mix the grass in with the other stuff? Donna asked.

"You make it sound so simple. You dismiss the *years* of study that went into this process."

"Right. So really, what are we supposed to do?"

"Okay," Arthur replied, holding up a sheet of lined paper with the recipe on it. "I think we've got everything here but the magic ingredient." Arthur laid the recipe on the countertop. "The grass should be in that plastic bag right over there."

Donna peered into the bag. "Is this supposed to be quality stuff? It could be Lipton's tea, for all I know."

"You never have been into drugs that much, have you?"

"Not before you. You've definitely been a negative influence on my life. I'll have to mention that to my father."

"You don't actually see your father that much, do you?"

"No." Donna shrugged. "Not lately."

"So what are you planning to do next year? I mean, after you graduate."

"I don't know. Nothing definite. Why do you ask?" Donna took a step back and placed one hand on her hip.

"I don't know. I was just wondering. It's nothing to get angry about."

"Who said I'm angry?" Donna demanded, placing her other hand on her other hip.

"I would be if I were willing to take my life into my own hands, but I'm not. Let's forget I brought it up. Sorry."

"I'm not angry."

"Fine. I wasn't trying to make you angry, I really wasn't."

"It's just that you're so hard to read at times," Donna said. "I can never tell what you're really thinking." She let her hands drop.

"Hard to read? I don't think so."

"You *are*. I have to pry everything out of you, and I mean everything. You haven't told me one personal thing about yourself that I haven't had to drag out. It makes me wonder sometimes."

"About what?" Arthur asked, now thoroughly confused. "I thought I told you everything. I've been more open with you than anyone I've ever known."

"Open, more open? If you say so. Maybe it's just the way you are."

Arthur didn't say anything.

"Some people are like that," she mumbled, mostly to herself. "They keep everything bottled up inside."

"Do you really think I'm keeping something from you?" For the first time, Arthur's inflection revealed a trace of concern. He wondered if she knew about Billie Lee.

"No, it's not that, exactly," Donna replied, sounding exasperated.

"Good, because I'm not keeping any secrets."

"It's just that . . . well, we've slept together a number of times now, and you've never told me how you feel about me."

"Oh." Arthur sighed, relieved that Billie Lee was apparently not the issue. "Well, I care a lot about you. I thought you knew that. I thought you could tell by the way I act around you."

"I know you like the sex, but do you like *me*? Do you like being with me? Do you see any kind of future for us, or is this just a passing fling for you?"

"Are you talking about something permanent?" Arthur looked at her intently. "I really haven't given it a lot of thought, but I—"

"No, I wasn't talking specifically about that. I just meant agreeing to be there for each other now. Today. It doesn't have to be something formal, like getting married, at least not at this point."

"If you want, you can move in with me at any time. Seriously, move in this afternoon," Arthur said.

Just then, their conversation was interrupted by a series of loud knocks at the front door. Arthur grabbed the bag of marijuana, looked frantically around the room, then stuck it in the freezer. "If that's the police, they'll need a warrant to search the place," he explained. Standing with Donna behind the closed front door, trying to sound intimidating, he called out, "Who is it?"

"Your father. It's raining out here," came the reply.

Arthur opened the door. "Hey, Dad, great to see you. I want you to meet a friend, Donna Will."

"A very pretty girl," Arthur's father said, nodding at her.

"Come in and sit down. It's been months. How are things going? How's Mom?"

Arthur's father stepped in, looked around, took off his raincoat, and handed it to Arthur. He then took a seat in the easy chair, putting the canvas bag that he had been carrying on the floor next to him. After hanging up the raincoat, Arthur and Donna sat down on the couch, facing him. "Your mother is fine, but she's not too happy with me right now."

"Why?"

"I just got orders for 'Nam. I ship out the first of the month." Arthur's father looked pleased.

"How did that happen? I thought you were slated to stay at the Pentagon until you retire. I thought the whole thing was carved in stone."

"I volunteered. That's why your mother is so upset. But I couldn't stand being on the periphery any longer. The war is being lost, the troops are coming home, and nobody wants to do anything about it except bury their head in the sand."

"What are you going to do over there?"

"I'm going to head up an intelligence unit. This isn't like World War II. I finally figured that out. This is guerrilla warfare, which means intelligence is the key to everything."

"It's been a guerrilla war all along."

"Yes, I know. But what we've had for the past five years is an absurd situation in which our troops have been labeled as the bad guys. No matter what our intentions, the South Vietnamese have viewed us as an invading enemy, which means we never know when an attack is going to take place or where a land mine is planted. We don't know a damned thing because we don't have the trust and cooperation of the South Vietnamese people—the peasants in the villages, the ones who know what's going on and could help us if they wanted to. This whole thing comes down to winning the people over and getting from them the information that we need to be effective."

"Trying to win the hearts and minds of the South Vietnamese goes back to the Johnson administration. It didn't work," Arthur said.

"We didn't have enough of the right kind of people over there then. Too many just going through the motions, too many amateurs."

"And you think you can change all that?"

"I can't do it all, but I can lead. I can show others how it's done. I can go over there and set up an intelligence network that produces vital information, information that in turn results in victories on the battlefield. And once that pattern is set, once that pattern is duplicated, the war will be over within months. It's like everything else—primarily a matter of execution."

"Why would the South Vietnamese suddenly start cooperating with you? You're of a different race, from a completely different culture. You represent a country that has been burning their villages and turning them into refugees."

"It's a matter of winning their respect. Respect that comes from knowing an individual's true character, one on one. Don't ever underestimate how important that is. Once that respect is established, it will grow. Strong relationships will form naturally. The result will be trust."

"I don't know," Arthur replied.

"During World War II we had that respect from the Germans. Even though they were our enemy, they respected us because they knew us, knew what we were made of. Now we have to win that kind of respect from the Vietnamese."

"That may not be easy," said Donna, who up to that point had been listening quietly.

"Nobody said it would be," Arthur's father shot back as his head turned involuntarily in her direction.

"The Vietnamese are fiercely nationalistic," Donna continued. "The Chinese tried to dominate them for centuries, followed by the French and the Japanese. But the Vietnamese never gave up. Even after being enslaved for generations, they kept fighting, kept resisting, kept going until they got their independence back."

"The United States is not trying to enslave anyone," Arthur's father argued. "Just the opposite. We're trying to ensure their freedom, give them self-government, just like South Korea."

"I don't think the Viet Cong see it that way," Donna replied. "From their point of view, we're foreigners trying to impose our system on them. They don't want it. They think there are too many strings attached." Donna's voice remained soft and even.

Arthur's father let out a sigh, then looked at Arthur. "Before I forget, I brought something for you." He opened the canvas bag and took out an ammo belt with a black leather holster. He then pulled back the flap on the holster and drew out a German Luger. "I picked this up in Italy during the war. They were easy to get back then. I always thought I would give it to you or Tom when you were old enough, but I never got around to it. Semiautomatic. It's a nice weapon."

"Thanks, Dad," Arthur replied, grimacing slightly. "I don't know what to say."

"You'll need to keep it clean. Protect the metal. And I brought a box of shells, too. It's still quite functional."

"I don't think I'll have much use for it, but I'll take care of it."

"Good. You do that." Arthur's father stood up. "Well, look, I've got a plane to catch. I just stopped off here to say hello before I report for briefings."

"You have to go so soon?" Donna asked.

"Yeah. The Army never lets up, kind of like those Vietnamese patriots you were talking about." He studied her briefly, then turned to Arthur.

"How's Mom holding up?" Arthur asked, frowning a bit.

"As well as can be expected. She hasn't really gotten over Tom. Now she's afraid the same thing will happen to me."

"But you're not afraid of that?"

"I should have been killed five, maybe six, times during World War II. When you go through something like that, you learn not to worry about death so much. When your number's up, it's up. Otherwise, you keep going."

"You'd rather go down in combat than behind a desk."

"I wouldn't put it that way. I'm interested in contributing to the effort, not dying in battle. Despite what you may think, I don't have a death wish. I simply want to help the Army pull out a win."

"I suppose," Arthur mumbled.

After the door closed behind Arthur's father, Donna said, "I hope you appreciate the fact I didn't say a word about the Luger."

"It's always about winning with him," Arthur sighed, looking past her. "Sometimes he makes the war sound almost reasonable."

༖

Later that day, Susie-Q waited for Vic in the furnished apartment that he had rented, having moved out of his home of twenty years in Oak Park. As she looked around, opening and closing closet doors and cabinets, Susie-Q could tell that the place had been refurbished recently and the faint smell of new carpeting still lingered. Continuing her tour from one room to the next, she reflected on her association with Vic and concluded that he was basically a very decent guy who simply needed help through a rough time.

Vic had moved into the apartment several weeks earlier, following an almost anticlimactic scene with his wife, Cathy. As the exchange began, he simply presented her with the private investigator's report.

"Okay, so you got me," Cathy said. "So I want something more out of life than being married to the goddamn FBI."

"Like what?"

"I want feeling. I want sharing. I want to be appreciated. I don't know; there's something so goddamn dark and gloomy about your life, and it's taking over mine. I can't stand that. When Denise was little, I guess I didn't notice so much, or maybe things were different then. I don't know. But being around you now is like living in a cemetery. It really is."

"And things are different with this Bob character?"

"Yes. When I go into work and see him, everything is exciting and full. Yes, the sex is great, but it's part of something bigger, part of feeling alive. And he really cares what I think, too. Can you imagine how different that is for me?"

Vic didn't respond.

"And he shares his feelings about everything, not just his well-formed opinions, but his actual feelings. It's hard to explain."

"I think you've explained it fairly well. You're having a cheap affair with your boss."

"God, what's the point in trying to talk with you?"

"What about family? What about Denise? People are attracted to each other all the time, but they don't rut like animals and throw away everything that's important. Family used to mean something."

"Yes, I know. Women used to sacrifice their happiness for all kinds of reasons, but times are changing. Women want fulfillment just as much as men, and that includes emotional fulfillment. I'm sorry, but I'm not going to throw away my remaining years by clinging to an ideal that isn't really true. I'm just not going to do it."

"Don't worry. Nobody's asking you to. It will take me less than a day to move the hell out of here and get a lawyer. Apparently, you already have one."

Once he had left his wife, Vic visited Susie-Q at the massage parlor as often as he could. And with each exhilarating session, he found his affection for her growing. In addition to her youth and good looks, and the incredible sex, she was easy to talk to, easy to open up with about anything. During his most recent visit, he had asked if she would consider spending the night at his place sometime, and to his surprise, she agreed immediately, spelling out exactly what the additional cost to him would be. Grateful for the opportunity to actually lay next to her for an extended period, Vic set a date right away, then closed his eyes as she lifted the towel. Half an hour later, following a particularly gratifying sexual release, he casually asked her what she would do when she grew tired of giving massages, not that it would be any time soon, he hoped.

"If I tell you, you have to promise not to tell anyone else."

"Who would I tell?"

"I know. But promise."

"Okay. I won't tell anyone."

"I'm working on a master's in psychology. And when I'm finished, I'm going for a PhD."

"No. Where?"

"Northwestern. My grades are good, too. I'm going to be an analyst."

"You'll probably know a lot more about human nature than most analysts."

"That's truer than you realize. Most of what I do now is actually mental."

"You really think so?"

"Sure. I create a sexual world for my clients, a world that is as close to their ideal as possible. That takes understanding and insight on my part. Take your situation with your wife. I make it possible for you to turn things around, to change a situation that isn't fair to you into one that's better than fair."

"You've certainly done that," Vic agreed quietly.

"I hope so, because that's my job. That's what I'm paid to do, to cheat nature at every turn. As I said before, nature is often terribly cruel and deserves to be cheated. I don't know why some people have such trouble recognizing that."

"And you see yourself doing the same kind of thing as an analyst?"

"Sure. Nature loves to play terrible mind games with people, creating all kinds of problems for them. My job will be to undo the mind games, to undo the suffering caused by natural reactions to bad things in life."

"So, you think life is naturally cruel and unfair."

"It certainly can be, more for some people than others. I think we're all programmed biochemically to need certain things like acceptance, respect, success, love, sex. But some people aren't able to get what they want or need."

"We're all . . . programmed biochemically?"

"Well, that's the way I see things. As an undergraduate, I had a double major in psychology and biological science. And while I've always thought the theories of people like Freud and Jung were interesting, I feel that most of our behavior is driven biochemically by what we call feelings, which to me is just another word for instinct."

"You think our feelings are instinctual?"

"Yes, in the sense that they are triggered chemically by hormones in response to various mental or physical stimuli. I mean, if you see something you want, there's usually an emotional component to that desire. And I think this makes us just as instinctual as the other animals. We like to think our behavior is more rational than that of the lower animals, but if you look around, you can see that that's not true. Most of our behavior is based on emotion. We may cleverly cover our motives with rationalizations, but if you dig deep enough, you'll find some emotional impetus."

"So we're all animals."

"Yes, but humans do have language, which, among other things, can help us understand the interaction between the chemistry going on in our brains and the things we face in the world around us."

"And sex is one of the things we need but don't always get?"

"Exactly. Just like all living things, we have a strong drive to reproduce. We don't know why, but it's there, no question about it. Sometimes, I think it's like we're all pawns in some elaborate game that we're not in on. And my job is to play the game—and cheat. Now, I cheat by helping guys get past social hurdles that prevent them from having sex. In the future, I'll cheat by helping people get past mental hurdles that prevent them from having peace of mind."

"Well, if I ever have any mental problems in the future, you'll be the first analyst I see."

୭

As Susie-Q continued to wait for Vic, she sat down on the living room couch, picked up a newspaper, and began reading. Suddenly, she heard the lock turning in the front door and assumed that Vic had arrived earlier than expected. "Vic, is that you?" she called.

"No," answered Denise as she entered the room. "I'm his daughter. Who are you?"

"I'm Susan. Your father said he was going to be here in about half an hour, so I thought—"

"You just let yourself in?"

"Yes, he gave me a key. We're working on a case together."

"Really." Denise sat down in a chair facing Susie-Q. "Do you mind if I ask you a question?"

"No, go ahead."

Denise cleared her throat. "How old are you?"

Susie-Q laughed. "Not that old. I'm twenty-four. But I do know I'm older than you are because your dad said you were in your second year of college."

"He's talked to you about me?"

"Sure, some, just in passing. Nothing personal though."

"And you work for the FBI?"

"Yes."

"You must have finished school then. I know you have to have a degree to get in, usually law or business."

"I have a degree in psychology. I'm helping your dad do some profiling."

"I see," Denise said, looking around the room.

"I don't work full time for the FBI. The thing with your dad is just a freelance assignment. Mostly, I'm doing graduate work in psychology. I'll be starting on a PhD soon."

"Really." Denise frowned. "I'm not sure I even want to finish my bachelor's degree. I'm thinking seriously about going back and dropping out."

"Why?"

"I don't know. I just don't fit in. So many silly games and so many people that are just plain mean."

"Well, yes, I think everyone feels that way at one time or another. But you can work your way past that."

"Maybe, but I want to find a place where I actually belong, where people are more enlightened and caring. I don't want to become a teacher and start a family as if nothing's wrong with the system. I want to be a part of something better first, something I can actually believe in. I need that."

"If you don't want to play other people's games, you need money. Money may not change the way things are, but with it you don't have to let the way things are affect you as much."

"You learned that studying psychology?"

"No, just observation."

"That seems a little cold to me, like trying to buy your way out. I want real relationships based on who I am and who other people are, not based on who has money."

"But if you have money, everything falls into place. You don't have to worry about getting along with people who do things you don't like. And you don't have to worry about *impressing* anybody. Money gives you the power to be who you really are."

"What about finding love? Money doesn't help you do that."

"Oh, like true love?"

"Yes."

"Well. In my opinion—again, just from observation—true love is an illusion. Not that we aren't attracted to each other from time to time. We are. But it never lasts, at least not usually. I mean, just look at married couples today."

"Like my parents."

"I wasn't talking about them, necessarily, but yes, I suppose they are an example. Like so many people, they found themselves in a marriage that doesn't work anymore."

"And money helps that?"

"Yes. Because money gives you the freedom to react honestly. If two people with money are attracted to each other, they get together. Then, if the time comes to break up, they simply do it. No financial entanglements, no dependencies, no hard feelings."

"What about kids?"

"Not a problem if you have money. A big problem if you don't, like a lot of single mothers these days."

"I don't know. I think there must be a better way." Denise stood up to leave. "Could you do me a favor?"

"Sure. What is it?

"Could you tell my dad I was here and that I'll see him later?"

"Okay, but he should be here any time. Are you sure?"

"Yes," replied Denise, turning toward the door. "I'm sure."

Chapter Twelve

Late the following Sunday morning, Donna reclined comfortably on the living room couch in Arthur's apartment, a phone to one ear, going over hometown news with her mother. Arthur sat nearby in an easy chair, leafing lazily through various sections of the *South Bend Tribune*. The faint aroma of coffee and rolls lingered in the air.

Donna had once again spent the night at Arthur's place but still insisted that she was unwilling to move in with him, preferring instead to maintain her independence despite the increasing number of sleepovers.

Suddenly, the doorbell rang, but neither Arthur nor Donna were startled by it. Donna continued with her conversation, while Arthur gathered up his newspaper, laid it aside, and looked at his watch. It rang again. Arthur rose from his chair and opened the door for Jeffrey and Cherrie, who greeted him cordially.

"Donna will be with us in a minute," Arthur said, glancing in her direction. "She's on the phone with her mother."

"So, I hear you finally made some brownies," Jeffrey said, rubbing his hands together.

"That's right. Come into the kitchen and see for yourself." Arthur led the way into the kitchen where the brownies sat in a covered dish. "So how do they look?" he asked, uncovering the plate.

"Appearance is not the important thing," Jeffrey replied. "Performance is where it's at."

"Okay then, go ahead and try one."

Jeffrey picked up a brownie, sniffed at it, then took a bite. "Not bad. Feels like just a touch of glass fiber has been added, but not bad. So what's on the agenda this afternoon? I believe you said something about Monopoly."

Donna entered the room. "Hi, guys. Yes, Monopoly. But I have to warn you: I have the home court advantage here. We're playing with the same set I used when I was a kid."

"Ho, ho," Jeffrey responded, his eyebrows raised "You're going to need all the advantages you can get."

Donna opened the hall closet and pulled the game off the top shelf. "I get to be the thimble," she announced. "That's always been my favorite."

"This is the same set you had as a kid?" Cherrie asked, smiling. "That's good karma, you know."

"I know," Donna replied, setting the game on a card table in the living room. "I remember playing with friends on stormy nights when I was young, next to the fireplace with the ocean crashing outside. It was a lot of fun."

Cherrie lit a joint, took a hit, then passed it to Arthur.

He took a deep drag and held it. "This stuff is really good," he said as he released the smoke. He studied the joint a few seconds, then passed it to Jeffrey. "A few more hits like that and I won't know when it's my turn to roll."

"It's laced with opium," Cherrie said.

"I see," Arthur replied. "I guess that's another first for me — opium."

"Don't start making excuses already," Jeffrey taunted playfully. "You have to stay competitive no matter what. It's all part of the game."

"I didn't think hippies were supposed to be into competition," Arthur replied. "I'm beginning to think you're more of a capitalist at heart than you let on."

"I think we owe a lot to the hippies," Jeffrey said, "but I've never seen myself as one of them. I'm more a part of what I feel is an emerging establishment."

"But you have to admit—you look the part, and you do drugs."

"Yes, but before long, everyone will have long hair and do drugs. It's all part of the social evolution."

"I don't know about that," Donna said, frowning. "A lot of people don't get that much out of doing drugs."

"You don't like getting high?" Cherrie asked.

"I don't see the point."

"That's easy. It makes you feel good. Don't you want to feel good?"

"Sure, but I like feeling good because something real happened, not because of some chemicals I took."

"But drugs can *expand* your reality," Jeffrey said.

"You think so?" Donna replied.

"Sure, like grass, it changes your perspective, helps you get into the funny side of things, keeps you from taking things so seriously all the time. And acid can give you deep insights into the things around you, can let you see how things really work."

"I think drugs play tricks on your brain," Donna said firmly. "So you think you have a better view of reality than you actually do. And I think getting into drugs too much can cause you to lose contact with reality altogether."

"I thought you and Arthur were into grass," Jeffrey replied. "I thought that's what the brownies were about."

"I'm into grass," Arthur said immediately. "It's just that Donna—"

"I don't mind if other people do grass once in a while," Donna said, "or have a drink now and then. I'm just saying—I prefer having my perceptions unaltered."

"That's fair," Jeffrey conceded. He took a long drag on the joint, then released the smoke. "But stoned or not, I'm not going to take any prisoners once we start playing."

"Dream on," Donna said, laughing.

As Arthur brought the brownies in from the kitchen and set the plate on the table, the phone rang. He picked it up without thinking but tightened his grip when he heard Billie Lee's voice.

"Hi," she said breathily, sounding particularly sexy. "Did I catch you at a bad time?"

"Kind of. I've...uh...been meaning to call you."

"I wondered about that. I haven't heard from you in weeks."

"I tried a couple of times," Arthur lied, "but you weren't there."

"Good. That makes me feel much better. It really does. So when do you want to get together? I've been thinking about you quite a bit lately. I hope you don't mind."

"Of course I don't mind, but I don't think I'm going to be able to get away any time soon. Things are pretty hectic here right now."

"How about lunch tomorrow? As it turns out, I'm going to be passing through South Bend on my way to Detroit."

"Oh . . . well, I guess we could do that."

"How about The Keg? Do you know that place? It's supposed to be good."

"Yes, it's good. What time?"

"How about a late lunch, say one thirty? We could avoid the crowd that way, if that works for you."

"That sounds fine." Arthur glanced over at Donna. She appeared to be engrossed in setting up the game with Cherrie and Jeffrey. "I'll see you then." He hung up the phone.

"What was that all about?" Donna asked. "Not bad news, I hope."

"No, just someone I knew from college. He wants to get together sometime."

"Someone from Illinois?"

"Yes. No big deal."

Arthur looked away from Donna, then around the room, then back at her. A brief pause followed, which was relieved by Jeffrey, who declared, "So, Let's play."

༄

At one thirty the next afternoon, Arthur sat at a back table at The Keg. As he sipped on ice water, Billie Lee walked in. She wore jeans, a camel-hair coat, black lace-up boots, and a yellow muffler that seemed to set off her blonde hair. She looked dazzling. "Whew, it's windy and cold out there," she said, tossing her head. "She took her coat and muffler off, revealing a red and white ski sweater, and sat down.

"Yes, winter is almost here, and from what I understand, this is the middle of the Snow Belt," he said.

"You sounded nervous on the phone yesterday. Almost like you wanted to get rid of me or something. It bothered me all night."

"No, not at all. I just had some people over, and it was hard to talk."

"Were any of them girls, by any chance?" Billie Lee twirled a strand of hair with her finger.

"Well, yes. There were girls there. Nothing heavy though. Just a few friends."

Billie Lee nodded. "I'm glad it was nothing serious. I wouldn't want to be in the way or anything."

"No. Don't worry about that. You're not in the way at all. Far from it."

"I hope not. I'm very attracted to you, in case you didn't know." She peered into Arthur's eyes. "In a way, being with you has helped me get past Joshua's death. But just in a way. As I said before, our relationship is very different from the one I had with him." As Billie Lee smiled at Arthur, a waitress stopped by and took their orders.

"So you still think about Joshua?" Arthur asked, after the waitress had gone.

"Oh, yeah, quite a bit. Sometimes I wonder what he would think about Vietnam these days. So much is changing, yet it keeps going on. Do you think about it much these days?"

"Sure." Arthur stroked his chin. "My brother was killed over there, and my father is on his way to Vietnam as we speak."

"Really? I didn't know your brother had been sent over there. When was he killed?"

"About three and a half years ago."

"And your father is going over? I would have thought he's too well connected for something like that."

"He volunteered."

"Volunteered? You told me he was hard-core, but I—"

"He couldn't wait to get over there. Can you believe that? He thinks he can make a difference. Some of these old guys just don't know when to quit. They can't concede anything."

"I know a lot of people in the government don't want to face the inevitable, but can that kind of stubbornness be used to justify thousands of additional casualties?"

"Maybe not. But war isn't rational. It just seems rational to the ones calling the shots."

"Yes, but that's no excuse. The people running this stupid war have let it go on for years and years. Sometimes I think they get off on it or something. Maybe it makes them feel important, who knows? But more and more of us believe that something needs to be done now, something to really shake these bastards up. It's pretty easy for Nixon and Kissinger to piss away time and lives. Nobody's shooting at them. No bombs are going off in their faces. They're leading damn good lives. But if they had to worry about devastation here at home like what's being carried out in Vietnam, I think we'd see some action pretty fast for a change." Billie Lee stared hard at Arthur. "And you could play a role in something like that. You really could."

"What kind of role?"

"A big one. Like I said before, our group needs plutonium to go ahead with the construction of the bomb, and we desperately need your help. I didn't tell you that before because I didn't want to pressure you. But we really need you."

"So you *are* planning to go ahead with the bomb idea," Arthur replied, frowning.

"Yes. It's just that with Joshua gone we don't have a way to get plutonium, and since his murder, it has taken us a while to get our nerve back."

"I don't know anything about making plutonium," Arthur insisted, shaking his head.

"You don't have to. One of our people would show you exactly what you need to do. All you would have to provide is your technical expertise and access to equipment."

"I don't know. You're talking about me getting involved with a bunch of people I don't know anything about. There are a lot of crazies out there these days."

"I would introduce you to the leader of the project right away. He would explain things to you very clearly, and I think you would find that he is quite sane. The whole idea is to bring sanity to the situation. And you would be working with me, too. If something didn't seem right to you, you could just talk to me about it. Nobody wants to involve you in something you don't want to do."

"But a nuclear bomb? Isn't that a little extreme? I mean, that sounds crazy."

"We're not going to set it off. We don't want to hurt anyone. We just want the government to take us seriously for a change, to stop thinking of us as a bunch of misguided, stupid shits."

"I don't know. I can see a certain logic in what you're saying, but—"

"Take some time to think it over. And remember, I want you to come over to Chicago to see me, no matter what you decide. I've already told you I've got the hots for you. That's not going to change." She leaned her head forward and looked into his eyes.

"Okay," Arthur said, feeling his face flush. "How about the week before Thanksgiving? Would it be okay if I drove over and saw you then?"

"Sounds perfect. That will give you some time to think over what we talked about today and decide one way or the other."

Arthur nodded.

"So, do you have any plans for this afternoon?" she asked with a mischievous smile.

"Nothing in particular, other than work. I should be getting back."

"That's too bad. I was hoping we could swing by your apartment, maybe share another bottle of wine." She smiled again and raised her eyebrows.

"I have to admit, that does sound interesting. You know, I haven't had that much time off since I got here. I guess I could check with Dr. Fischer and give it a try. Let's find a phone."

§

About an hour later, Arthur sat on the couch in his apartment sipping wine as Billie Lee, also holding a glass of wine, sat perpendicular to him with her legs resting on his lap.

"So are you in trouble with your boss?" she asked.

"No, I told him a friend had come into town that I hadn't seen for a while and asked if I could have the afternoon off. He said it wasn't a problem."

"Good. I really like this. It's like playing hooky. Sex in the afternoon on a workday, kind of naughty, breaking the rules, gets me kind of hot." She pressed her knee gently into his crotch.

Arthur gasped with pleasure and laid down with her. Just then, the doorbell rang. *Oh, no,* he thought. *Donna. Did she forget her key? She's supposed to be in class..* "Let's not answer," he whispered. "I wouldn't normally be here anyway."

The doorbell rang again, followed by pounding. "Arthur, are you there?" called a male voice.

Not Donna, Arthur thought. *Good.* He got up and after losing his balance somewhat, made his way to the door.

He opened it and found Jeffrey facing him, looking perplexed. "I saw your car and wondered if anything was wrong."

"Oh, no, nothing like that. I just decided to take the afternoon off."

As they spoke, Billie Lee swiveled around into a seated position on the couch.

"Do you mind if I come in?" Jeffrey asked, more or less pushing his way past Arthur. "Cherrie and I were wondering if you would like to—" Jeffrey caught sight of Billie Lee. "Oh, I'm sorry," he said quietly. "I didn't know anyone was here."

"That's okay. This is a friend, Billie Lee. Billie Lee, this is Jeffrey. He teaches drawing and painting at Notre Dame."

Billie Lee smiled at Jeffrey and said hello, but remained seated.

"I think Arthur mentioned something about you," Jeffrey said, taking a seat on a chair by the couch. "I believe he said you had a mutual friend at the University of Illinois."

Arthur sat down on the couch next to Billie Lee. *What the hell is he doing?* Arthur wondered nervously. Didn't he realize that anything that had been said about Billie Lee was not to be brought up in front of her?

"Yes, we both knew a grad student at Illinois named Joshua Taylor," she replied evenly.

"And he was killed?" Jeffrey asked.

Now, what? Arthur thought.

But once again Billie Lee appeared unruffled. "Yes, he was killed. The case is still open."

"Well, I'm sorry you had to go through something like that. There seems to be a lot of unnecessary violence and death these days, but when it's someone you know, it's still a tragedy."

"It would help if there were some kind of resolution, like maybe finding the murderer," Billie Lee said.

"Yes, I'm sure, but a lot of these cases go unsolved. Do you have any idea why anyone would have done something like that?"

"No, not at all."

"Well, I'm going to take off now," Jeffrey said as he stood up. "I was going to talk with Arthur a little, but that can wait."

"We can talk later, if you want," Arthur said as he got up and started walking toward the door.

Jeffrey turned to Billie Lee and said, "Nice to have met you."

"You too," Billie Lee replied. After Jeffrey left, Arthur returned to the couch. "I don't know about you, but that guy gives me the creeps," Billie Lee said.

"I know. I just mentioned you to him one time when we were smoking grass and drinking wine. I guess I got a little looser than normal, but that's the only time your name ever came up."

"Don't worry about it. I just don't like pointed questions about Joshua. I still think there's more behind his death than we know, and I guess that makes me a little more sensitive than I would be normally."

"Yeah, but I can't figure out where Jeffrey was coming from. Maybe he was trying to make conversation in an awkward situation. I don't know."

"What awkward situation'?"

"Well, the two of us here, playing hooky."

"So, do you still want to play?"

"Are you kidding? Of course."

"Great, let's see how ready you are." Billie Lee leaned over and spread her hand out on Arthur's crotch. "Okay, I just wanted to make sure," she grinned. "But remember, you can't talk to anyone about the plutonium, not even a friend you trust. And that definitely includes Jeffrey."

"Don't worry. I won't do anything like that again."

Chapter Thirteen

The following week, Arthur decided to shoot some hoops after work. Although the ground had been covered with frost that morning, the afternoon temperature had risen to the high forties, and enjoying the remaining autumn weather while he still could seemed like a good idea. Arthur retrieved his basketball from the trunk of the Porsche and tossed it into the back seat. A lot like being a kid again, he thought: playing outside, sunshine, fresh air. He imagined meeting his brother somewhere for a pickup game with friends, something he had actually done not all that long ago.

As he slid behind the wheel, Arthur's thoughts turned to Billie Lee. The incredible sex. Those long tan legs. That flowing blonde hair. But her interest in plutonium . . . *Jesus*. And making a nuclear bomb to end the war . . . *God almighty*. The plan that she had outlined seemed almost plausible one minute, then too bizarre to even consider the next. Still, working closely with Billie Lee would be exciting, no doubt about that. She'd said she would continue seeing him, even if he didn't join the project, but Arthur had to wonder if that were true. *Probably not*, he concluded.

And what about Donna? How could he enjoy great sex with Billie Lee and still maintain a serious relationship with her? He imagined explaining to each of them why he was seeing the other one. She's so sexy, he would say to Donna. Listen to that accent. Look at that blonde hair. She's so sweet, he would say to Billie Lee. Look at that face. Look into those eyes. He smiled as he pictured both of them fighting over his father's Luger to see who could shoot him first.

When he arrived at the basketball court, Arthur was surprised to see Jeffrey and Cherrie there by themselves, under the far basket. Jeffrey stood frozen in a stationary pose, his basketball pressed hard against his hip, engaged in what appeared to be a deep conversation with Cherrie. Arthur climbed out of the Porsche and bounced his own basketball a few times to announce his presence. Jeffrey and Cherrie turned to him and glared, giving him the unmistakable impression that he was very much the intruder.

"What's going on?" Arthur asked cautiously.

"Not much," Jeffrey answered, sounding annoyed. "What's going on with you?"

"Nothing unusual."

"That's too bad," Cherrie replied, sounding almost hostile. "I could get into something unusual about now."

"Take it easy," Jeffrey said, addressing Cherrie. "There's no reason to go crazy."

"Is something wrong?" Arthur asked. "Did something happen?"

"You might say that," Cherrie said. "First of all—"

"Okay, okay," Jeffrey interrupted. He turned to Arthur. "I might as tell you. I'm out at Notre Dame."

"What do you mean?"

"I got busted." Jeffrey tightened his lips.

"How?"

"One of my students. I don't know. I don't know. Basically, he's a good kid, but he deals a little, and I bought some stuff from him. He's from one of the Chicago suburbs and has some connections there. Anyway, his roommate got pissed off at him about something and turned him in."

"Wow."

"Yeah," said Jeffrey, shaking his head.

"So, how did *you* get caught up in it?"

"Someone from the South Bend police department, someone from the intelligence unit, called this kid and told him to come down to the police station right away or they would send a car out and arrest him. Of course when he got there, they tried to scare the living hell out of him. They told him he was in deep trouble and had better hand over the names of his customers right away or they would send him to prison for a long time and ruin his life, the whole bit. They told him he had been under surveillance for months and they already knew who some of his customers were, so trying to hold out on them would be a big mistake. Of course, he broke down right away, and when they got my name, they were ready to celebrate. I guess a lot of the townies really hate the people at Notre Dame, which isn't that surprising if you stop and think about it."

"What's going to happen to you?"

"It depends. From what I can tell, they don't have anything really solid on me. It's his word against mine. At least that's the impression I got when they interrogated me. And of course, I didn't admit to anything."

"Did they arrest you?"

"No, they just called me at home this morning and told me to come down to the station. Then, when I got there, they told me about busting Jerry and said that the only choice I had was to cooperate fully. But like I said, I didn't break, so they offered me a deal. I can avoid an investigation and charges if I resign from Notre Dame immediately. Apparently, the whole situation was discussed earlier this week with Notre Dame officials. Of course, Notre Dame wants to keep this thing as quiet as possible, so I have until tomorrow to decide. I meet with the cops and Father Cassano in the morning."

"What are you going to do?"

"Probably resign. If they do investigate, some of my friends will get burned for sure, and I could end up with a record that would kill any chance of me getting another teaching job. Sergeant Cooper emphasized those points heavily this morning, the bastard." Jeffrey looked at Cherrie. "She thinks I should stay and fight it out, but I don't think that's such a good idea."

"I think they were bluffing," Cherrie said. "What do they really know? If they had anything on you, they would have arrested you right away. You would be in jail right now."

"I'm just thinking in terms of damage control. If they look for evidence, they'll find it, and other people will be implicated. Sergeant Cooper was right about that."

"So you're going to give up everything, just like that?"

"I don't have any choice."

Cherrie looked away.

"Why don't we go back to my place?" Arthur said. "I have a bottle of Scotch we could crack open. I think it's still legal to do that."

"I could get into something like that," Jeffrey said. "This has been one hell of a day."

Several hours later, while sitting around the dining room table, Arthur, Jeffrey, and Cherrie had pretty much killed a fifth of Johnny Walker Red. Donna had also joined them but drank only lemonade.

"So what's going to happen to the student who turned you in?" Arthur asked. "Are they going to prosecute him?"

"No," Jeffrey mumbled, now slurring his words. "They put him on probation and sealed his record, then kicked him out of Notre Dame forever. That was his deal."

"Getting nailed out of the blue like this is kind of rough."

"It's not so bad. So I start over again. So what? There are lots of colleges in California. My mistake was coming to the Midwest in the first place, to a conservative Catholic school, at that."

"I think the dream is dying," Cherrie said, her head weaving slightly. "A few years ago, I thought it could really happen, but not anymore, not anymore."

"What do you mean?" Jeffrey asked.

"I thought the white culture was softening. I thought people were becoming less materialistic, more spiritual, less militaristic. Music was changing; art was changing. Even clothes were changing. People were turning on and looking for a simpler, more holistic lifestyle. But that's all going away. I can feel it inside."

"Why do you say the white culture was changing?" Arthur asked. "Why just whites? It's like the only ones who ever did anything wrong were white."

"Because whites are the ones who needed to change the most," Cherrie insisted. "They've been the ones bent on getting power and money at any cost. That's what I thought was changing."

"I don't know if I agree with that," Arthur replied. "People of all colors want power and money."

"Look at U.S. history. It's a story of hundreds of years of white greed and aggression," Cherrie persisted.

"Well, of course greed is part of it, but this country was founded on idealistic principles. Equal opportunity, personal freedom. I'm not saying it has always worked out that way. No system is perfect, but the guiding principles were good."

"You're not serious, are you? Have you noticed the race riots taking place across this country, the burning and destruction and killing? Have you heard of the Black Panthers? Why do you think all of that is happening?"

"There have been some injustices. There are cases of discrimination, but not all whites are at fault. And things are getting better. The framework, the Declaration of Independence and the Bill of Rights, is—"

"The Declaration of Independence? Are you kidding? White Anglo-Saxons writing about equality and the pursuit of happiness, while at the same time bringing African slaves to this hemisphere to work land that they had stolen from native peoples. Of course, that was before the white migration west, more Indian wars, the Trail of Tears, and white-led wars to drive Mexican Americans from their homeland. White men may write very eloquently about the nobility of man, but what they actually brought to this continent was superior weapons, military organization, and greed. And of those things, the level of the white man's greed was the hardest for the native peoples to comprehend." Cherrie finished her Scotch. She reached for the bottle, then frowned when she saw that it was empty.

"That was a long time ago. Things have changed a lot since then," Arthur said.

"It wasn't that long ago, and you're still benefiting from what happened. Don't you see that? You have personal freedom. You have choice." Cherrie exhaled strongly. "I mean, have you ever thought about what it's like to live on an Indian reservation or in a ghetto? Have you thought about the very minor difference between living in places like that and living in a concentration camp? And what about Vietnam? Isn't that your white culture trying to colonize a native people yet again? Yes. I'm afraid it is. But there is a difference this time—a big difference. The Vietnamese have weapons and military strategies that are just as good as the white man's. And they're far more motivated than the whites because they're fighting to keep their homeland."

"We have a lot of black soldiers fighting over there as well as whites," Arthur replied evenly.

"Which only proves that slavery is not really a thing of the past in this country," Cherrie shot back.

Donna looked around the table. "Would anyone like some coffee?"

"Please," Cherrie said. "Thanks." She turned back to Arthur. "Look, I'm not trying to say that you personally are responsible for all the crimes that white men have committed over the years. Of course, you're not. It's just that I thought things were really changing in a fundamental way, and now I see they're not."

"Don't be so sure," Jeffrey broke in. His words were now badly slurred. "When we get to California—"

"The sixties are over," Cherrie insisted.

৯০

The next morning, after thoroughly cleaning every possible surface, Arthur turned off the vacuum and sat down on the couch. "That should do it," he said to Donna. "Everything has been either flushed or vacuumed or pitched out. If the cops do show up, they're not going to find anything."

"Do you really think they'll show up?" Donna asked as she sat down next to him.

"I don't know; they could. They may tell Jeffrey they're not going to investigate his friends, then turn right around and investigate the hell out of everyone he knows. I don't want to take any chances."

"You're probably right. Besides, I think it's time we stopped fooling around with drugs altogether. They may be fun once in a while, but they're not worth the risk. I think they've really hurt the credibility of the Movement, too. Who wants to listen to someone talk about ending the war when he looks like he might be zonked out on acid?"

"You never did get into drugs that much, did you?"

"No. Just grass once in a while and a little wine now and then. There are other good reasons to stop, though."

"Like what?" Arthur wrinkled his brow.

"Just . . . reasons."

"What reasons? Once this whole thing blows over, I don't see anything wrong with doing a joint once in a while."

"That's not what I mean," Donna replied. Her voice now had an unusual edge. "Look, I have something I need to tell you." She swallowed hard.

"Go ahead. What is it?"

"I'm seeing a doctor this afternoon." Donna's face turned red. Her eyes fell. "I think I may be pregnant."

"What? Pregnant? I thought we . . . what makes you think . . . I mean I know what makes you think that, but are you sure? Am I... I mean—"

"If there is a baby, you're the father," Donna replied evenly. "And no, I'm not sure. That's why I'm going to see the doctor." She raised her eyes to meet his. "You don't have to worry. I'm not going to try to force you into anything you don't want to do."

"Do you want me to go with you to the doctor?"

"No. I would prefer doing this by myself. I really would. I'll let you know the results as soon as I get them."

"Well, if we have to get married, I think—"

"Let's not worry about that now. We still have plenty of time."

That afternoon, having taken off from work an hour or so early, Arthur watched as Donna pulled into the driveway. Climbing slowly out of the car, she paused briefly and rolled her eyes toward the sky. It was in that instant that Arthur knew she was pregnant. He opened the front door for her.

"The test was positive," Donna said.

"Yes, I see."

"I *don't* know. I don't know what to think." She shook her head.

"Look, we're in this together—wherever it takes us."

"You mean like . . . marriage?" she asked.

"Yes. You don't have to give me an answer now, but yes."

Donna sat down in the nearest chair. "Are you sure? If it came right down to it, I think my family would help me raise the baby."

"I'm sure. Let's just give the idea some time to sink in."

"My mother is going to kill me."

"Well, we'll give her some time, too. She'll probably come around."

"She's not going to have much choice." Donna stood up and put her arms around Arthur's neck. He encircled her waist with his arms. They stood silently in this embrace for several minutes, neither really wanting to move.

⊱

Later that week, at about two in the morning, the telephone next to Vic's bed rang.

"Hello, Daddy?" asked the voice on the other end, sounding uncharacteristically sheepish. "Did I wake you? I know it's late, but I thought . . . I thought I should give you a call."

"Denise. Thank God you called. Your mother and I have been worried sick about you. Are you okay? It's been almost a week. Where are you?"

"I can't tell you exactly where I am, but I'm in Canada."

"Canada? Why?"

"Warren lost his student deferment, so we came up here."

"I thought he was doing okay in school."

"He was. But last semester he became more involved in the Movement, protests against the war and everything, and ended up getting a couple of Ds and dropping a course, which put him on academic probation. When his draft board found out last summer, they reclassified him 1-A, but he didn't get an induction notice until last week. Of course, he was back in school by then, so he asked for an extension to have a chance to pull his grades up. But they told him it was too late for something like that. They told him he'd better show up for his induction on time, or he would be facing federal charges. So, we came up here to Canada."

"So you're giving up your life and your future because this Warren character doesn't want to face up to his military obligation."

"We want to be together."

"I know. I understand that. There were a lot of couples who wanted to be together during World War II, but they decided to do the right thing. They put their personal lives on hold for a while to meet their obligations. If you want to live in this country, you have obligations. And so does this Warren character."

"Yes, but the whole student deferment process is so unfair. Some schools are easier than others. Some majors are easier, and the draft boards just do what they want."

"What do you mean?"

"Well, Warren knows this one guy, for example, who flunked out of school completely. He was out for a whole semester—four months. But he was from a small town, and his mother was friends with someone on his draft board. They played bridge together or something. So he never got drafted. He was reclassified 1-A, but amazingly enough, he never got called up. Then, he got back into school and got his student deferment back as if he'd never been gone. So he flunked out but never got drafted, while Warren *does* get drafted, just for going on probation. It's not fair."

"I agree. It doesn't sound fair, but lots of things in life are unfair. You just need to—"

"I mean, at first a married guy with a kid could get a deferment. So a lot of guys got married and had a kid. Now they're talking about doing away with student deferments altogether and going to a lottery. How are we supposed to plan our lives? It's like there are rules, but there are no rules. I don't know. If he could have just made it to the lottery, maybe he—"

"I don't think running off to Canada is the answer, I really don't. Are you sure you're okay? Really?"

"Yes, basically."

"What does that mean?"

"Well, we're sharing a house with two other couples, and there isn't much money. And I guess with the holidays coming, I feel a little homesick. But overall, there's a kind of mellow feeling in the house that I like. And we feel like we made the right decision, even though I know you don't agree."

"Do you need money?"

"No, but thanks. Thanks for everything. I really mean that. And I'll call you again, I will. So don't worry, please. Goodbye, Dad."

The receiver clicked, and Vic sat motionless for almost a minute listening to the dial tone.

&

That evening at about six thirty, after another busy but seemingly pointless day at work, Vic entered his empty apartment. Another day down the drain, he thought, another day out of his life gone. But at least Susie-Q was scheduled to come over that evening. He ambled into the kitchen and considered having a quick drink before she arrived but decided against it. Hard knocks from life had already left his head spinning. He didn't need a drink.

What he did need was a way to collect himself, to regain his equilibrium. Maybe Susie-Q's sexual favors would do the trick but probably not. His problem wasn't that he was horny or that he felt a need to avenge his wife's betrayal yet again. His problem was depression. His life was falling apart. He had to wonder if continuing on even made sense anymore. *Suicide*, he thought. A simple enough solution. But he knew he wouldn't actually try something that drastic because there were too many unknowns associated with an act that final. He didn't understand life well enough, or death either, for that matter, to toy with his own existence. Yet another discouraging thought to ponder.

So maybe it was time to face facts, he thought. His life had changed. His wife had deserted him for another man. His daughter had left him and his way of life for God knows what kind of situation in Canada. The two people who had meant the most to him were now gone. And the world itself had changed. The young people with their strange music and hostility toward established values. Not to mention some members of his own generation, trying to act hip, trying to prove they still had it. Things just weren't the same anymore, whether he liked it or not.

His only course of action, he concluded, was put his head down and try to make it through another day, keep doing his job and hope that his personal situation would eventually clear up on its own. Until then, he would be a middle-aged man who had played the game straight his entire life but now didn't seem to fit in.

When Susie-Q rang his doorbell, he almost wished she hadn't shown up for the appointment. Getting up from his chair to answer the door seemed to be almost too much. But when he finally did let her in, Susie-Q seemed as effervescent as ever. "You look a little stressed," she said with a smile. She slid out of her coat and handed it to him. "I know how to take care of that.

Let's go right to the bedroom. You get undressed, stretch out on the bed, and I'll give you a deep massage, guaranteed to bring you back to life."

"Whatever you say. You're calling the shots tonight." In the bedroom, Vice pulled the bedspread and covers back, took off all his clothes, and lay face down on the sheets with his forehead buried in a pillow. Without saying anything, Susie-Q climbed on top of him, her bare legs straddling his hips. She had obviously taken off her pants. Vic wondered what else she had taken off.

"Here," she purred, leaning forward, resting her weight on her hands as they pressed against his shoulder blades. She then sat back and kneaded his shoulders and neck. "See? Sometimes I actually do give my clients a massage."

"I have to admit; today a massage probably feels better than sex."

"Oh, my God, poor baby," she laughed. "What's wrong?"

"Everything, except maybe you being here with me now."

"So why don't you tell me about it?" She continued kneading as she spoke. "I'm going to be an analyst in a few years, and this might be a good time to start gaining experience."

"Don't you need more school? I mean, before you're ready to start working as an analyst?"

"I need more credits before I can become certified, and I have to have at least a master's degree under my belt. But I think I already have a pretty good grasp of how things work and how I can help people."

"You're going to give massages while you delve into their psyches?"

"No," she drawled as she reached back and lightly slapped his right hip. "Don't be like that. I'm going to become completely legit."

"And you think you know how life works well enough to do that right now?"

"Sure, that part's not hard at all."

"Well, I have to admit, things don't make a whole lot of sense to me now. So, if you have some insights, maybe you could clue me in."

"Okay, I'll share with you what I have observed." Susie-Q climbed off Vic and lay next to him on the bed. He glanced over and saw that she was completely naked herself. Lying on her back, she stared pensively at the ceiling with her hands clasped behind her head, seemingly gathering her thoughts. He took the opportunity to take in her pert breasts and rich pubic area. "I guess we could start with why we're here," she said. She took a deep breath, then slowly asked the question, "So why are we here?"

"That sounds like a good place to start. I certainly haven't figured that out yet."

"It seems to me that our overriding reason for being here is to perpetuate life, just like all the other living things on this planet. I mean, if you think about it, we're born; we mature with support from the preceding generation; we reproduce ourselves, or at least try to; we take our turn as parental figures to help the next generation mature; and then we die. The main thing is that life goes on, and we all seem to have a role to play in that process, even those of us who aren't actually parents."

"I guess that makes sense. The perpetuation of life. Life does seem to go on, no matter what."

"But that's not a very satisfying explanation, is it? I mean as to why we're here."

"Not particularly."

"That's because we don't know why reproduction is so important. There definitely seems to be an agenda—procreation—but we're not in on why it actually happens. We're not in on the big picture. We're just little biochemical units being manipulated by forces greater than ourselves, kind of like ants busily carrying out our assigned tasks without knowing why." Susie-Q inched closer to Vic.

"So how does this picture of life help you treat people with problems? It sounds like you're saying we don't control much of anything."

"Okay, we'll tie everything together later. But next we have to consider is what having problems really means. And based on what I've seen, I think we're actually talking about feelings. When we say we have a problem, we're actually saying we feel bad about something."

"Feelings?"

"Yes, feelings are very important, both good and bad. Sometimes, I think we're so used to being directed by feelings, we don't recognize how significant they actually are."

"You don't think reasoning plays a role in what we do?"

"Not a major role, no. Not as much as some of us would like to think. Once we're motivated to do something, we may use reasoning to help determine the best way to accomplish what it is that we're trying to do and also to rationalize why we're doing it. But the real driving force, the need to do the thing in question, is usually based on emotion or feelings."

"I don't know if I agree with that."

"Well, why am I here now?" She slid her right ankle up and down over the back of his right calf.

"Okay, we may do some things because of feelings, but not everything."

"More than just some things. And I think most of the problems that people experience, at least the problems I'll be treating, are caused by an inability to deal with bad feelings. Remember, my premise is that the purpose of life is procreation. And it seems to me that Mother Nature pushes us in that direction at every turn. She does this by making us feel good when we're doing the things that lead to reproduction and by making us feel bad when we get off track."

"If you're saying nature makes us feel good about having sex, I can agree with that much."

"Well, there you go," Susie-Q said. "Very good; that's very insightful. I'm impressed with your grasp of the obvious."

"Okay, okay," Vic replied.

"But since you brought it up, let me ask you, have you ever thought about how sex works?" Susie-Q asked.

"You mean the mechanics?"

"No, I'm thinking more about the mental aspects. I mean, take me, for instance. What about me turns you on?"

Vic cocked his head to one side and surveyed her nude body. "Your breasts, your legs," he answered slowly. "If you turned over, your ass would definitely be a turn-on.."

"But everyone has breasts and legs and an ass. Old people, children, men, women—we all have those things. Are mine really that different in shape?"

"I'm not turned on by old people, or children, or men."

"But that's the point. I'm sure I could find men, say, with legs and a butt that are close in appearance to mine. But you wouldn't have any interest in them because the fact that I'm female and in a certain age range makes all the difference. You're programmed that way; you didn't learn that. It came very naturally to you, like eating ice cream. And even when I'm dressed, it's my aura, my hair, my eyes, my laugh, my voice, my personality, even my perfume that reinforces your programmed desire for me. But you'll notice I never said anything about your desire being rational. It's not something you decided to pursue as a result of logic."

"I think we can agree that the desire for sex is natural enough."

"But my point is, Mother Nature doesn't stop there. There's a lot more to reproduction than just wanting to have sex. Nature also causes us to feel good about doing the things that lead to sex, like achieving a respected place in whatever social setting we find ourselves in, or making ourselves physically attractive to members of the opposite sex. These things make us feel good about ourselves when we succeed, but conversely, we feel bad when we come up short. And that's when we sometimes do things to make ourselves feel better that take us even farther off course. That's when we can have real problems."

"Like what?"

"Aggressive behavior, withdrawal, perversions, criminal acts, drugs, all sorts of things. And that's where I'll come in. I'll help people feel better about themselves and their situation by working through it with them and by helping them avoid problematic behavior."

"So how does all this work? Exactly how does nature make us feel good when we're on the right path?"

"Biochemically. I think we talked about this once before. Research is beginning to show that chemicals similar to morphine are made in our body and light up our brain when certain stimuli are received. These chemicals make us feel good under what are thought of as positive circumstances, like a mother comforting her baby, or when a toddler says its first word, or when a pretty girl smiles at you. The thing is, though, all of this happens automatically. In a sense, we're all chemically programmed to respond to certain social or natural cues. With animals, we call this instinct. And from what I can see, we're just as instinctual as all the other animals. The only real difference is, we can talk about it."

"But if we're all operating out of instinct, directed by our biochemical programming, how are you going to be able to help people with their problems by just talking? It seems like you're going to be up against some pretty powerful forces."

"Once you see how Mother Nature operates, you can try to beat her at her own game."

"But isn't it nature's job to keep us on the right path? Isn't she on our side?"

"She is, but only in a sense. Mother Nature deals in averages. She doesn't care about individuals at all. She simply gives you a genetic package, shoves you into the game, and then turns her back on you. She may have made you appear cute as a baby so your mother or some other adult would feel a desire to pick you up and take care of you. But if that doesn't work out, Mother Nature has no answers."

"Hmm," Vic responded.

"And if pretty girls don't smile at you once you've grown up, Mother Nature shrugs her shoulders. But I can help by intervening. I can find a surrogate mother for babies who need one, and I can help you find at least one girl to smile at you."

"What if I'm too hapless to get even one?" Vic asked, feigning a frown.

"I don't think that's the case with you, *necessarily*." Billie Lee smiled as she drew out the last word. "But if it were, I would try to help you adjust to the limits of your particular situation. Maybe help you learn to feel good about occasional smiles or nods from pretty girls, instead of easy sex at every turn."

"It still sounds like helping people with their problems could be quite a challenge."

"Oh, I'm sure it will be. And I'm sure I won't always be successful. But at least I know what I'm up against. And I should be paid well." Susie-Q patted his leg.

Vic rolled his eyes. "I guess that's the important thing," he mumbled under his breath. "It's always about the money."

"Hey, I should be paid well. I'm going to help people fight nature's cruel system of biologically manufactured emotions, which often leaves them feeling bad about themselves, or the situation they're in, through no real fault of their own."

"So if it's all biochemical anyway, why not just use drugs to help people feel better about things and call it good?"

"A lot of people do use drugs to accomplish exactly that, both prescribed and otherwise. But drugs don't get at the underlying cause of the problem."

"Yeah. I keep thinking about my daughter's boyfriend. I wouldn't be surprised if he's on drugs. He certainly looks like he is. And he's probably trying to get my daughter hooked as well. I don't know what it is about kids today."

"Well, they have a lot to deal with, but I very much prefer a clear-headed approach to taking on life's issues. I like seeing things as they are and trying to deal with problems directly."

"So the idea is to feel good about yourself by following the path laid out by nature as much as possible."

"Kind of, but not exactly."

"What does that mean?"

"We've already seen that Mother Nature can be cruel and unfair, but the problem is, she can also be stupid."

"How?"

"In a lot of ways." Susie-Q furrowed her brow. "Take dominance, for example. Nature often rewards dominance with good feelings, particularly for males. Again, I think it's tied to procreation. But dominance can easily get out of hand. Look at all the wars and misery caused by leaders who want to be in control. Nature rewards certain behaviors with good feelings, but she doesn't have the perspective to be followed blindly. My job will be to help people navigate a sometimes cruel and not necessarily intelligent system of existence, while helping them feel good about themselves at the same time."

"Maybe you should continue as a masseuse, that is, if you want to make people feel good. Not that you wouldn't do a good job as an analyst, but the challenges you describe seem almost overwhelming." She didn't reply. Vic sensed that he had said something wrong.

"Do you wonder why I do this?" Susie-Q asked evenly, still stretched out naked, her hands still behind her head.

"You said your reasons were financial. You said you wanted to get your advanced degrees from Northwestern without going broke or into debt in the process. I wasn't serious about you continuing as a masseuse. I know you have plans for better things in the future."

"But for now, you think my reasons for doing this are strictly financial."

"I guess."

"That's only partially true. There's more to it than that."

"Like what?"

"Sexual arousal, for me."

"Really?" Vic looked at her closely.

"Yes. I like feeling attractive to members of the opposite sex. Like we said, it's a natural enough thing. And I particularly like to see well-educated, good-looking guys, guys who could easily get a lot of girls through normal means, anxious to pay me for my favors. We were talking about the need to dominate getting out of control. Well, the need to turn people on sexually, to be a sexual object, to feel good about being a sexual object, can also get out of control. Actually, I think that is a form of dominance. And the good feeling that comes from it is very powerful."

"How does something like that happen? I mean, how did you become a masseuse in the first place?"

"I think it had to do with breaking down boundaries. Once you start behaving in a way that's outside the norm, it becomes easier to continue doing things like that, more and more. The whole thing just accelerates."

"So did you start having sex when you were too young or something?"

"No, just the opposite. When I was young, my family, especially my father, was very strict, very religious."

"How young *were* you?"

"I guess I'm talking about junior high and then high school. I couldn't date boys or go to parties all through that time. I didn't even go to my junior or senior prom. I remember girls who had been my friends in junior high school, girls who didn't do that much socially at that time, branching out and becoming more active as we got older. It really hurt. They were doing the things I wanted to do but couldn't. It was if they were leaving me behind."

"Your father didn't approve of interaction with boys your own age at all?"

"Just group activities at church."

"So when did things change for you?"

"When I went away to college. Once I got out from under my father's control, I went crazy. I would meet a guy and have sex with him right away."

"Right away?"

"Yeah, yeah. In his car, in his room, on the football field, it didn't matter. Sometimes, I didn't even know the guy's name.

It was like I was trying to make up for everything that I had missed."

"And then you became a masseuse?"

"After my freshman year I couldn't go home again, not even for the summer."

"You felt guilty about how you had been living?"

"No. I couldn't stand the thought of being under my father's roof for even one night. I had noticed that there were ads in some of the papers for masseuses, so I answered one of them and stayed in Chicago that summer. I enjoyed the guys, some more than others, the money was good, and I liked the sense of control I had over the situation. I've been doing it ever since."

"So you actually enjoy what you do?"

"Yeah, I actually do."

"Do you ever get off yourself, I mean while you're giving hand jobs or anything?"

"Hey, that's kind of personal, isn't it?" Susie-Q sounded amused.

"Come on. How many times have I climaxed right in front of you? I mean, talk about personal, not that I'm complaining or anything."

"All right, all right, I'll tell you about it. Maybe it will turn you on. Not that that's ever been much of a problem." She grinned and slapped his butt. "After I've had a good session with a guy, maybe later that night in bed, I'll think about it and masturbate. Okay, I have a vibrator. I like to think about the different guys— how they feel when I touch them, their facial expressions, how excited they get while I'm doing it for them, how grateful they are, how much they genuinely appreciate the whole experience, and it doesn't hurt if they're good-looking." She laughed softly.

"It sounds like you really get into this."

"I know, I know. Isn't it awful?" She laughed again.

"And you plan to give all this up when you become an analyst?"

"Yeah, I'm afraid so. This is just a phase. Once I feel good about having made up for my repressed adolescence, I'll pursue a normal life."

"Like what?"

"I don't know — marriage, kids, a career, a home in the suburbs. I'll try to experience the more normal highs associated with the reproductive game myself."

"Will you tell your future husband about your wild days as a masseuse?"

"Oh, no, no. My goal, both professionally and personally, will be to help people get past bad feelings or avoid them altogether. Causing bad feelings myself is definitely not part of the plan."

"Don't you think it's important to be completely honest with your mate? Don't you think that's key to forming a really solid bond?"

"I guess it depends on the guy. I'd like to be completely honest. I like talking about this now with you. That's one of the reasons therapy works, by the way. Talking about things that have been bottled up inside usually helps relieve the pressure, helps facilitate healing. But I have to be realistic. Most guys, most husbands, couldn't handle it. Again, I think they're programmed that way, a dominance thing tied to reproduction."

"I don't know."

"Well, what about your wife? If she came back to you and said she had made a big mistake, that she wanted to get back together, would you listen to her?"

"I don't think that's going to happen."

"I know, but what if it did?"

"I guess I would listen to her. But the damage has been done. It's not like we just met and were talking about her sordid past. We had been married for twenty-two years, but that didn't mean anything to her. She just threw that away to be with someone else."

"You say the damage has been done. But to what? To your ego? That's what I've been talking about. Nature has programmed you that way, to become filled with resentment and rage when you've lost your position of dominance with your mate, even if it's just temporary."

"I wouldn't say that that was just a male reaction. There are plenty of jealous females out there."

"That may be true, but from what I've seen, it seems harder for males to get past infidelity than females."

"So if you're saying that everything I do is driven biochemically by nature, the idea of me having a will of my own must be an illusion."

"No, although your drives occur naturally, you *can* control them. You *do* have a will. And to a great extent, your will is directed by strong moral and legal influences, usually imposed by others. I should know. That's where I ran into trouble myself. My father loved using his own version of moral authority to justify controlling everything I did."

"Dominating you made him feel good about himself."

"Exactly."

"And now you get back at him by flaunting yourself at his moral principles."

"Sure, kind of like how you're getting back at your wife's infidelity with me."

"But you also ran away from your father's way of life."

"Yes, just like your daughter and her boyfriend are running away from what seems to them to be an unreasonable situation."

"Do you think it's me she's running away from? Was I too controlling?"

"No. I met her once, and I didn't sense any hostility toward you at all. And I'd have to say that that's the kind of thing I'm pretty well tuned in to."

"Still, she's gone." Vic sighed heavily.

"She'll be back as soon as she can. The war isn't going to last forever, and Canada isn't that far away."

"And what about Cathy?"

"Oh, your wife. I don't know. But things will change with time, one way or the other. Maybe she'll come back. Maybe you'll find someone else. No matter what, things will get better for you than they are now."

"Sometimes my situation seems hopeless, and at other times the whole thing seems almost funny. I must be cracking up."

"No, most people have mood swings. Being able to see the humorous side of things can be a big help."

"Just lying here with you now, talking about things, has made me feel a lot better. At times like this I see life as one big comedy."

"I think humor, seeing the funny side of things, helps us cheat nature, helps us get by all the biochemical programming."

"Could that be one of the things that separates us from the lower animals? I know you think we're all pretty much the same, but I've never see them laugh at anything. I had a dog once that seemed to smile a lot when she was pleased, but she never came close to laughing."

"Humor probably depends on an awareness that the lower animals don't have, I'll grant you that. I hope that makes you feel good."

"As a matter of fact, it does. But have you ever tried to figure out why some things are funny? I mean, what does being funny even mean?"

"I think the point of all jokes is the same."

"Really? There are so many different kinds of jokes."

"I know, but for me, the bottom line of every joke is you shouldn't take life too seriously, because life doesn't take you too seriously. I think that when we acknowledge this, even briefly, there's a burst of relief that makes us feel very good, and we end up laughing."

"You know, I think you're going to be a pretty good therapist." Vic closed his eyes as he felt the tension leaving his body.

≫

About one week later, Arthur sat in his easy chair after a busy day in the lab, nodding off as he waited for Donna to return from an SDS meeting. Suddenly, the phone rang. As he reached for it, Arthur imagined Donna on the other end, letting him know that the meeting was running long and that she was going to be late. But when he picked up the receiver, he was quite surprised to hear Cherrie's voice.

"Hello, Arthur, I was wondering if I could come over and talk with you about Jeffrey."

"Jeffrey? Sure, I guess. Is he having more problems with Notre Dame?"

"No, no, or I should say, I don't really know. I haven't seen him lately." Her voice sounded uncharacteristically edgy. "I don't know where he is. I'm starting to become concerned."

"I haven't seen him either, not since that evening you were both here. You can certainly come over if you want, but right now I don't know how I can help you."

"Good, thanks. I have just a few questions. I won't take much of your time. I can be there in about ten minutes, if that's okay."

"Sure, if that's what you want."

A short time later, as they sat in the living room, Arthur asked Cherrie if she would like something to drink.

"No thanks. I'm just very confused by this whole thing. Something isn't right. Something is funny."

"Like what? I mean, he's been through a lot; we know that. He may just be keeping a low profile while he figures out what he wants to do."

"That's what I thought at first. But he hasn't been at his apartment for almost a week now, and his car hasn't been there either. So finally, I stopped by the Art Department office to see if anyone there knew where he was. But they said they had never heard of him. I started with the main secretary. She told me his name didn't sound familiar, and when she showed me a faculty list for the department, his name wasn't there at all. It simply wasn't there. Then, I talked to an administrator who showed me a schedule of the art classes for this semester and who taught them. His name wasn't there, either."

"That really is odd. You don't think they're trying to cover up the fact that he got in trouble and is no longer on the faculty, do you, like something from *Nineteen Eighty-Four*?"

"Not really. The schedule was printed at the beginning of the semester. No, I think it's something else. It has to be something else. I mean, I have to wonder if this whole thing about him being an art professor was some kind of lie. What else could it be? Maybe his real thing was dealing drugs."

"But didn't you model for him?"

"Yeah. That's how I met him, in fact. He called me one afternoon and said he had gotten my name and number from the Art Department. He said he was looking for a model for a painting that he was going to do. He told me that he was an art professor at Notre Dame and wondered if he could schedule some evening sessions with me. I said sure and met him at one of the studios. He did some nude sketches of me holding different poses, and we went from there. After the first session, we had some coffee together and talked a lot. It was like we had known each other forever. We seemed to really meld. So I continued seeing him as a model and then started becoming more of a girlfriend. But now, I don't know what to think."

"Didn't you also model for other art classes at Notre Dame?"

"Once in a while, yeah."

"Did you ever see him around the department then?"

"No, I never did. I never saw him teaching or anything like that."

"You know," Arthur said, "when I first met Jeffrey, he was playing basketball with some of his students."

"How do you know they were his students?"

"He said they were his students. I guess I didn't have any reason to question what he told me."

"But now, maybe you do."

Chapter Fourteen

A few weeks later, Arthur and Donna pulled up to his mother's new townhouse in a Lincoln Continental, one that he had rented at the D.C. airport. "I can't believe how nervous I am," Donna moaned. "My hands are actually tingling. What if your mother doesn't like me?"

"Don't worry. She will."

"What if she doesn't like the way I look or something? What if she thinks my hair is too long or my skirt is too short? What if she thinks I'm some kind of weirdo?"

Arthur glanced at the knee-length pleated plaid skirt that Donna was wearing. "She won't think you're some kind of weirdo. But if you want, I'll tell her you're pregnant and we're living together. That should help smooth things over."

"For heaven's sake, don't even joke like that. You'll end up saying something like that in front of her."

"I'll try to control myself," Arthur deadpanned.

"I don't know about *your* mother, but my mother is going to go absolutely apeshit when she finds out that I'm pregnant. And if she knew that we were living together, oh, God . . ."

"You're just nervous because of my dad. He always comes on too strong. My mother's not like that at all. You'll see."

"God, I hope you're right."

"I know you want to wait, but we could actually tell my mother about you being pregnant now, and it wouldn't be a problem."

"Sure. I'll introduce myself, shake her hand, and say, 'By the way, Mrs. Weiss, I'm pregnant with your son's baby.' That should go over big. Just promise me you won't say anything now. We have to wait at least a couple of weeks before telling her. We have to give her some time to get used to the idea of us being a couple."

"Eventually, she is going to be very happy about this. Trust me."

"What religion is she?" Donna asked, looking panicked as she suddenly realized that the subject had never come up.

"Southern Baptist," Arthur answered as he turned off the ignition. "That's how she was raised. Her whole side of the family is Southern Baptist. Dad hasn't gone to church with her for years, though. She usually goes by herself."

"She's Southern Baptist, and I'm Catholic. Oh, my God."

"Don't worry about it. She's not going to ask you anything about your religion, and you're not that religious, anyway."

"You don't know how religious I am. And you don't know if she's going to ask me anything about it or not. God, I hope the subject doesn't come up."

"I think you'll be okay once you meet her. Don't worry so much. It's going to be fine."

At the door, Arthur's mother greeted Donna with a warm hug and appeared genuinely pleased to see her son.

"This seems like a nice place," Arthur said, looking around the front of the townhouse. "How do you and Dad like it?"

"It's okay for now, or it will be if they ever get it finished. They just papered in the kitchen last week. We'll get something more permanent when your father finally retires." As Arthur nodded, his mother added, "Well, come on in. It's cold out there. Here, let me take your coats."

After carrying their coats off to one of the bedrooms, Arthur's mother invited them into the living room and sat down with them at the coffee table. "Your father has never cared much about where we live. For him it's always been just a place to hang his hat. But I've always wanted something more." She turned toward Donna. "I wanted a place where I could plant things and fix things up my way, like the house I grew up in when I was a girl. My father was a family doctor, in a small town in Indiana, not too far from Indianapolis. I grew up in a huge Victorian."

"That sounds wonderful," Donna said.

"It was. During the Depression money was tight, but things didn't cost that much, either. And the house was paid for. I really feel bad about not having had a secure place like that for the boys when they were growing up, but their father being in the Army and all made that impossible."

"You and Dad did fine," Arthur said. "Tom and I were like any other kids, except we saw a little more of the world."

"I worry about you not having any roots. I know how important roots have been to me. Then again, here I am living in this ultramodern townhouse, next to neighbors I don't even know, trying to put together a traditional Thanksgiving dinner like I was back on the family farm or something." She shrugged and smiled, then turned toward Arthur. "At least your Aunt Clara is coming, all the way from Muncie, just to help me cook. She and Charles are driving out."

"Really? Driving out?"

"Yes. They should be getting here tomorrow morning sometime." Arthur's mother turned back to Donna. "So what do you do? Arthur hasn't told me anything about you, of course."

"I'm a student at Saint Mary's."

"That's a sister school to Notre Dame, isn't it?"

"More or less. A lot of people think of it that way."

"What subjects are you taking there?"

"Mostly liberal arts. A lot of history and literature. I may take some education courses next year."

"So you're thinking about becoming a teacher?"

"Possibly. I haven't decided yet."

"That would be nice. At least you could stay in one place and settle down if you wanted. Of course, things are so different these days; kids are so independent and opinionated. I think it's the war. There's so much protest against it. Sometimes, I think that's all that's on the television anymore." Mrs. Weiss frowned. "I suppose you don't have much protest at St. Mary's though, do you?"

"Saint Mary's is a conservative school. There isn't much student activity there."

"I wish it would all stop—the war, the protests, everything." Arthur's mother turned to Arthur and established eye contact with him. "Your father's been over there for almost a month, but I haven't heard a word from him for ten days now."

"He's probably involved in some covert operation or something," Arthur replied. "I'm sure he'll call or send a letter as soon as he can."

"We communicated by mail for nearly four years during World War II," Arthur's mother said with a sigh, "and for almost two years during Korea. I thought those days were over a long time ago. I don't know if I can go through something like that again. I'm getting too old to be a pen pal."

"Dad should be back from Vietnam after one year at most, one tour of duty and out. That's the way it typically goes. At least there's an end in sight this time."

"I was so shocked when he said he was going over. He had said practically nothing to me about the war for months. Then he showed up one day with orders in his hand. No warning, no discussion, nothing. Another mission, another tour of duty." Arthur's mother shook her head and looked out the window. "I don't know why he wanted to go so much, but I do know he had to pull some strings to get the assignment. Word got back to me that some of his friends think he's trying to use the war to advance his career, maybe get a star or something before he retires. But I don't think so. I think it goes deeper than that, a lot deeper. I think it has something to do with Tom." She turned to Donna. "Tom was Arthur's older brother."

"I know."

"Yes, I suppose you do. Well, let's change the subject to something more pleasant, shall we? So tell me, Arthur, when are you two going to get married?"

"Mother! What brought that on?" Arthur exclaimed as his head lunged forward and his eyebrows raised.

"I can't be serious all the time," his mother, laughed. "Cut me some slack."

ﾟ

Late the following Sunday night, after a much-delayed flight home, Arthur and Donna finally reached their apartment. Having parked the Porsche in the driveway, they sat and talked a bit before getting out. "I really enjoyed the visit with your mother," Donna said, yawning. "You were right. I think she likes me. She'll probably be happy to see you settle down, too."

"Don't act so smug, or I'll tell her what a leftist radical you really are."

"She'd never believe you. Especially once the baby comes. I am glad you asked me, though," she added, sounding more serious. "To marry you, I mean. That was nice, by your mother's fireplace and everything."

"I wanted to do it right," Arthur said. "So we'd have some memories of this time."

"I'll remember."

"You know, I thought I was going to spend the next few years of my life playing the field, a different girl every night. Then I meet you, and everything changes. I never can catch a break."

"You've never been so lucky."

"I guess," Arthur replied, taking the key out of the ignition. "That really didn't seem much like Thanksgiving though, I mean compared to previous Thanksgivings."

"What was so different? It seemed fine to me. It was perfect."

"I don't know. It was such a small group this time. Just us, my mother, Aunt Clara, Uncle Charles."

"Your Aunt Clara was funny as a stitch. I'm really glad she was there." Donna got out of the car and stretched her arms and legs. "Wow, we're finally here. I feel like sleeping for a week."

"I know what you mean. I thought that flight was going to last forever. My ears won't stop ringing." Once inside, Arthur set the suitcases down in the bedroom and stretched out across the bed, still fully dressed. "I'll unpack in the morning," he muttered with his eyes closed. "I don't have the energy to do it now."

"It won't be any easier then," Donna said, her shoes off, her hands on her hips. When Arthur didn't respond, she sat down on the edge of the bed beside him. "Tomorrow, I have to talk to Father Tom about the wedding. I can tell you I'm not looking forward to that."

"I suppose not. Let me know if he wants to meet with me too."

"He will; don't worry about that. And of course, I also have to call my mother tomorrow."

Just then the phone rang. "God, no! Let it ring," Arthur said. "I don't want to talk to anyone."

"We'd better answer it. It could be important." Donna picked up the receiver. "Hello? Yes, just a minute." She handed the receiver to Arthur. "It's your mother. She sounds funny."

With renewed energy, Arthur sat up and spoke into the phone. "Hello, Mom? We just got back. What's up?"

"I've been trying to get you all night. I got the telegram right before noon. Your father's been killed."

"What?" Arthur's face contorted immediately into an expression of disbelief. "Are you sure?"

"Yes. Colonel Franklin stopped by and confirmed it this afternoon. He wasn't killed in battle or anything. He was flying in a helicopter and got caught up in one of those terrible storms they have over there. I guess he was killed instantly."

"Are you all right? I'll get a plane back out there as soon as I can."

"Don't push yourself. There's no need to rush."

Chapter Fifteen

Arthur placed the phone in its cradle but continued to stare at it. Donna sat down next to him, then asked gently, "What's wrong?"

"My dad's been killed. I'm going to have to go back tomorrow."

"Oh, God, I am so sorry. I should go with you." She put her hand on his forearm. "I'll call Father Tom first thing in the morning and cancel."

"I don't know." Arthur pulled his arm away. "You can come with me if you want, but my mother is going to have a lot to deal with. I don't want to make it any harder for her than it has to be."

"I guess it's up to you," Donna said slowly, a trace of disappointment apparent in her voice. "I only want to help, but it's up to you."

"It's not that I don't want you there. It's just that the two of you just met, and I don't want my mother to have to worry about being polite or anything. And I don't want to put you in an awkward situation, either."

"You don't have to worry about me. I can certainly stay out of the way if I need to. I would only be there to help."

"I know. It's just that I—"

"You don't have to be so stoic all the time. If I went, you would have someone to talk to, especially late at night. That could be important."

"Let me think about it. Everything seems to be closing in on me right now. I need some time to let my head clear. I need to close my eyes for a while. If I don't, I won't be able to function at all tomorrow."

The phone rang again. "Now what?" Arthur groaned as he picked up the receiver. It was Billie Lee.

"Hello, Arthur," she began gently. "I know it's late, but we need to meet. Can you get away for a while?" To Arthur, she seemed a bit more intense than usual, despite the lightness in her voice, despite her heavy accent.

"I don't think so," Arthur replied, giving Donna a wild look. "This is an extremely bad time for me. Extremely bad. To begin with, I have to make a reservation for a flight out of here tomorrow. Things are insane right now."

"I know this is a bad time. But this won't take long, and it is extremely important that I see you. How about meeting me at Sherrile's at midnight? That's not far from where you are, and they're open all night."

"I just can't do it. I know I missed getting together with you last week. I called and told you I was sorry I couldn't make it, but I just can't do anything right now. Maybe in a few weeks."

"I'm afraid that won't work. I know things are bad for you right now, but the project is heating up. We have to get together tonight, if at all possible."

"I can't make it," Arthur replied angrily. "Something's happened here. It's very personal. I'm sorry, but I don't want to talk about it now."

"I know," Billie Lee said quietly. "I know. I was sorry to hear about your father. I may have disagreed with him politically, but he was a good man."

"How did you happen to know about my dad?" demanded Arthur.

"It was on a newscast this afternoon. Apparently, he was flying with a South Vietnamese general or something when it happened."

"Oh," Arthur replied, speaking more calmly. "That sounds like my dad, rubbing shoulders with the brass."

"I hate to push at a time like this, but the project involves other people, and we're going to have to act quickly to get things to work out the way they should. Can you spare me just fifteen minutes? That's all I ask, just fifteen minutes."

"Why not discuss it now?"

"We can't do it on the phone. You never know who else is listening."

"Right." Arthur sighed. "Right. Okay, I give up. I guess I can always sleep on the plane."

"Thanks. See you at midnight. I really appreciate you taking the time to do this."

Arthur started to respond but simply hung up instead.

"Who was that?" Donna asked.

"Nobody important. Someone from the lab with a technical problem. I may have to go in for a few minutes, if you can believe that." Arthur ran the heel of his hand over his forehead, then spread his fingers out on top of his head. He stood for a moment staring at the wall, then said, "Okay. I'll call the airline and get two tickets for us. Which do you want, an aisle seat or the window?"

Later that night at Sherrile's, Arthur was staring a cup of hot coffee when Billie Lee came in and sat down across from him.

"Again, my condolences," she said.

"Thanks."

A waitress showed up immediately and took Billie Lee's order for coffee.

"One thing about your father," Billie Lee continued. "He knew what he believed in and was willing to fight for it. So many young people these days go through the motions, but you have to wonder if there's anything behind what they do. You have to wonder if they would really be willing to put themselves on the line."

"Not like you."

"Not at all like me. I'm willing to do what I have to because I think our objectives are critical to the future of this country. I

don't know if you realize it or not, but we have an opportunity
to make history, to change the direction of the most powerful
country in the world, to literally save it from itself."

"Sounds pretty heavy when you put it that way," Arthur replied flatly. "You have to wonder if it's worth the effort."

"Of course it is. Many lives could be affected." Billie Lee
frowned.

"That's what I mean. What difference do all these lives
make? What difference do any lives make? We live for a while,
we take everything so seriously, and then it's over. All the things
we cared about so much don't matter in the least. My dad's a
perfect example."

"You're down right now. That's understandable. Things will
look different tomorrow."

"I'm not so sure. If you think about it, we're nothing more
than animals trying to survive and mate. Some people are into
dominating other people, but that's just their way of pushing
death away, of feeling immortal for a while. Drugs do the same
thing. So do sports, movies, music. Lots of things, lots of diver-
sions to avoid thinking about death."

"I never thought about it that way."

"I have. Denial is supposed to be the first stage of the dying
process, which is probably true. But I think it starts a lot sooner
in life than most people realize."

"Maybe. I don't know."

"Have you ever noticed how much we look like fish?"

"No, not really. Look, I—"

"You don't think of us as animals?"

"I know we're animals, but I don't think we look like fish.
Apes a little, maybe."

"Just think about our heads. Imagine that we have no neck
or body, just heads swimming in water. Our ears could be our
fins. If you picture the people in this room that way, they look
like fish, treading water or swimming through. And in the end, I
think that's about all we amount to. Life is really nothing to get

excited about." Arthur sipped his coffee.

"Life is all we have. Some of us believe it's our duty to make it as good as we can."

"By threatening to destroy it?"

"We're not threatening to destroy all life. We're just trying to deal with the government by speaking their language. Unfortunately, the threat of nuclear bombs is one of the few things they seem to understand."

"Don't you think it's odd that the evolution of science has brought us to this point?"

"To what point?" Billie Lee closed her eyes briefly without altering her facial expression.

"To the point of nuclear stockpiles, to the point of total destruction. It's almost as if we realize on some level that the world would be better off without us. And since we all have to go sooner or later, why not end the whole ridiculous thing with one big blast?"

"I don't think nuclear war is inevitable, if that's what you mean. But if it did happen and human life was wiped out, other forms would be left to carry on and evolve."

"Yes, exactly. But the other forms wouldn't be intelligent enough to see the absurdity of the situation, at least not at first, and that would make them far more in harmony with the planet than humans ever were.

Billie Lee studied Arthur's face for a moment. "So are you going to make the plutonium for us?" she asked,

"I don't know." Arthur pressed the fingertips of his right hand against his forehead and closed his eyes. Even with the death of his father, her presence seemed strong, energizing, sure. "It's just, I don't know, hard to imagine really doing something like that. Do you see what I am saying?"

"I know, but we have to overcome inertia. We're dealing with a time crunch. To start with, let's say I supply you with twenty pounds of uranium, which, by the way, I can do. After you've received some training, your job would be to convert the uranium into plutonium and deliver it back to me. I would then take it to the next stage where it would be used to make the nuclear bomb."

"Isn't there a danger that the plutonium could fall into the wrong hands? I mean—"

"No, everything has been carefully worked out."

"So what would you do with the bomb once it's made?"

"It will be strategically placed, and its location will be given to the government right away, to show we're not bluffing and to reduce the chance of some kind of accident. But the government will also be told that plans exist for other bombs to be planted around the country, and the only way for them to prevent this from happening is to end the war immediately. No more negotiations, no more talk, just pull the troops out. This would put tremendous pressure on the government for a change. Of course, we would do everything we could to minimize any chance of the plutonium being traced back to you."

"The whole thing sounds so risky. How do I know the people making the bomb are actually responsible enough to pull something like this off?"

"They are."

"But how do I *know*? You said yourself there are a lot of people in the Movement these days who aren't very mature. I don't want to put nuclear materials in the hands of people like that."

"Don't worry. The people behind this thing are heavyweights in every sense of the word. If you knew who they were, you'd agree with me, believe me. But we obviously can't tell you who they are, because we need to protect their identities, and we need to protect you from knowing too much as well. Knowledge can be very dangerous. The FBI isn't the joke everyone thinks it is. They can be very sophisticated when they have to be."

"That may be true, but how can I turn a batch of plutonium over to people I don't know anything about? And as long as we're being honest, I don't really know anything about you. You could be a Russian agent, as far as I know."

"Or I could have the best interests of the United States at heart, like I say I do. Look, if I were to reveal the identity of some of the people involved, you couldn't turn back, even if you wanted to. And there would be a certain amount of personal risk to you from that point on. That's just the way these things work. But this is a step we could take if you want."

"How would something like that happen?"

"Okay. Okay." Billie Lee paused and looked at Arthur closely. "Let's make this simple. Are you ready to take this step? Are you ready to meet some of the people involved and commit to the project?"

Arthur stared at her before answering. She returned his gaze but said nothing. Her mesmerizing eyes left him feeling light-headed. "Why not?" he answered at last. "This stupid war has already wiped out my family and changed my entire life."

Billie Lee scooted her chair back. "Wait here. I have to make a call." She walked to the front of the restaurant and disappeared. As Arthur sat quietly at the table, he felt a deep sense of loneliness. It occurred to him that his father's influence on his life had probably been much stronger than he had realized. The one entirely predictable force.

After a few minutes, Billie Lee returned. "Good news," she reported. "You're going to meet our team leader."

"Who's that? Not some student activist, I hope."

Billie Lee looked around the room before leaning forward and speaking softly. "No, the man's name is Alan Dorfmann, *Doctor* Alan Dorfmann. He's a physics professor at the University of Michigan. We'll go to Ann Arbor and meet with him next week after your father's funeral. I think you'll get along fine with him. He's a research scientist like you."

"He does sound a little better than what I had pictured. But how will I know he's the real thing?"

"You'll be seeing him in his element. You'll talk; you'll get to know him. I hope you realize what a big step this is. Whether you fully appreciate it or not, you are now part of the team. You are committed to the program."

"Let's see how the meeting with this Dr. Dorfmann goes. If you're right about him, I'll do what I can."

℘

The following morning, Vic met with Bono in the Chicago office. His boss was once again in full FBI uniform: short hair, business suit, white shirt, conservative tie, and wingtips. "We got some more information on Billie Lee," Bono said while leafing through the folder spread open in front of him. He took a sip of coffee. "Looks like she's getting ready to meet a physics professor at the University of Michigan, a Dr. Alan Dorfmann.

"She seems to like the scientists," Vic commented dryly.

"Yeah, but this one is a real concern. He's been active in campus protests and has strong ties with SDS. The local agents think he may be part of the new Weathermen faction, which could make him more dangerous than most."

"That's all we need—a physics professor helping the Weathermen. Talk about irresponsible. Of all the antiwar activists out there, these academic types piss me off the most. They spend their whole life in an ivory tower and then imagine they have all the answers for the rest of the world. What a load of bullshit."

"That may be, but we have to figure out what Billie Lee is up to."

"How do you know she's going to see this guy?" Vic asked.

"Dorfmann's office and phones have been bugged for over a year now. She called him last night and said she had someone for him to meet. Didn't say who, though."

"You know, I can't figure out why the Bureau is so interested in her. She never was that much of a leader in SDS. And since she graduated, she hasn't been active at all. Maybe she just has a thing for scientists."

Bono raised his eyebrows. "It could be a CIA thing," he said. "She was close to Joshua Taylor when he was active, but during that time she also traveled quite a bit internationally. That seemed to get the CIA's attention. And ever since Taylor's death, they've insisted that we monitor her activities. So maybe they know something we don't. I guess we're just here to follow orders."

"I guess, but I don't see where the CIA's coming from, either," Vic said.

"Well, in addition to her international travel, and Joshua Taylor turning up murdered, she *has* gone out of her way to meet other *disaffected* scientists. There could be something there."

"I suppose."

"So, have you heard anything about your daughter lately?"

Vic winced as Bono asked the question. He had explained Denise's situation earlier to Bono, not because he wanted to, but because he felt it would be prudent to be upfront about it before any bad news about her boyfriend surfaced. "Not since she called. I just hope she isn't messing her life up too much."

"Were you able to trace the call back?"

"Yeah. She called from some phone booth in Toronto, which doesn't tell me much. I hired an investigator to look around the Toronto area for her, but that's just a shot in the dark."

"Times are changing. Young people seem to have minds of their own these days."

"It's that stupid boyfriend she has. He can't fit in, so he doesn't want her to fit in either. I don't know. I remember when I got out of the Army and joined the Bureau, I was really proud to be a part of things. But kids today turn their back on everything."

"Maybe it's the war," Bono said.

"Everything can't be blamed on the war."

Chapter Sixteen

While Donna rested in their motel room, Arthur sat woodenly by himself at the funeral parlor, watching a parade of military men pay their respects to his father. For the most part, the men stood only a few moments at the side of the closed casket, then fell into small groups around the room, engaging in quiet conversations about everything from the latest football scores to their days back at the Point.

"Your father was very proud of you," a raspy voice to the right called out. Arthur turned and saw an older man wearing a coat and tie seated a few spaces down. He had very short blond hair and seemed to have a permanent scowl on his red, weather-beaten face.

"Thank you," Arthur replied, barely looking up.

"No, I mean it," the older man said. "You and your brother were *it* as far as your dad was concerned. When you got that PhD in chemistry, everyone in the Pentagon knew about it. That's all he could talk about, for Christ's sake. For a while there, I thought he was going to pass out graduation pictures."

"He didn't make a big a deal out of it at home."

"No, he wouldn't," observed the older man, compressing his lips, forming what appeared to be a smile. "He never was one for direct compliments. But behind your back?" The older man rolled his eyes.

"How did you know him?"

"North Africa. We fought together for three and a half years over there—Tunis, Sicily, Anzio, Rome. Then when we got home, we kept bumping into each other, serving together off and on for years. I knew your dad well."

"He never talked about the people he worked with, at least not to me. I wouldn't recognize your name if you told me."

"Don't worry about that. I know he liked to leave his work at work. He was very compartmentalized that way. But like I said, he and I go way back." The older man cleared his throat. "I'll never forget the first time we saw action together. Jesus, what a catastrophe. We were supposed to take this position where the Germans were dug in real deep, and we were supposed to take it fast. It seemed damned near impossible to me. But by God if we didn't do it, and in a little over three hours at that. A more experienced outfit would have taken days, maybe weeks."

"What do you mean?" Arthur asked, feeling a need to be polite.

The older man appeared to smile again. "That's right. You haven't seen combat, have you? Let me tell you a little something about it. If a commander has a tough objective, like we did, and he has to get it done fast, and he has his choice between experienced troops and green troops, he'll take the green troops every time, if he knows what he's doing."

"Why?"

"Because green troops don't know enough to use their heads. They just charge in, no matter how many casualties they take, and get the job done. Period. Then, when it's over, the survivors look around at all the death and carnage and realize they don't ever want to do anything that goddamn stupid again. But of course, by that time they've taken the objective, and the commander comes out looking brilliant. That's what happened to your dad and me. After our first time in combat, we were heroes. We even got bronze stars." The older man paused, looked over at the casket, then dropped his eyes momentarily. "But we couldn't forget all the guys who were dead, and we knew deep down that the only difference between us and them was dumb luck."

"But in the end, it doesn't seem to matter that much," Arthur said. "My dad is just as dead now as they are. Sometimes, I had the feeling he actually wanted to die. It was like he felt guilty about having survived when so many others he knew didn't."

"That's a pretty typical reaction. In fact, I don't know anyone who lived through combat that hasn't felt that way at one time or another."

"Yes, but his whole life was built around combat. World War II, Korea, Vietnam."

"I take it you and your dad didn't see things quite the same way."

"We had our share of disagreements."

"Well, I could tell you something about your dad that you probably don't know."

"Like what?"

"He wouldn't have bothered challenging your opinions if he hadn't respected you." The older man raised his eyebrows, took a deep breath, then blew it out slowly. "So you're starting a career in radiation chemistry at Notre Dame?"

"That's right. How did you happen to know that?"

"Word gets around. Sounds like an interesting field." They both fell silent. After a somewhat uncomfortable pause, the older man said, "Well, look, I have to shove off now, but I'm glad I got the chance to meet you. At your age, you probably can't imagine what something like this means to me. But you gave your dad something to be proud of, and your dad was one of the few men I've ever known that I truly respected."

"Thanks. I appreciate that." The older man stood up, nodded once at Arthur, then turned and walked away.

As Arthur turned back to the front of the room, Billie Lee suddenly appeared. She looked around quickly, then sat down next to Arthur. "I can't stay, but how are you? You holding up?"

"I guess. There's something kind of bizarre about all of this. Someone's alive, then they're dead. I don't know how we're supposed to take any of this seriously."

"Death is inevitable. But what I can't stand is the way the military tries to glorify it. They try to make dying in uniform seem so noble, no matter how wrong the cause is, no matter how many innocent people are slaughtered along the way."

"Maybe we're supposed to go down fighting. Maybe that's better than dying of old age," Arthur said.

"Not unless you're fighting for the right thing."

༈

The next day at the cemetery, a windy late November morning, Arthur stood next to his mother as his father's remains were lowered into the ground. Donna stood on the other side of Arthur with her head down, trying to appear inconspicuous. A few moments earlier, the occasion had been commemorated by a brief eulogy and an echoing twenty-one-gun salute. In addition to family members and friends, a contingent of military men stood solemnly at attention.

"Doesn't seem like much," Arthur's mother said quietly as she turned toward Arthur.

"What doesn't?"

"The ceremony, the grand finale. Your father must have seen something in it that I don't."

"Most things don't live up to expectations. Not that it matters."

"Look at all the dignified men on display," his mother continued. "There's something about all of this that makes them seem so full of purpose, as if they were on some kind of higher mission. But when you know them like I do, you know better. They're nothing more than a bunch of little boys itching for a chance to get into trouble again—another war, another affair, another night out drinking."

"Was being an Army wife that bad?"

"No, not for me. Not at first, anyway. Not when I thought World War II was going to finally end most of the fighting in the world. But since then, it's been one war after another. Big ones, little ones. I've come to the conclusion that it's part of men's nature to go to war. I don't think it has much to do with politics or government. I think it's genetic."

"Not all of us men want to go to war."

"I know, but you would if it was over something that seemed important to you. The predisposition is always there."

ം

Following the burial, back at the motel, Donna busily packed for the return flight to South Bend while Arthur lay sprawled across one of the double beds with his shoes off, watching her. "I can understand you wanting to spend some extra time with your mother," Donna said. "But we do have to get started on the wedding, too. Do you want me to begin making arrangements?"

"If you want. I'll be back next week."

"I can't put off telling my mother about this much longer, either. I should probably call her today, but I really don't feel like doing it."

"Call her now. Get it over with."

"I guess I could. It would probably be better than thinking about it all afternoon." She sat down on the side of the other bed and dialed her mother's number. "Hello?" she said with a gasp.

"Donna? Is that you? Are you all right?"

"Yes. I was just surprised to get you so easily, that's all."

"Well, you sound funny. Why?"

"I don't know. I was just surprised."

"You don't usually call during the week. Is something—"

"I have something to tell you."

"Oh, I knew it. Problems at school?"

"No, things are fine at school."

"Are you sure?"

"Yes. It's just that I—"

"It's not that SDS, is it? You didn't get arrested, did you?"

"No, nothing like that. It's this boy I've been seeing. We're getting pretty serious. In fact, we want to get married."

"Oh, my God, you're pregnant."

"Well, yes. I may be. In fact, I'm sure I am."

"Have you seen a doctor?"

"Yes, I went to a doctor. I'm still in my first trimester."

"Is he any good? I mean, some doctor in Indiana—"

"She seemed okay."

"Have you thought about an abortion?"

Donna was taken aback. "No, I don't want to do anything like that."

"Are you sure? Who's the father?"

"His name is Arthur. He's very nice. He comes from a military background. His father was a—"

"*What* kind of background?"

"A military background."

"You know, Bill McCormick was asking about you just the other day."

"I never liked him. I told you that."

"Hmm. Well, don't be so quick to say no to an abortion. Why don't you give it some serious thought before you—"

"No. I'm not going to think about it. I want to start making wedding plans."

"Well, you can't have a big formal wedding. You remember what happened when Sandy Wassermann got married six months pregnant. People never stopped talking about it. Just the other day —"

"Then we'll have a small wedding in South Bend. I would prefer that anyway."

"This is going to break your father's heart. You know that, don't you? You've always been the perfect daughter to him, no matter what."

"This will not break Daddy's heart. Don't say that. If we just—"

"When are we going to meet this boy? You can't get married to someone we haven't even met."

"We can all get together at Christmas. I'll bring him out. We can have the wedding at the first of the year."

"Are you sure he even wants to marry you? Have you talked about an abortion with him?"

"No, we never talked about that. He wants to marry me."

"Are you sure? Did he say that? How do you know?"

"I know he wants to marry me, and I want to marry him."

"Why don't you ask him what he thinks about an abortion? You can still marry him if you want, maybe later."

"No, I'm not going to ask him that."

"I'm just trying to be realistic. You have to look at your options. Is getting married really the best thing for you right now? You don't want to make a huge mistake, do you?"

"Look, this is going nowhere, and I've got to make a flight."

"A what?"

"A flight. It's a long story."

"Where are you going? What are you going to do?"

"I've got to go now. I'll call you back tonight. Say hello to Daddy for me."

Donna hung the phone up and turned to Arthur. "She didn't take it very well," Donna said, looking much relieved despite her assessment of the situation. "She wants me to ask you what you would think about an abortion."

"It never came up, with you being Catholic and all."

"I know we never talked about it, but what do you think now?"

"I don't know. There's a lot to consider."

"You don't *know*?" Donna looked stunned. "God, I don't have *anywhere* to turn."

"It's your decision," Arthur replied, trying to recover. "I'm not going to ask you to do something that you don't want to do."

"Yes, it is my decision." Donna's face was flushed. She appeared to be on the verge of tears. "The only question is whether you're going to be a part of it or not, or anything else in my life, for that matter."

"I made a commitment to you. That hasn't changed."

"But now you don't know?"

"Look, you just caught me off guard, that's all. I have a lot on my mind right now." Arthur got off the bed, walked around to Donna, and sat down beside her. "Go back to South Bend.

Talk to Father Tom. Start making arrangements. I'll be back next week. I want you to marry me. I want you to have our baby."

"Are you sure?" Donna asked, her eyes filling with tears.

"That's the only thing on this planet I am sure of."

That night, having seen Donna off at the airport, Arthur returned to the motel room that they had shared the night before. As he lay rigidly across one of the beds, unable to relax, the television across the way cast the only light in the room, playing an old movie that he had no interest in.

Then, the phone rang. *Now what?* he thought. Not that he had been close to falling asleep. For almost an hour, his thoughts had been flashing from one issue to the next—his father's death, his mother, Donna, Billie Lee.

He picked up the phone and was greeted immediately by Jeffrey. "Hi, Arthur. I got the phone number for your room from Donna. When I called your apartment to see how you were doing, she answered and told me you were still there."

"Yeah, I decided to stay over for a while to make sure my mother is okay and everything. How are things going with you?"

"Okay, I guess. I was sorry to hear about your dad, of course. But as for my situation, the worst is over now. My ties with Notre Dame are officially broken."

"That must have been hard."

"At this point, more of a relief than anything else. I'm actually starting to become optimistic about the future again."

"You know . . . uh . . . Cherrie was asking about you."

"She was? I haven't seen her in a while, but I think things might be pretty much over with her as well. I'm not sure yet, but that's the way things go sometimes."

"She said you hadn't been at your apartment recently, and when she tried to track you down at Notre Dame, they acted like they never heard of you."

"I don't know who she talked to, but they're probably trying to distance themselves from me. I guess that's understandable."

"She said you weren't even listed as an instructor on the class schedule for this semester."

"That doesn't mean anything. There were some last minute changes after the schedules were printed. It sounds like she's still having trouble dealing with the situation."

"That could be. She seemed pretty confused."

"She and I have both been through a lot lately, but life goes on. Of course, you have your own issues to deal with."

"Yeah, things really seem to be piling up on me now. I was just lying here trying to sort it all out."

"So what's going on with you? I mean, now that the funeral is over and everything."

"Well, let's see. My dad's dead now, and I don't know how much support my mother is going to need. Donna is pregnant, so we're going to do the right thing and get married. And then, there's Billie Lee. She wants to proceed ahead with the uranium conversion. She says it can't wait. Of course, when all of these things finally do settle out, if they ever do, I have a full-time job at the Radiation Lab that I should probably give some attention to if I want to continue working there."

"It sounds like you have a pretty full plate, I'll give you that. So Donna is pregnant, and you're going to get married. Despite everything, it sounds like congratulations are in order. I think that's going to turn out really great for you. Congratulations."

"Thanks. We're going to get married at the first of the year. I'm meeting her parents at Christmas, which could be kind of tense. But once I get through the holidays, things should start coming together. I 'm actually looking forward to starting a new life with her."

"And I'm sure you'll work out something with your mother as well. Helping her adjust to her new life will probably take time, but the opportunity to see her new grandchild will help, I'm sure."

"Yeah, probably."

"So that just leaves Billie Lee and the plutonium. Maybe the best thing for you to do is to forget about the whole deal. I know

Billie Lee is great in bed, but you are making wedding plans now with someone else. You know, you can't be a stud forever."

"I know what you're saying. But the thing with Billie Lee is not really about sex anymore. It was, that's for sure, but now it's the project itself that seems important. Besides, it may be too late to back out."

"Why?"

"The whole thing is just accelerating. This weekend, I'm supposed to meet the group leader for the project. He's a professor at the University of Michigan."

"Professor of what?"

"Physics, and it sounds like there are a number of other well-educated people working on this thing as well. I guess I feel I should do my part. I know my personal life is starting to come together, but sometimes you have to look at the bigger picture."

"Is Billie Lee going with you?"

"Yes. She stopped by the funeral home briefly, then said she had to take care of some things before we head out. We're going to fly into Detroit together Monday, then drive into Ann Arbor from there. I don't know where she is now, but like I said, this isn't about spending time with her."

"So what are you and this professor going to meet about?"

"He's going to train me on uranium conversion procedures. But this will also be an opportunity for me to gain some insight into the people running this thing, and if something doesn't look right, I may still try to get out from under it."

"Well, for your sake, I hope that's an option."

Chapter Seventeen

The following Monday, Billie Lee and Arthur set off for the University of Michigan in a small car that Arthur had rented at the Detroit airport. As Billie Lee drove, Arthur quietly recalled past interactions with his father and his brother, dismissing what now seemed like trivial disagreements with them, seeing them both as bigger than life. His father, a military man who did more than talk. His brother, an all-conference football player who always did what was expected of him and then some. Their lives pissed away for a lot of political hot air. But as the stretch of silence continued, Arthur's thoughts turned to the disturbing dichotomy that his life had become—trying to build a relationship with Donna while converting uranium into plutonium for Billie Lee. *What am I doing?* he asked himself. He wanted to marry Donna, wanted her to have their baby, wanted a family with her. But he also wanted to support Billie Lee's effort to end the war, to shock the government, to make the shallow bastards scramble. He had to admit he found the idea of threatening the government highly satisfying, if for no other reason than to make the loss of his father and brother felt by the idiots responsible.

"Do you mind if we pull into this rest stop?" Billie Lee asked. "We're about fifty miles from Ann Arbor, and I need a break."

"I can drive if you want," Arthur replied. "We can change places in the rest stop."

"No, I just want to break the drive up a little. It can get a little boring at times." The rest stop was not crowded. Billie Lee pulled into a parking place at the far end and unbuckled her seat belt. "Do you want to fool around a little?" she asked, placing her hand on his arm.

"Here? What if someone pulls in next to us?"

"We'll give them a show," she answered with a wide grin and bright eyes. "No, really. I wasn't thinking of anything too heavy, maybe just a hand job. We could put my coat over your lap if that would make you feel more comfortable."

"I don't know. This seems so public," Arthur said, looking around the lot.

"Look, if anyone pulls in next to us, I'll stop and become the model of decorum." She smiled again at him.

As she took off her coat, Arthur unbuckled his pants and slid them and his underwear down to his knees.

She looked at his erection and said, "So far, so good." She then covered his penis with her coat and grasped the shaft with her right hand. "Does that feel good?" she whispered provocatively, moving her hand up and down.

"Yeah, this was definitely a good idea."

She cupped his testicles in her left hand, gently squeezing them as she continued the steady rhythm with her right hand, her eyes focused on his face.

"You'd better move your coat," he gasped after several minutes had passed. The back of his head was pressed against the seat, and his body arched forward as he climaxed.

"Wow, you needed that,'" she commented softly. She released her grip on his penis and fished around in her purse for some tissues. "You should be a lot more relaxed now when we have the big meeting." After cleaning up, she placed the used tissues in a small plastic waste bag.

"That's for sure," Arthur replied as he pulled up his pants. "Do you want me to do something for you?"

"No, this is a bad time, but thanks."

"That was really great. I didn't even ask you for it or anything."

"I know. I just thought it would be fun."

"Well, it was fun for me, that's for sure, but it was kind of one-sided."

"That's okay. I like watching you. I like watching when you get excited."

"Why?"

"I guess it's because I like you a lot. And when we have sex, I get the feeling that we're really close, that you really want to be with me, that we're part of the same thing. It's a good feeling."

"It *is* a good feeling," Arthur said, nodding his head.

Billie Lee started the car.

Once they arrived in Ann Arbor, Billie Lee drove slowly around the perimeter of the campus looking for a place to park. As she did, Arthur observed what seemed to be a ubiquitous population of student hippies, most of them with long hair, most wearing jeans, some with headbands, some wearing boots. The scene seemed almost dreamlike, and he imagined that he was on a sightseeing bus in a foreign country, witnessing the emergence of a previously unknown culture. "Not much like Notre Dame, or even the University of Illinois," he said.

"What do you mean?"

"I mean, long hair everywhere you look."

"Oh, yeah, I don't even notice these days."

"Wonder where they'll be ten years from now?" Arthur asked with a slight frown.

After leaving the car in a parking garage, Arthur and Billie Lee walked five blocks to the physics building, then up two flights of stairs to the third-floor office of Dr. Dorfmann. Billie Lee knocked at the door, which was already ajar, and leaned in. Dr. Dorfmann put down the journal he had been reading and smiled at her. He appeared to be about thirty-five, had shoulder-length brown hair, wore a loose open-collared shirt, and sported a handlebar mustache with heavy sideburns. "Good morning!" he said, pushing his chair back and standing. "I've been expecting you. Come in, come in. Billie Lee, you're looking good, as usual. And I see you brought someone with you."

Although startled somewhat by Dr. Dorfmann's youthful appearance, Arthur stepped forward and introduced himself, noting that Dorfmann was about five-nine, had a slight build, and looked like many of the students that he and Billie Lee had just passed outside. But as he looked farther into Dr. Dorfmann's eyes, he saw an intensity that most of the students seemed to lack. Stepping from behind the desk, Dr. Dorfmann shook hands with Arthur and Billie Lee energetically, then reached for the office door. "Here, we'd better close this. Can't be too careful these days. I don't think the office is bugged, though. At least, I haven't found anything, so far."

"As you know," Billie Lee began, "we stopped by here today so you two could meet each other and hopefully establish a good working relationship."

"Sounds like a *great* idea," Dr. Dorfmann replied. He returned to his desk and said, "Have a seat." Billie Lee and Arthur sat down across from him. "So. Arthur. I understand you're going to make some plutonium for us."

"As far as I know," Arthur replied, "but I don't know much more about it than that."

"Don't worry. We'll fill you in. But first, let me say I'm glad you decided to join us. I can't emphasize that enough."

"Why?"

"Well, for one thing, we need people who can handle radioactive materials. People who aren't afraid of them."

"Can't anyone do that with a little training?"

"Oh, probably, but we need people with more than a cursory knowledge of the materials involved. We need people who can anticipate problems and prevent them from occurring."

"What materials are you talking about? What exactly do you want me to do?"

Dorfmann pursed his lips for a moment before answering. "Okay. Tell you what. I'll give you a quick synopsis of the plan. Then, you tell me what you think. I'm very interested in your opinion, by the way. You're not just another warm body around here."

Arthur shrugged.

"To start with, I'll provide you with a tungsten target and ten uranium-238 specimens shaped in the form of disks. Your job will be to irradiate the tungsten in the presence of these disks, using a small chamber that has been designed to hook up to a Van de Graaff like the one in your lab at Notre Dame. Now, as you irradiate the tungsten, a significant amount of adjacent uranium will be converted into plutonium-239 and fission by-products. What we want, of course, is the plutonium-239. Then, once you've converted all the disks, you'll carefully pack them up and give them to Billie Lee. She'll be responsible for delivering them back to me. So you see, we need someone with a scientific background for this, someone with access to hydrogen ion beam equipment who can do the irradiation and then handle the resulting plutonium responsibly." Dorfmann leaned toward Arthur. "What do you think so far?"

"I don't know," Arthur replied. "To be honest, I haven't worked with radioactive materials that much. Do you have written procedures for all of this, something that spells out in detail how to convert the uranium into plutonium and how to handle the plutonium after that?"

"Oh, sure. We've put a lot of thought into this. You wouldn't believe. We'll provide you with very specific procedures for everything, along with protective equipment."

"What kind of equipment?"

"Nothing unusual: a self-contained breathing apparatus, safety gloves, a safety suit, foil bags. We'll also give you a steel container to keep the chamber and plutonium in and a van to transport everything. You'll be driving the van home from here, by the way."

"Okay. It sounds like you have it pretty much worked out. But again, I've never done anything like this."

"Don't worry. We'll give you complete training while you're here and some hands-on experience. The written procedures will have all the specifics like exposure time, beam distance, cooling, everything. We'll also give you a Geiger counter to make sure you don't generate too much fission byproduct, like plutonium-240."

"How much of a problem is that?"

"Well, above a certain level, plutonium-240 is too hot to work with. And we certainly don't want any nuclear accidents, which is why I'm saying we need someone very conscientious, someone like you, to carry this project out."

"What happens once Billie Lee delivers the irradiated disks to you?"

"Oh, we'll separate the plutonium out and purify it. We have a version of the Purex process that we're going to use."

"What's that?"

"It's a common extraction procedure using water, acids, and solvents. So, what do you think so far?"

"Well, I have another question, if that's all right."

"Sure. Anything."

"I don't mean to question how you're doing things right away, but your plan seems almost too elaborate. Have you ever thought about simply stealing some plutonium? You must know people with access to it, either in research labs or at nuclear power plants. Why not just take what you need instead of going to all of the trouble of making it yourself?"

"That's a fair question," Dorfmann said, leaning back in his chair. "I guess I'd have to say there are a couple of reasons. First, security at nuclear power plants and research labs is pretty tight. I'm not saying it's so tight that we couldn't pull off a theft if we had to, but we would probably compromise some people we know, which, of course, we don't want to do.

"But—" Dorfmann lowered his voice. "There's a better reason for making the plutonium and the bomb ourselves. We want to show the government that our organization has the technical capability and the will to make nuclear weapons from scratch, without stealing anything. We want them to know that they're not dealing with a group of amateurs with pipe bombs. We want them to know that we have the sophistication and connections to make big things happen, that we have the wherewithal to plant nuclear devices across the country, if it comes to that. This is going to be absolutely key to our negotiating position."

"I guess that makes sense."

"It does if you're as serious about this thing as we are. By the way, I understand you lost your father and a brother in Vietnam."

"Bad news travels fast. My dad was killed about a week ago."

"Is that why you're joining our effort? The fact that you've been affected in such a personal way? Sometimes, it takes something like that."

"To some extent, but I've been opposed to the war for a long time."

"I know what you mean. Sometimes we know something is wrong, but we don't really *feel* how wrong it is until our lives have been directly affected by it."

"So have *you* been directly affected by Vietnam?" Arthur asked.

"No. Not Vietnam so much, although I have known people who were killed over there. A couple of former students just last year, for example. I guess my involvement has more to do with who I am, with my heritage."

"Your heritage?"

"Yes. I'm a Jew. My parents died in a concentration camp during the last war. They got me out before it was too late, but they didn't make it themselves. So as a result, I can't stand the idea of remaining passive while the government goes completely insane again. It happened in Germany in the thirties and forties, and it's happening here now."

"This war isn't about anti-Semitism, of course. Jews aren't being persecuted."

"No, not Jews." Dorfmann paused and rubbed his eyes. "But in Vietnam, our military is turning ordinary villagers into refugees and prisoners of war by the thousands. Their homes are being torched, the people are being killed indiscriminately, and their lives are being turned upside down. It's not that different from what the Nazis did in Eastern Europe."

"Except that you see our soldiers as the warmongers this time."

"In a way, but I don't think it's quite that simple. Our soldiers, the ones who are doing the actual fighting, are as much victims of this thing as the Vietnamese. Some people have asked me how the Jews could let themselves be led off to slaughter by the Nazis thirty years ago. I would ask those same people how they can let their sons be led off to slaughter by the United States government today. Last year, we had two hundred and eighty U.S. soldiers killed every week in Vietnam. Every week! To say nothing of the enemy body count and the South Vietnamese killed on a daily basis. And most of these kids, at least the ones from the United States, had no idea why they were dying. So as I said, I can't simply stand by and watch this time."

"Dr. Dorfmann will actually construct the bomb," Billie Lee said softly, "with the plutonium that you provide."

"And some help here and there," Dorfmann added.

"Couldn't you irradiate the uranium samples yourself?" Arthur asked. "It seems like you could do it here as well as I can at Notre Dame."

"Not really. For one thing, I'm being watched far too closely these days. I'm afraid I've been a little too vocal with some of my antiwar sentiments. Plus, the entire school is being scrutinized more. We're considered a radical campus, you know. That's why we need a more secluded place to do the irradiation, a place like Notre Dame."

"But you're not worried about constructing the bomb here?"

"No, not at all. Once we have the plutonium, making the bomb can be done anywhere. It's a fairly simple process. All we need are some common chemicals and a few pieces of apparatus. Actually, these things have already been rounded up and are in a private house not far from here. All we need now is the plutonium."

"Just out of curiosity, how do you make a nuclear bomb? I know the principles involved, but I don't know any of the specifics."

"Like I said, it's surprisingly easy." Dorfmann leaned forward in his chair. "You start by making two hemispheres of plutonium metal, each one about the size of a half a grapefruit." He held his hands out in front of him and cupped them to illustrate the idea. "Typically, we would use a ceramic crucible as a mold and an electric furnace as a heat source. These items can be bought anywhere. Then we bring the two grapefruit halves together and put a small amount of initiator at the center." Dorfmann brought his hands together.

"What do you use as the initiator?"

"Radioactive material. But don't worry. That we already have. So then, we cover the plutonium grapefruit with a beryllium shell."

"Why beryllium?"

"Because of its density. It makes an excellent neutron deflector. I'm sure you know that beryllium has more atoms per cubic centimeter than any other element, so it's a good neutron scatterer, too. Using a beryllium reflector, instead of a more common metal, means we need less plutonium. So the plutonium core can be smaller."

"That makes sense."

"Yes. So anyway, the next step is to form a second shell around the beryllium made out of plastic explosive. Again, we can buy plastic explosive anywhere. We plan to use the kind that has the consistency of putty, and when the time comes, we will simply work it by hand over the beryllium until the second shell is formed."

"Don't you have to worry about accidentally setting the bomb off?"

"Yes, as a matter of fact, we do. We have to be very careful. Too much explosive packed on the outside, for example, can make the device too hot inside, too many neutrons reflecting back into the plutonium. To make sure we're okay, we push a wire through the plastic explosive until it touches the reflector. Then we use a Geiger counter to see if the core is too near criticality. If it is, we have to start over."

"Sounds like that could be a fairly tense operation."

"That's why we need competent people. People who are detail oriented and willing to work carefully. But the final product is well worth the effort. The destructive power of one of these devices is amazing, and the mechanism is so simple."

"Just a matter of nuclear fusion."

"Right. Once a bomb is detonated, the plastic explosive creates a shock wave that slams into the reflector. The reflector acts like a piston and drives into the plutonium. At that point, if we've managed to set it up correctly, the density of the plutonium increases almost to the point of criticality. Then the shock wave hits the center, and the plutonium is compressed to the point of being supercritical. This is when collisions take place between free neutrons and the plutonium nuclei, resulting in implosion, which results in a nuclear fireball."

"You sound a little excited when you talk about it."

"I am. I absolutely am. I'm astounded by the power that's unleashed. There's nothing like it. When an implosion device is detonated, the temperature in the core reaches several hundred million degrees in one hundred millionth of a second. That's hotter than the temperature at the center of the sun. And the pressure produced by an implosion device can be as much as one hundred million atmospheres, which means that, initially, the core expands at a speed of five million miles per hour. That's faster than anything that we know about in our entire galaxy except atomic particles traveling near the speed of light. When I think about the destructive force of nuclear energy, everything else about our self-absorbed lives pales into insignificance."

"I've got to be going," Billie Lee said. "I think you two can take it from here."

"Are you sure?" Arthur asked.

"Yes. I'll drive back in the rental car, since you'll be taking the van back."

"Okay," Arthur replied, his head swimming. He felt himself sinking deeper into a situation that seemed both dangerous and eerie.

Dorfmann smiled. "We have a lot to do today."

That evening, Dorfmann dropped Arthur off at a nearby Holiday Inn where Billie Lee had reserved a room for him. Arthur was exhausted. Familiarizing himself with tedious processing procedures, absorbing detailed technical explanations, and acquainting himself with the reference material that he would use later had worn him out. Without undressing, he stretched out across the bed and closed his eyes. But about an hour or so later, Arthur awoke from a troubled sleep, feeling very much alone. He had agreed to call Donna later that evening at about eight, but he didn't feel like waiting. He needed human contact right away. Without really thinking about it, he dialed Billie Lee's number. He didn't know if she would be home yet, but it was worth a try. The phone rang, but there was no answer. He hung up and stared at the blank television across the room, now feeling more alone than ever.

Suddenly, the phone rang. Arthur answered with an awkward, "Hello?"

"Hi," Billie Lee piped brightly. "Did you call me just now?"

"Yes, I did. How did you know?"

"I thought that may have been you, so I went to the public phone downstairs to call you back. This way we can talk without worrying about Big Brother listening in. So are things going okay?"

"I guess so. There's a lot to take in. I'll probably feel better after I've practiced on the equipment they have here."

"You have the whole week to get on top of it. And if you need more time, we'll take more time. We want you to feel completely comfortable about this conversion thing by the time you go back."

"I'll try, but I feel kind of disoriented here. I don't really know anyone or where anything is. I'm like a fish out of water."

"You're probably just homesick. That will change over the next few days. I'm sure you'll be a lot more acclimated by the end of the week. I'm planning to stop by there Friday night, by the way. I have a meeting in Ann Arbor on Saturday. I hope you'll have some time to see me. You already have a room." She laughed in a way that was both soft and seductive.

"You know, I'm starting to feel better about the whole thing already," Arthur replied, picturing Billie Lee with him on the bed. "Maybe you *are* what is missing here."

"I could have probably stayed there with you, you know, but I didn't want to be a distraction. I realize things are a little hectic for you now, but if you stay focused, everything will fall into place, including you and me."

"I still wish you were here, though."

"I have to say, you sound a little horny. Maybe I should have stayed after all." She laughed again, slowly, knowingly, ending in a low register.

Arthur found himself excited by her laughter, by her voice, by thinking about his intimate moments with her. He pictured her blonde hair moving as she turned her head and smiled. When she smiled, her eyes lit up the room. Doing whatever it took to see her smile always seemed well worth the effort, seemed to make life worth living.

"You know," she continued, interrupting his thoughts, "once we've actually put this device together, once we've proven that we can do it and have begun talks with the government, cooler heads in Washington might actually prevail. They may come around instead of continuing a war that never made any sense anyway. But if they don't, they will have to face the reality that more bombs will be made, followed by more demands for peace. And if they decide to continue on with their stubborn prosecution of the war, eventually one of those bombs may actually be detonated. I guess that's the crux of our argument—why not stop before things get even worse?"

"So you have negotiators lined up?"

"Oh, yeah. I can't tell you who they are, but I think you would be impressed. We're talking about three very well-established academics with doctorates and lots of publications. One of them is a physicist, one is a psychologist, and one is a historian."

Arthur remained silent.

"And then, rounding out the team is the chief spokesman, an attorney with a background in international law. When this thing starts happening, the negotiators will all be located in another country, not on U.S. soil. There's no point in taking unnecessary chances. And a key part of our strategy will be to include the media from the beginning. We want the public to know that a bomb was planted, where it was planted, and why we planted it. We think that public pressure could be critical to our success."

"It sounds like you're playing a dangerous game. Do you really think it's going to work?"

"I do. I think people are tired of the war. I even think that most of the people in the government want to see it end, and I think our plan may be just enough to tip the balance."

"If you're not taken out by the FBI first."

"That is a real possibility. That's why my time with you is so important."

"What do you mean?" Arthur asked.

"I mean our time together—the sex, holding each other. I don't know where this ride is going to take me. I may end up dead. I may end up in jail. I just don't know. But I do know that each time we're together could be our last. Being with you is like taking a break from the insanity. It's like feeling what a normal life would be like, at least for a while, and I love the feeling."

"I thought you were optimistic about the whole thing."

"I am, but I'm still living on the edge. And I can't just forget about Joshua."

"I guess not. So you're going to be here Friday?"

"Yeah, I'll just stop by your room. We can take a break from all this political bullshit and enjoy the natural side of being human."

"That sounds great. Just thinking about you being here will be enough to keep me going this week."

After saying goodbye to her, Arthur stretched back across the bed. *Does this plan make any sense,* he wondered, or was this just some farfetched scheme that would never get off the ground? *And how did he get up to my neck in something like this, anyway?* He certainly agreed that the war made no sense, and the war *had* taken the life of his father and his brother. But trying to threaten the U.S. government? He shook his head. Did his participation in this plot have more to do with his opposition to the war, or was it the incredible sex with Billie Lee? He could easily come up with solid reasons for not doing something this crazy, but all he had to do was see Billie Lee or simply hear her voice, and the reasons flew out the window. *I don't know. I don't know,* he thought as he fell back to sleep.

At a little before eight, Arthur forced himself to regain consciousness and shook his head briskly. He picked up the phone and called his mother.

"Arthur, are you okay?" she asked.

Arthur sensed more concern in her voice than normal. "Yeah, sure. I was just wondering how *you* were doing at this point."

"Well, I got a call from Donna today, asking for you. She seemed to think that you had stayed over here with me."

Shit, another curve ball, Arthur thought as his face flushed and his ears rang, aware now that he was going to have to come up with a new story for Donna. "I'm actually in Ann Arbor, Michigan," he said, trying to sound calm, reminding himself that this new lie should be as close to the truth as possible to avoid slip-ups. "A friend of mine on the faculty here, Alan Dorfmann, is having personal problems right now. His marriage is falling apart, and I'm doing what I can to help him through the transition. Originally, I did plan to stay over with you for a while, but then this suddenly came up. I'm going to talk with Donna later this evening. I'll fill her in then."

"Good. She sounded worried. Sounds like you two are becoming an item."

"Yeah, we are. In fact, we may make things permanent before too long."

"That's wonderful. She seems like a very nice girl. I hope things work out with her. I really do."

"Thanks. But how are you doing? I feel kind of guilty about not being there with you now. That's why I called."

"I don't think it's really hit me yet," his mother sighed. "I'm kind of used to living on my own from time to time, and your father was overseas when he was killed. I know it's stupid, but unless I think about it, it feels like he's still over there and I'm still waiting for him to come home."

"Well, if you need to have family closer by, just let me know, and we'll work something out."

"I appreciate that, but for right now I don't see any reason to change anything."

"Well, no matter what happens, the offer is going to stay open."

After he had said goodbye to his mother, Arthur climbed off the bed, filled a glass with tap water, drank it, and then called Donna.

"Where are you?" she asked immediately. "I thought you were going to stay over with your mother."

"I'm in Ann Arbor. A friend of mine, Alan Dorfmann, is going through some rough times and needs help."

"What kind of rough times?"

"Marital problems. He's having trouble dealing with it." *Don't say too much*, Arthur thought to himself. *The less you put out there, the less you'll have to remember.*

"Marital problems? Are you kidding?? You have a mother who just lost her husband and a girl carrying your baby who needs your help with marriage plans. Couldn't you have simply told him that you were too busy to help right now, that he should probably try finding a counselor or somebody like that to work with him?"

"I just talked with my mother. She seems to be doing okay, for now, anyway. And I'll be back this weekend to help with the wedding. Don't worry about that. It's just that things seemed to hit all at once."

"I don't know. Something sounds funny. I didn't even know you had a friend in Ann Arbor."

"Well, I do. Just try to be patient. This is a crazy week, but once it's over, things will work out."

"I hope so."

"Don't worry, they will."

☙

Three days later, Vic met with his supervisor in the Chicago office. "We finally got the transcript of their meeting with Dorfmann," Bono said, resting his hand on the file on his desk. "Get this. It looks like they're planning to build a nuclear bomb."

"Oh, come on. A nuclear bomb?" Vic leaned back in his chair.

"Yeah. Dorfmann is showing Weiss how to convert uranium into plutonium using radiation equipment. Then, Weiss is supposed to take ten uranium disks back to Notre Dame and do the conversion on them in his lab there. When he's done, he passes the plutonium on to Billie Lee, who passes it on to Dorfmann. Dorfmann then uses the plutonium to make a small nuclear bomb."

"How long are we going to let this continue before we do something about it?"

"That's a good question. I don't know. The problem is, things aren't exactly as they appear."

"What do you mean?"

"For one thing, Billie Lee is not an antiwar activist. Never really was. She passed herself off as one, and the CIA let us believe her story. But she's not. She's an arms dealer. And right now, she wants all the plutonium she can get so she can sell it to the highest bidder."

"How did you learn that?" Vic asked, leaning forward.

"The CIA finally clued us in. They let us think she was politically motivated so we'd keep tabs on her for them, but what they're really after is information about the organization behind her, the people with connections. Apparently, they have quite a network." Bono clicked his pen a few times on his desk.

"What a bunch of assholes," Vic replied. "They could have had the professional courtesy to let us know what was really going on."

"The only reason they let us know now is they don't want us upsetting the applecart. They don't want us arresting her before they learn where she's supposed to deliver the plutonium and to whom. One thing for sure, it won't be to Dorfmann."

"So Weiss and Dorfmann are just a couple of dupes?" Vic asked, his shoulders raised.

"Yeah, all the way. She batted her eyes at them, and they couldn't wait to climb into bed with her."

"She was sleeping with both of them at the same time?" Vic raised his eyebrows.

"No, Dorfmann first, then Weiss. Last summer, Dorfmann had agreed to convert the uranium for her, but then he balked, so she used him to help recruit Weiss. And now, the CIA thinks she may even try to have Weiss make additional batches for her once the first one is done."

"I guess sex still works."

"It does with these nerdy science types."

"Why did Dorfmann stop sleeping with her?"

"He's married and finally broke things off with her. Felt guilty, I guess."

"But he's still working with her."

"Oh, yeah. He still believes in SDS and the Movement and thinks she's part of it all." Bono clicked his pen on the desk again.

"But he didn't want to convert the uranium."

"Right. He knew he was being watched and didn't want to risk it."

"So she recruited Weiss to do it."

"Yeah. With him I think it was mostly sex, although his father's death may have pushed him over the edge."

"So what's going to happen to him?" Vic asked.

"Well, that's another thing." Bono shook his head. "Weiss's dad had some friends in high places, so the situation has become very delicate."

"Very *delicate?* God. Nobody's accountable for anything anymore. How about a simple bullet in the head? I don't care who his dad was."

"That can't happen. Washington was very clear about that. We have to handle Weiss with kid gloves."

"What about Dorfmann, then? Does he get off, too?"

"Probably. The CIA may offer him a deal in exchange for his testimony against Billie Lee. Once he finds out that she's an arms dealer, he'll probably cooperate fully."

"Of course. Why not? So did you find out why Joshua Taylor was killed?"

"Yes. Apparently, he changed his mind and told Billie Lee he didn't want to go through with the plan to make plutonium. It sounds like he may have even figured out that something was wrong with her story. At any rate, the organization behind her decided he knew too much and killed him. She may have even pulled the trigger."

"Did he sleep with her, too?"

"Of course. That's how she works."

"So Taylor is dead, Dorfmann and Weiss walk, and we wait for the word to move in on Billie Lee."

"That's about it."

"Now all we have to do is find a way to pin this whole thing on the Black Panthers." Vic sighed.

"Don't make jokes. There are people in Washington who want to do exactly that."

Chapter Eighteen

By the end of the week, Arthur felt more confident about his ability to complete the daunting task ahead. The hands-on experience that he had gained through repetitive exercises, accompanied by Dorfmann's patient instructions, had greatly lifted Arthur's spirits. But as the week progressed, Arthur couldn't help feeling that Dorfmann had become more distant. Despite their frequent interaction, the exchanges between them had become almost exclusively technical. It was as if Dorfmann was afraid to let his guard down, especially after he learned that Arthur's father had worked at the Pentagon. The only time their conversations did take a personal turn, it seemed to Arthur, was when Billie Lee's name came up. Dorfmann appeared to be keenly interested in the nature of Arthur's relationship with her, for some reason. It was if he were fishing for personal information about her because he had a crush on her himself.

That Friday evening, Arthur sat in his room at the motel, waiting for Billie Lee to arrive. When she finally knocked on the door, he jumped up and opened it wide. "God, it's good to see you," he said.

She put her arms around him and hugged him tight. "Can we stay here awhile?" she said. "I'm kind of tired from the drive." Ten minutes later they were both naked in bed, writhing in heated passion.

"I've thought about this all week," Arthur murmured as he buried his face in her breasts.

"Me, too," she replied, caressing his buttocks. "It feels like I've been away for a long time."

Half an hour later, Arthur was beginning to fall asleep, with one side of Billie Lee's face flat against his chest.

"So how is your girlfriend doing?" she asked casually, startling Arthur awake.

"You mean Donna? How did you happen to know about her?"

"I saw her at your father's funeral. Are you two serious?"

"No, I wouldn't say we were serious. We see each once in a while, but I don't think it's going anywhere."

"I take it she doesn't know about me."

"No. If she asked, I'd tell her about you, but I'm pretty sure she's seeing other guys, herself," Arthur lied.

"So does she know anything about the plutonium or anything?"

"No. I haven't told anyone about that."

"Good. The most important thing right now is to stay on course. I like having sex with you, because there isn't anyone else, at least not anyone that I'm attracted to."

"That doesn't have to change, as far as I'm concerned."

"Good." She breathed in deeply and squeezed his arm.

The next morning, before heading back to South Bend, Arthur stopped by Alan Dorfmann's office. Dorfmann waved him in enthusiastically, and Arthur took a seat across from him at his desk. "Here are the keys," Dorfmann said, sliding them over to Arthur. "The van's in my parking space in the lot behind the building. I'll walk you out to it when you're ready. So, do you have any questions?"

"No, I think we covered everything. And we certainly practiced enough."

"Good. I think you'll do a good job. Remember, Billie Lee is your contact now. She'll let you know when to start the conversion, and she'll arrange the pickup afterwards."

"She's really key to this whole thing, isn't she?"

"Definitely. She has a way of getting things done. No question about that."

"Did you work with her much before this project?"

"No, not at all. She just showed up one day and asked if I wanted to join a major effort to end the war. I was already active in SDS, so I said I was open to anything that made sense. We talked for a while and seemed to hit it off. Very compatible right off the bat, maybe too compatible." A wistful expression passed briefly over his face. "She almost broke up my marriage, but that's another story."

"I see," Arthur said, almost stunned by the revelation. Later that day, as he took the Highway 31 exit off the interstate, Arthur couldn't stop thinking about Billie Lee and Dorfmann. So she had slept with him. That had to be what he meant. As sleet now pelted the windshield, Arthur glanced up at the gray sky and began recalling the many times that Billie Lee had given him the impression that he was the only one who mattered to her.

But how honest had she been? he wondered. Was sleeping with guys simply her way of manipulating them into doing what she wanted? Was the attraction she claimed to feel for him just a line? *Possibly, possibly,* he thought. Then again, maybe she was simply drawn to the guys she worked with. *Not so unusual.* But if, in fact, she *was* using him, the cheating on Donna would eventually stop, which would actually be kind of a relief.

Back at the apartment, Arthur parked the van in the garage and locked it up. He was not supposed to move it again until he received word from Billie Lee. When he entered the living room, he found Donna curled up in a chair, surrounded by textbooks. She was wearing blue jeans, a bulky knit sweater, and red wool socks. She looked terrific. As Arthur walked over to her, she stood up without saying anything, and the two embraced. "So, you made it back," she said softly as the kiss dissolved. She let her hands slide down his arms. "How is your mother doing?"

"As well as can be expected."

"And how is your friend in Ann Arbor?"

"He's doing better."

"Good. We'll have to spend some more time with your mother as soon as we can, but for now, we have to see Father Tom first thing in the morning."

"That should be fun. I hope he's not going to be too judgmental. By the way, I drove back in a rented van. I'll return it in a couple of days."

"Okay. Just remember, the thing with Father Tom is honesty. When he asks questions, just be completely honest."

"You don't think I was planning to lie to him, do you?"

"You'd be surprised how easy that is to do."

❧

That evening, while Vic was working the *New York Times* crossword puzzle in his apartment, his telephone rang.

"Hello, Vic?" said Cathy, his estranged wife. Her inflection was soft and earnest.

"Yeah," Vic answered curtly. "Now what?"

"Denise just called. I thought you'd want to know."

"Of course I want to know. My God. What did she say?"

"She wants to come home." A slight pause followed.

"Great. That's great. Where is she? I'll go pick her up now."

"She's in Toronto, but she's coming back on a bus."

"A bus? That's crazy. I'll go up there and drive her back myself."

"No, she doesn't want that. I offered to do the same thing, but she said no. She said she wants some time by herself to stare out the window and watch things pass by."

"How do you know she won't change her mind?"

"I don't, but I think crowding her right now would be a big mistake. Let's just let her do it her way."

"All right, all right. What happened, anyway? Why did she decide to come home? Did something happen?"

"Yes, something happened. She got off early from her job one afternoon and found Warren in bed with one of the girls who lives in the house with them. Apparently, the girl's boyfriend was out at the time, too. Anyway, later, when he and Denise were alone, he tried to act like nothing was wrong. He tried to tell her it was all part of the free love thing, that it was just physical, that it shouldn't affect their relationship. So she thought about it for a while and then called me. She said that she wanted to come home. It sounds like she's really through with him."

"Thank God for that. I always thought he was a piece of shit. So when did all of this happen?"

"Her first call was a couple of days ago. Then she called me back this morning to let me know that she had gotten her bus ticket and should be here tomorrow evening."

"Well, I'm so glad you finally got around to telling me about it."

"It was hard for me to call you. I had to think about things first."

"What the hell was there to think about?"

"I don't know. The thing with Warren sounded so cheap and sleazy . . . and familiar. I guess it made me think about what I was doing with Bob."

A pause followed before Vic responded. "I thought Bob was romantic and exciting."

"He was. At least, I thought he was. But I think a lot of the excitement came from doing something forbidden, something to get back at you. Then, as the divorce proceedings actually started, a lot of the excitement seemed to fade away. And when I heard Denise talking about what Warren did, the thing with Bob seemed like a big mistake. I don't know . . . What do you think?"

"I think we should get Denise back before anything else. The rest of it, anything between you and me, I think we should take real slow. I think we've already made enough mistakes. We certainly don't need to rush into anything now."

"I guess that's true. I'm meeting Denise's bus at seven fifteen tomorrow at the Chicago terminal. We could meet her together if you want."

"I'll be there."

Vic pushed the receiver button down, then dialed Susie-Q's number. She answered on the third ring. "Hello. How's it going?" he began, trying to sound casual.

"Fine. Is anything wrong?"

"What do you mean?"

"Nothing. It's unusual for you to call me like this, and your voice sounds a little different, that's all."

"Well, nothing's wrong, exactly. It's just that I have to cancel tomorrow's appointment, if that's okay."

"Sure. You let me know in advance. That's all I ask."

"It's not that I *want* to cancel; it's my daughter. I'm going to meet her tomorrow. She's coming home."

"Oh, that's really cool. I know how worried you've been about her."

"Yeah, I can't wait to see her."

"So, do you want to set up another appointment?"

"I don't know. I'm so busy right now. It's hard for me to commit to anything definite."

"We're not talking about a commitment, just an appointment."

"I know, but I have so much going on now."

"I see…Well, when things settle down for you, maybe you could give me a call."

"Sure, I'll call. Don't worry about that."

"You know, I only have five clients now. I'm only working with people I like."

"That's very flattering. You make me feel bad about canceling."

"Don't worry about it. In a few years I'll be a therapist, and all my clients will be new. But anyway, I hope things work out for you and your daughter. I really do."

"Thanks. I'll call you soon."

"Any time…Goodbye, Vic."

∽

Over the next few days, Arthur received no word from Billie Lee. But the presence of the van under his roof weighed heavily on his mind. In the light of day, Arthur was able to suppress his anxiety, but at night, the van seemed like a ticking time bomb. He imagined cops knocking on his door, looking for drugs but finding the uranium instead. He imagined the story making national news and the media camping out on his front lawn. He pictured himself trying to flee the country on the sly to start a new life, only to be apprehended at the border.

In a recent nightmare, Arthur dreamed that he was being tried for treason in a court presided over by his father. Wearing a flowing black robe, Arthur's father was deliberate and fair, but the disappointment in the old man's eyes was almost unbearable. As the proceedings came to an end and the gavel slammed down, a prison door swung open, and Arthur entered with his head hung low. Then suddenly, a firing squad materialized, led by Dr. Fischer. His boss ordered Arthur to snap to attention, and as he did, Arthur saw that his brother Tom was one of the uniformed soldiers holding a rifle aimed at his chest. As Dr. Fischer dropped his hand, the firing squad unloaded on Arthur, and a giant mushroom cloud immediately formed, followed by a series of tremendous explosions that destroyed most of the planet.

What am I doing? Arthur thought, sitting up in bed, blinking his eyes, and running his fingers over the cold sweat that had formed on his chest and shoulders. *Plutonium? Plutonium for a nuclear bomb?* Arthur looked over at Donna as she slept peacefully next to him. *This is getting too heavy,* he thought. *Way too heavy.*

The next morning, Donna sensed that something was wrong and observed that Arthur had become more withdrawn with each passing day. She didn't find his behavior unsettling, however. She assumed that he was simply nervous about getting married and becoming a father. "You're not getting cold feet, are you?" she asked, smiling, taking hold of his arm, looking into his eyes.

"No, I don't think so, but I can't say I'm looking forward to meeting your family, especially your mother."

"Why? She hasn't done anything to you, at least not yet."

"I know, but I'm sure she sees me as the commoner who had the audacity to steal her daughter. I know I'm not what she wanted for you."

"That may be, but you *are* tall. That must count for something." Donna grinned and laced the fingers of Arthur's hand with her own.

"Your mother likes guys who are tall?"

"I don't know. I never asked her, but I had to come up with something to make you feel better."

"Thanks."

"Don't mention it. Any time." She pulled him close.

Later that week, while trying to relax in his easy chair after work, Arthur heard a knock at the front door. Donna had gone shopping, and he wasn't expecting anyone. Feeling a familiar wave of paranoia, Arthur considered not answering before finally pushing himself out of the chair. Swinging the door open wide, he saw Jeffrey, standing alone, shifting his weight from one leg to the other in the cold.

"How's it going?" Arthur asked.

"Fine."

"Good, good. I'm glad you stopped by. I really am. It's been a while, hasn't it? Come in. So, what's been happening with you these days?"

"I'm moving to Arizona. And how are you doing?"

"Well, the funeral was a week and a half ago, but it's like the whole thing hasn't sunk in yet. I don't know if it ever will. But what about you? Arizona? Here, sit down. Tell me about it." The two young men took seats in the living room.

"The good news is," Jeffrey said, "a friend of mine got me a job at the University of Arizona as an art instructor. It could turn into something like I had here eventually. I don't know. But the main thing is, I'll be able to paint outdoors. The colors and natural formations in the desert are incredible. I can't wait to get down there and get started. I can see some major work coming out of all this."

"And Cherrie?"

"She's not going with me. I talked with her about it, but she doesn't graduate until this spring. Besides, she's been accepted at Stanford Law School for next fall. I guess we're going in different directions now. It was probably inevitable."

"Law school? I thought she was an art major."

"No, history."

"Things are changing fast."

"It's kind of ironic," Jeffrey observed. "She's leaving her cultural heritage to pursue causes within the white establishment, and I'm leaving a comfortable white lifestyle to pursue Native American values in the Southwest."

"That does sound ironic. I hope you find what you want."

"At least I can slip into Mexico if I need some psychedelic inspiration. Well, I'd better go. I just wanted to see you before I left. Funny how things turn out, though."

"Yes," Arthur said. "Yes, it is."

After they stepped outside and Jeffrey had begun walking away, Arthur noticed a piece of mail in the mailbox. *Late in the day for mail,* Arthur thought. Lifting the mailbox lid, he took out a heavily taped letter with his name and address on it, but no postage. He carried the letter inside and opened it. The message he read was brief and to the point:

Arthur,

I understand things went well in Ann Arbor. Please proceed as agreed. When you have finished, I will contact you. After you have read this note, please destroy it immediately.

There was no name or signature at the end. Arthur was relieved to get word that he could finally begin working on his part of the plan, but the surreptitious nature of the note bothered him. *Why the indirect communication?* he wondered. Was he being watched? Who else knew about this thing? Was it too late to back out? Thoughts of Joshua flooded his mind, leaving him anxious. *Who really killed him?* he wondered. *The government?*

After mulling the situation over for most of the evening, Arthur decided to proceed with the plan as soon as possible, if for no other reason than to get the damned thing over with. The next morning, Arthur scheduled beam time on the Van de Graaff for ten o'clock Saturday night, a time when the lab would likely be vacant. In addition, he decided to be as truthful as possible with Donna and told her that he planned to meet a colleague at the lab late Saturday. Thankfully, she didn't seem to suspect anything.

Following two long days and nights of waiting and another round of nightmares, Saturday finally arrived. As the day wore on, Arthur became increasingly nervous, spending most of his time alone in the bedroom. Early that evening, to help alleviate the stress that was now pounding in his ears, he lay across his bed and forced himself to review the lab procedures one more time, even though he knew them all by rote, even though he was in no condition to assimilate new information. At nine thirty, Arthur said goodbye to Donna, took the van keys out of the vase in which they had been hidden, backed the van out of the garage, and drove to the lab.

After parking in his normal space, Arthur proceeded carefully through the cool night air, hauling the insulated steel case that Dorfmann had given him at his side. The case contained the lab procedures, safety gear, a Geiger counter, the reaction chamber, the lithium target, and the uranium disks that were to be converted into plutonium. Later, he was to use the case to carry the transformed disks back to his apartment. Once inside, Arthur looked around carefully but saw no one. He carried the case downstairs, through the small room that housed the Van de

Graaff controls and into the adjoining heavily insulated room where the Van de Graaff itself sat. He recalled that the controls were separated from the instrument because of the potentially lethal amount of X-rays produced during heavy metal irradiation.

Arthur took a deep breath. *Have to stay cool,* he thought. He opened the case and methodically put on the safety suit and accessories, then checked once again to make sure that everything he was going to need was present and accounted for. Holding his arms out in front of him, he felt like a spaceman in a 1950s science fiction flick. Under less pressing circumstances, he might have been amused by this image, but not now, not now. Arthur's stomach was queasy, his hands were shaky, and his ears were ringing from the unrelenting fear of getting caught red-handed. His career, his future, his life were all on the line. *Calm down, calm down,* he thought. If someone did happen to see him, he could try to bluff his way through it, doing as Alan Dorfmann had suggested, saying as little as possible while insinuating that he was working on a classified government project. *But what if that didn't work?* What if he ended up being charged with conspiracy to overthrow the U.S. government, or treason? What if he ended up in prison for life or even executed?

And as if these concerns didn't generate enough tension, there was the physical danger posed by the plutonium itself. Exposure to a few milligrams, a barely visible speck, would cause certain death in a matter of months, and it would probably be a painful death. Arthur pictured himself lying in a hospital bed with Donna at his side as alpha rays bombarded the linings of his lungs, creating scar tissue that would soon choke off the oxygen to his blood. Even exposure to a lesser amount, a few micrograms, an amount not even visible, would very likely cause lung cancer in ten to twenty years.

But enough. He had to convert the uranium disks without exposing himself to radioactive material and without getting caught. It was as simple as that. Arthur breathed in deeply as he approached the Van de Graaff, but he couldn't help feeling that the instrument looked different somehow, more imposing, almost intimidating. He set up the process chamber, then retrieved one of the disks from the metal case and placed it in position near the lithium target for ion beam transformation. Returning to the control room, Arthur closed the doors to the Van de Graaff room, which activated the safety switches. He then turned the power on and waited for the electronics to warm up and stabilize. This took a long ten minutes. As he waited, he watched the entrance to the control room, looking for any colleagues or graduate students who might be stopping in. But nobody came.

Next, he switched on the selsyn power and gas, and after another anxious ten minutes, set the voltage at 2.5 MeV and adjusted the gas pressure. *Turning lead into gold,* he thought. *Nothing to it. Nothing to it.* As he continued to work, the routine nature of the procedures he was following began to calm him somewhat, eventually enabling him to relax to the point that he became almost unaware of the time. And after nearly six hours of irradiation and cooling, as he set the last of the disks up for conversion, he suddenly felt a burst of optimism, a growing confidence that this assignment was going to be completed successfully after all, despite all his initial misgivings. By four thirty that morning, the job was done, and Arthur was elated. He placed the equipment he had used in the steel case and made sure the irradiated disks were all inside as well. Next, he locked the case and took it out to the control room. He then removed the self-contained breathing apparatus, the safety suit, and the gloves and placed them carefully in the foil bags that had been provided.

Feeling immensely relieved, he carried the case and bags outside. As he made his way to the parking lot, he looked around but saw no one. He then set the case and bags in the back of the van. It was now close to five. Through the darkness, the campus looked still and beautiful. A gentle breeze seemed to celebrate his accomplishment. The mad excursion had finally come to an end. He felt like a G.I. back from war, on his way home.

Back at the apartment, Arthur pulled the van into the garage slowly. After climbing out, he carefully scanned the street and surrounding apartments. No cars, no people, nothing. Just a quiet Sunday morning. He closed the garage door and locked it, then carried the steel case and foil bags to a large storage cabinet located next to his workbench and locked them securely inside. He patted the side of the cabinet. *Mission accomplished.*

Arthur then proceeded to the bathroom, where he took a long, steamy hot shower. But as he stumbled into the bedroom and collapsed on the bed next to Donna, his eyes closing, his mind beginning to drift off into blissful sleep, he was suddenly startled by the sound of her voice.

"Where have you been?" she asked, sounding wide awake. "You've been gone all night. Don't tell me you were at the lab all that time."

"But I was," Arthur replied. "It just took more time than we thought."

Donna moved into a stiff upright position with her back against the headboard. Wearing a simple blue cotton nightgown, she folded her arms in front of her. "You were out all night, then come dragging in after five in the morning and take a fifteen-minute shower. Why would you need to shower so long? Did you get dirty?"

"No, I just felt like a shower. You know hot showers help me relax."

"I get the feeling that something is going on. Last week, I answered the phone twice, and the person on the other end hung up on me. Are you seeing someone else? Just tell me if you are."

"Come on. It was just work. There isn't anyone else. This kind of research gets very involved at times. That's all."

Donna looked at him but didn't say anything. She then lay down on her side with her back toward him. Arthur started to say something but closed his eyes instead.

༄

Later that morning, the phone by Vic's bed rang. He answered after the third ring.

"Vic, this is Frank Bono. Sorry to call on Sunday morning. I hope I didn't wake you."

"Good morning. What's up?"

"Well, apparently we lost Billie Lee. That's what's up. We watched her for months without a problem, and now, all of a sudden, she's disappeared. Maybe we got too comfortable. I don't know."

"You want me to look for her?"

"No, that's not it. We already have people looking for her. The thing is, we're supposed to arrest her when she passes the plutonium on to her contact. The CIA wants to know who that contact is, who's making deals these days, who's buying this stuff. And we're responsible for determining that, for pinning that down. But now we're going to look like a bunch of idiots who can't handle anything because we don't even know where she is. If we don't turn this around fast, the CIA will never let us live it down. Never. Washington is really upset."

"So what do you want me to do?"

"We know that Weiss made the plutonium last night, but he hasn't passed it on to her yet. You need to pay him a visit as soon as you can and put the fear of God in him. You need to let him know that his life depends on us knowing exactly when and where she's going to take possession of the plutonium. We can still pull this out if we get full cooperation from him. I'm depending on you to take care of that."

"I'll do what I can."

Five minutes later, Vic's phone rang again. "Hello?" he answered warily.

"Good morning," a raspy voice replied. "You don't know me, but I work at the Pentagon, and I want to talk with you about Arthur Weiss."

"Who?"

"Don't worry. You don't have to acknowledge anything. I just want you to listen to what I have to say. I was a close friend

of Arthur's father, who, in case you didn't know, had a very distinguished military career and was killed recently in Vietnam."

"What does any of this have to do with me?"

"I'll tell you what it has to do with you. I want to be sure that
you understand that Arthur's safety is first priority. First priority.
His brother was killed in Vietnam, and as I said, his father was
killed there, too. At this point I don't want to see his mother going to any more funerals."

"I can't really talk about this kind of thing on the phone. I
don't even know who you are."

"I know. But the point is, I know who *you* are, and I'm going
to hold you personally responsible for Arthur's safety. I know
you already have orders to keep him safe, but I want you to understand, you're going to have more accountability than you can
handle if anything happens to him."

"I don't appreciate being threatened."

"Nobody does. But sometimes it's important to make priori-
ties clear before starting an operation. That's all I'm doing here."

"Anything else?"

"No. That should do it."

There was a click. Vic set the receiver down and shook his
head. *I have to get out of covert operations.* he thought. *I need
something that makes more sense.*

Chapter Nineteen

The vague sound of a doorbell ringing intruded upon Arthur's dreams. "What?" he muttered. His body jerked involuntarily from a deep sleep into an upright position in his easy chair. He glanced at his watch. Ten thirty. Still Sunday morning. The doorbell rang again. As Arthur struggled to regain full consciousness, he recalled that he was alone, that Donna had gone to mass. The doorbell sounded yet again. Still groggy, Arthur rose slowly from his chair, snapped off the television, and stumbled to the door. He opened it halfway.

"May I come in?" Vic asked tersely. Arthur found his gravelly voice unsettling, almost menacing. "We met at the Radiation Lab. I work for the FBI."

"Oh, yes, I remember. You asked me about Joshua." Arthur pulled the door open farther.

"Right," Vic replied, brushing by him. "Come with me." Vic led the way back to the living room and sat down uninvited on the couch. Arthur followed and sat down across from him.

"What's going on? Why are you here?"

"As I said, I'm with the FBI. And as you well know, there's one hell of a lot going on."

"What do you mean?"

"I mean, you recently made plutonium for an international criminal who uses the alias Billie Lee. I mean, you're planning to turn this material over to her with the understanding that a certain disaffected physics professor at the University of Michigan, a Dr. Alan Dorfmann, will use it to make a nuclear bomb and threaten the United States government. I mean, Dr. Weiss, that life as you know it is over."

"You can't prove anything," Arthur replied weakly, now experiencing unrelenting waves of panic.

"Of course I can. Not that I need to. When someone's screwed up as much as you have, their situation is often handled directly, no questions asked."

"Are you threatening me?"

"We're a little beyond that, but if you want to call the police, feel free. Or maybe you would prefer going over my head at the FBI. I can give you either number." Vic sat back on the couch.

"I want to talk to an attorney," Arthur insisted with his eyes nearly closed.

"Are you having trouble understanding what I'm saying?" Vic replied harshly. "You want to talk to an attorney? My God." He shook his head, then fixed his eyes on Arthur. "Look, you're going to do exactly what I say, when I say, exactly how I say to do it. Is that clear?"

"No," Arthur answered, summoning up as much courage as he could. "I'm not going to do anything for you or any other government thug. If this comes down to getting killed, then that's what it comes down to. I'd rather go out like that than sell out to someone like you."

"I see. Well, before you conjure up any visions of yourself as some glorious martyr for some highly worthy cause, let me fill you in on a few facts. Billie Lee is not a member of any elite political group, as you were so easily led to believe. She's part of a ring that deals arms on the black market, plain and simple. And right now, she's after plutonium, plutonium that can be sold in the Middle East for one hell of a lot of money."

Vic paused. Arthur said nothing.

"You might be wondering," Vic continued, "why I'm meeting with you now, as opposed to running you in or simply eliminating you from the scene."

"I haven't had time to give it much thought," Arthur answered softly. He passed his hand through his hair.

"No, I guess not." Vic started to smile, but didn't. "The fact is, we need your cooperation, which makes you lucky, very lucky."

"I see," Arthur replied, feeling dazed. "So what . . . what do you want me to do?"

"We want you to help us locate Billie Lee. We don't know where she is right now. My guess is she's lying low because she realizes we're on to her. So we need your cooperation in helping us find her, which could make things go one hell of a lot easier for you down the road. And as you know, you're in some pretty deep shit."

"I haven't seen Billie Lee since we were at the University of Michigan."

"She'll contact you, because she still wants the plutonium. And when she does, I want you to call this number and let us know." Vic handed Arthur a piece of paper with nothing but a local telephone number written on it.

"How do I know you're telling me the truth? The only thing I know for sure is that somebody is lying to me."

"You'll figure it out. But in the meantime, you need to do what you're told. You know, I could have threatened you more than I did, but fear alone doesn't usually get the job done. That's why I took the time to explain things. We need to take Billie Lee out of circulation. The foreign government that she plans to sell the plutonium to is potentially a lot more dangerous than a whacko like Dr. Dorfmann."

"What exactly do you want me to say to her when she calls?"

"Whatever you would normally say. We want you to go along with her like nothing is wrong. Agree to meet her whenever and wherever she wants, but then call us. Keep in mind that once she has the plutonium, the simplest thing for her to do is kill you. And she won't hesitate, either. Especially if it means keeping things neat. Remember Joshua Taylor? She's the one who killed him. And she'll kill you, too. So one way or the other, you're going to need our help down the stretch, which means you'd better start cooperating with us now. And that includes keeping me informed."

"I guess I don't have any choice."

"That's a real understatement."

Late that night, as Donna slept soundly, Arthur slipped out of bed and crept into the living room. He turned on a light, then went to the phone, but he didn't sit down. He was too nervous; his stomach was churning. Instead, he placed a telephone call to the residence of Alan Dorfmann. He assumed Dorfmann's line was tapped, but he made the call anyway.

"Hello," groaned a woman's voice. "What is it?"

"Yes," replied Arthur, clearing his throat. "Could I speak with Dr. Dorfmann, please?"

"I'm afraid he's indisposed at the moment. May I take a message?"

"This is very important. It's imperative that I speak with him now. Could you tell him it's Arthur?"

"It's very late. Are you one of his students? If you are, his office hours are posted. He's usually—"

"I'm not a student. I need to speak with him now. Please."

"Just a moment. I'll see if he's available."

After what seemed like an interminable pause, Dorfmann's voice came over the line. "Arthur, is that you?"

"Yes. I know we agreed not to have any contact with each other, that everything was going to be handled through a third party, but something's come up."

"You know, this is probably not the best means of communication. I would suspect that we have a security issue. You might want to be very careful about anything that you say. In fact, it might be better if we agreed to meet somewhere to discuss what's on your mind. Can we do that?"

"There's not enough time, and I don't think we have anything to lose. I've given this a lot of thought," Arthur replied.

"Really? I hope you know what you're doing. But I'm afraid I'm going to reserve the right to hang up on you at any time. I hope you understand."

"I understand. Actually, I have just two questions. First, are you familiar with a former activist named Joshua Taylor?"

"No. Of course, there are so many people in the Movement now, but no, I don't know a Joshua Taylor."

"Okay. My other question is, have you worked with anyone else on this project besides the person who introduced us?"

"I have to tell you, Arthur, I'm *this* close to hanging up on you. Can you tell me what's going on?"

"Please answer that one last question. If you answer it, I'll let you go."

"Just her," Dorfmann replied after some hesitation. "When we met, I was quite active politically. I had been interacting with a number of people, but on this project? Well, she's the liaison. She has the contacts. So what's—"

"So you aren't really the team leader. You don't have *any* other contacts on this project."

"That's right."

"Damn. I was afraid of that. Okay, please listen, and don't say anything. The FBI knows everything. The project is finished. Billie Lee is not who she says she is. You need to destroy any tangible evidence linking you to the project as fast as you can. Then, you need to get the best attorney that you can find. I know it's hard to accept bad news like this over the phone, but I'm trying to help you. And this is the best I can do."

Arthur placed the receiver into its cradle. Beads of sweat ran down his face. He turned off the light in the living room and sat down in the easy chair, trying to calm himself. But his mind was racing. Some time later, he fell into a troubled sleep, dreaming at one point that he and Billie Lee were fleeing hand in hand from a swarm of FBI agents. But the faster they tried to run, the slower they moved. After a few hours, Arthur woke up in the chair feeling cold and unsettled. With a sense of resignation, he decided to get up and get ready for work. *Might as well go in early,* he thought. *Can't sleep now anyway.* But as he entered the garage to leave, Arthur was startled to see Vic with his backside against the front fender of the Porsche, arms folded.

Vic looked up as Arthur approached. "You're running a little early this morning," Vic began. " Have trouble sleeping?"

"What's going on? Did you hear from Billie Lee?"

"You can do better than that. You know why I'm here."

"What do you mean?"

"Your friend Dr. Dorfmann was picked up this morning. We couldn't take a chance on him tipping off Billie Lee. And for your information, the case against him is airtight."

"So my phone is bugged."

"Not necessarily *your* phone. But I am curious . . . What possessed you to call Dorfmann like that?"

"I wanted to understand Billie Lee's role in this thing better. I wanted to see how honest you had been. And if you had been straight about Billie Lee, I wanted to warn Alan. I figured it was the least I could do."

"No matter what the consequences to you?"

"What are the consequences to me? Is that why you're here now, to take me in?"

"No. We still expect Billie Lee to contact you, and we still expect you to cooperate. But if you pull another stunt like the one you did last night, we're going to shut you down hard and fast. That you can believe. So you might want to ask yourself where that would leave Donna and the baby." Vic paused and gave Arthur a hard look. Arthur didn't say anything. "You'd better get to work, doctor," Vic added dryly. "You don't want to be late."

Later that morning, while Arthur was staring at an open lab notebook on his desk, trying to focus on what he should complete that day, the phone rang. *Now what?* he thought. He picked up the receiver before the second ring. He didn't want to answer at all, but he was afraid to take a chance on missing any critical information that might affect the surreal ride that his life had become.

"Hello?" Arthur answered weakly.

"Hi, this is Jeffrey. Could we get together for lunch today? I have something I need to talk with you about."

"I thought you were going to Arizona," Arthur fired back, feeling nearly overwhelmed, thinking the last thing he needed was lunch with Jeffrey. What was there to talk about, Arthur wondered. *Drugs? God, no.* "I'm really busy right now," Arthur said anxiously. "Could we do this in a few days?"

"Well, like you said, I'm going to Arizona, so we have to do this now. And this really is important. Why don't you meet me at my apartment at eleven thirty? I'll pick up some sandwiches, maybe make some lemonade."

"No wine this time?"

"No. You definitely need to be thinking clearly. This is more about you than about me."

Although the meaning of this last statement wasn't exactly clear to Arthur, something in Jeffrey's voice seemed compelling. He couldn't pinpoint what it was specifically, but he didn't want to stay on the phone any longer than necessary. He was still afraid the subject of drugs might come up, and God knows who else might be listening in or even taping their conversation. Finally, yielding to the building pressure, he let out a sigh and replied, "Okay, eleven thirty."

At the appointed time, Arthur knocked on the door to Jeffrey's apartment. Jeffrey opened the door right away and led Arthur into the dining room, where a plate with sandwiches and a pitcher of lemonade sat on the table. "So how are things going these days?" Jeffrey asked amiably as they took seats across from each other.

"Kind of crazy, to be honest."

"I can imagine. Here, have a roast beef sandwich." Jeffrey placed a sandwich on a napkin and passed it to Arthur. "You're kind of sitting on a bomb right now, literally. I understand you made the plutonium."

"How did you know that?" Arthur asked, looking startled.

Jeffrey looked directly at Arthur but didn't say anything right away. Arthur felt his heart pounding, and his mouth was dry. He filled a glass with lemonade and took a long drink.

"I'm not really an art professor," Jeffrey said at last. "I don't know if you figured that out or not. You might have. But the truth is, I'm a CIA agent. I developed a relationship with you because of the Company's interest in Billie Lee."

"Really?" Arthur closed his eyes and felt the room starting to spin. *Stay calm,* he thought. *Stay calm.* He opened his eyes. "But I . . . saw you do drugs. You had a girlfriend, students, the whole works. Are you saying that none of that was real?"

"It was all a cover. I've had extensive training on how to handle the drugs you saw me do, or at least thought you saw me do, and the guys you saw posing as my students were actually agents themselves."

"What about Cherrie? Is she an operative, too?"

"No. She's just a girl I met, a student and part-time model who seemed to fit the image I was going for. Although she is good in the sack, and I am still human." Jeffrey smiled. "The main reason we created that story about me getting busted for drugs and kicked out of Notre Dame was to make leaving her smoother. We didn't want her to know or suspect anything. I'm not sure we were completely successful, but we wanted the break with her to be clean. When you're operating undercover, like I was, it's important to be thorough when taking care of the little things. It's the little things that can really trip you up. We didn't want her asking too many questions."

"So you just used her."

"Of course. We use people all the time. It's part of the job. I liked having sex with her, but come on."

"That seems kind of cold, don't you think?"

"Sure. Big deal. That's just the way it goes sometimes. But don't get me wrong. I really did like her, and we had a great time. It's just that the relationship could never be long term, and when the time came, it had to end."

"I don't think I'd want a life like that, a life built on deception. Don't you ever just want to be yourself?"

"I am myself. It's just that deception is part of who I am. But that doesn't make me all that different from everyone else. None of us are completely honest in our daily lives. We all say and do things that are at least somewhat dishonest to get what we want. Take your relationship with Billie Lee. What do you think Donna would have to say about that?"

Arthur looked down briefly, shook his head, then looked back up and made eye contact. "That's a long way from assuming a completely false identity just to get information for the government."

"But at the end of the day, I know what I've done and why. I don't get lost in the little games most people play."

"Well, I have to give you credit. I really thought you were an art professor. Did you study art in school at all, or was that just part of the act?"

"I majored in economics and then went to law school, although I did dabble in art from time to time."

"Jesus. And I really bought the whole thing. I thought you were a true believer in counterculture values."

"It was an easy role for me to play."

"Why?"

"Because some of my personal views do overlap with those of anti-establishment types."

"Really. What views?"

"The desire to beat the system, to get past all the bullshit rules."

"So, you're a liberal at heart."

"No, not at all. A lot of people in the Movement think they can beat the system by simply ignoring it. What they don't realize is, they need the system to survive. If they want to eat and live in a decent place with a roof over their head, they have to play the game. They simply don't have the wherewithal to be truly independent. Some of them are sheltered from this reality by their parents' money, but for most of them, that's not going to last forever."

"So you beat the system by working for the CIA."

"Exactly. I beat it the only way it can be beaten, from the inside. As long as I carry out my assignments, the normal rules don't apply to me anymore. The Company doesn't live by rules. We live by results. You would be amazed at what I can get away with, what I do get away with."

"Why is that so important to you?"

"It's just the way I am. I never did like being one of the sheep. In school, I was a jock. I was the star of the high school basketball team and good enough to start for three years for a major college. I got the girls. I mean, we're talking really hot chicks, and I routinely got preferential treatment along the way. It was great. All because I played basketball. Kind of stupid, isn't it?"

"I suppose." Arthur sighed.

"But the problem was, I wasn't good enough to play in the NBA. Most college players aren't, which means the good life comes to a crashing halt. And it certainly did for me. So, I went to law school, graduated, and got a job with a firm. But then, I was just another guy in a suit. I'm not saying it was all bad. It wasn't. I probably could have had a nice little conventional life, going home to the wife and kids every night, playing golf on Saturday. Probably a better life than most ex-jocks have. But it would have been nothing compared to my glory days. No real excitement, no sense of being part of an elite group. So one day, on a lark, I decided to send my résumé into the CIA. And now, three years later, here I am."

"So a sense of patriotism wasn't exactly the driving force in your decision to join the CIA. I mean, it wasn't about Vietnam, or protecting the United States from some supposed Communist threat, or anything like that."

"Nope. But I'm not alone. I think you could take most of the agents in the CIA and exchange them with corresponding agents in the KGB and not miss a beat."

"Everyone is in it for themselves."

"That's right. Everyone. And that includes bureaucrats and political leaders of every stripe."

"And it doesn't bother you that you've chosen to lead a life of deception?"

"Sometimes you have to use deception to get to the truth."

"Why?"

"Because the people of interest, the people with important information, typically lie all the time. And some of them are so self-deluded that they couldn't recognize the truth if they tried. So you position yourself to interact with these people and then piece together the truth yourself."

"So, what about the war? Do you actually support it?"

"No, I wouldn't say that I'm for the war. I believe it's stupid, more than anything else, because we can't win and it's costing us a fortune. It reminds me of the Roman Empire trying to conquer the world and going bankrupt in the process." Jeffrey took a long drink of lemonade. "I believe it makes sense strategically to have a military presence in Vietnam, to keep Russia and China off balance if nothing else. But the fact is, it's not worth the cost. We're simply in over our heads with no end in sight. Unfortunately, the current administration can't seem to admit that, which is just another example of foolish military strategy based on saving face."

"It does seem hard to get past the human element."

"Yes, it does. You know, many people see the CIA as cold and analytical, and I hope we are. I really do. Because it makes a lot more sense to be cool and objective when dealing with important issues like war than it does to be led down the path by petty emotion."

"So if ideology isn't the driving force behind the CIA, what is?"

"Quality of life. Right now, the United States has access to more natural resources and manufactured products than any other country on the planet. But if we're not able to protect our interests on a worldwide scale, other countries will be more than willing to grab those things away from us. That's why our defense system has to be strong. We have to leave other countries with no choice but to respect our lifestyle, which, among other things, allows hippies and idealists of every kind the opportunity to express their views."

"So it's really all about materialism."

"Right. And that's the point that liberals miss. You know, it's hard to be altruistic when you're cold and hungry."

"So why did you want to see me? Why are you telling me all this?"

"Well, some of us were wondering if you might be interested in a career with the Company yourself."

"You're kidding."

"No. You have a solid academic background. And you have guts, or you wouldn't have gotten yourself involved with this crazy bomb plot. And a lot of times, disillusioned idealists make the best operatives."

"What makes you think I'm disillusioned?"

"You're not stupid. You know the things I've been saying are true. You know the Movement is going nowhere. You know the real power structure that controls everything is not going to take notice of long-haired dreamers chanting in the street."

"So why not join the winning team? Is that what you're saying?"

"Exactly. You wouldn't have to worry about who's right or wrong in Vietnam. Most of the leaders involved are corrupt as hell anyway, no matter which side they're on. You would only have to concern yourself with carrying out your assignments, possibly undercover. You could do that if you wanted. And I must say, operating that way gives you a great sense of autonomy, a sense of independence and pure freedom. And the money is very good."

"I already have a job."

"But for how long, given your involvement with Billie Lee? You don't really think you're going to be able to go back to work at the Radiation Lab when this is all over, do you?"

"I hadn't thought that far ahead."

"Well, give it some thought. You know there are those in the FBI who will want to take you out quietly when this is finished. The Company could be your ticket out of that situation. And I might as well let you know—this offer is only possible because of some influential friends that your father had. So this might turn out to be one break you can't pass up."

"I don't have to decide now, do I?"

"No. You'll have some time, but please use that time to give my offer some serious consideration. And while we're meeting here, I'm afraid I have some bad news for you."

"What now? Not anything to do with Donna, is it?"

"No, but your friend Dr. Dorfmann has been killed."

"How can that be? The FBI picked him up this morning. They didn't say anything about him being killed."

"Who gave you that information?" Jeffrey asked.

"An FBI agent, Vic. He was waiting for me this morning in the garage by my car."

"Well, it sounds like Vic was mistaken. The FBI found Dorfmann this morning in his office, dead, shot through the head. They're holding a suspect, a black guy named Melvin Clark. He's out of Detroit, a Black Panther. I don't know all the details, but apparently, Dorfmann was having issues with the Panthers. The story is, they felt he was influencing black dissidents on campus to join SDS instead of the Panthers, sort of stealing them away, and the Panthers didn't like it."

"That sounds like bullshit."

"I only know what I was told. If you're saying the FBI is lying about it, I'm not going to insult your intelligence by saying you must be wrong."

"You know, in the past few years, a number of people that I've known personally have been killed because of the war, either directly or indirectly. People like my dad, my brother, Joshua Taylor, Alan Dorfmann. Doesn't this kind of thing get to you after a while? The CIA is known to be behind assassinations and killings. Doesn't that bother you?"

"It's just the way the world works. In many places, death is a way of life. It only seems abnormal to you because you've been insulated from the darker side of things by the security this country provides."

"But doesn't working undercover make you feel detached from life, in a way? Always living in the shadows, not really a part of what's going on?"

"When I see all the games people play, I don't feel bad about not being a part of it. I feel relieved."

"What kind of games?"

"All the power trips, ego trips, men of very average ability trying desperately to prove how superior they are by putting other people down."

"And you've found a better way."

"Right. I sometimes picture myself working in a jungle teeming with wild and dangerous animals. My job is to help take down the ones that have been identified by the people I report to as a threat. I have the training and skills to provide this service, and I am well compensated for my efforts. Besides which, I can remain independent. I don't have to play the game like everyone else. I just have to provide results."

"Have you ever killed anyone?"

"Yes, and I can tell you it felt good. Squeezing the trigger felt like hitting a twenty-foot jump shot to win the big game."

"Really?"

"Really. Once you've done it, you find it's not as hard as you thought it would be. It can be a real rush, too."

"So if I joined the CIA, I might be expected to kill someone."

"Not necessarily. Most assignments don't require anything like that. I'm just trying to be open with you now. I'm trying to cover all the possibilities to help you decide down the road."

"It's hard to think about something like that right now. There's just too much going on."

"I know. You're under a lot of pressure. We can work through any future plans when this mess you're in now is cleared up. My main objectives today were to let you know that you have future options and to make sure that hearing about Dr. Dorfmann's death doesn't create additional concerns for you. His murder, no matter how it happened, doesn't imply that you're next on some list somewhere. You have friends, including me. Also, I wanted to make it clear to you that Billie Lee poses a very serious threat to this country, one that we simply can't tolerate. It's very important that any ambiguity about Billie Lee be cleared from your mind."

"Yeah, I guess she really played me."

"Yes, she did. And despite what you might think, now that I've gotten to know you, I want to see you and Donna come out of this thing okay. But you are going to have to cooperate with the FBI as much as possible when they try to nail Billie Lee."

"I don't seem to have any choice."

"That's very true, but you may also have to show some initiative yourself."

"Like what?"

"I don't know specifically, but a lot of times these things don't go as smoothly as we would like. You may have to step up and take control at some point, which means you have to have confidence in who you are and what you're trying to accomplish. I know. I've been there."

Chapter Twenty

That afternoon, Arthur decided to leave work an hour early. He was too distracted by his current situation to get anything done, and he felt a pressing need to sit down and talk things over with Donna, a need to let her know that his future, their future, was spinning out of control. Arthur didn't want to share any of the gory details with Donna, especially anything that might be used later to implicate her, but he had to let her know that she would probably be better off going back to her mother's house to have the baby, at least until things cleared up. He briefly wondered if he was going to lose Donna but couldn't bring himself to fully consider that soul-numbing possibility.

Arthur stopped by Dr. Fischer's office and told him he needed to go home early because he wasn't feeling well. Dr. Fischer offered no objections.

At his apartment, the lights were out and Donna was gone. *Probably at the library,* he thought. He turned on the lights and noticed that a sealed envelope was on the coffee table. His name was printed across the envelope in big letters. He opened it and read the typed note inside:

Arthur,

We have Donna, so do exactly what you're told. Meet me at Notre Dame at seven this evening. Wait for me in the student parking lot, the one near the football stadium. Bring the plutonium. And don't be stupid enough to call Vic if you want to see Donna again.

Billie Lee

Just then, the phone rang. Arthur answered it immediately. "Yes," he said anxiously.

"How's it going?" asked the voice on the other end.

"Vic? What can I do for you?" Arthur closed his eyes and tried to regain his composure. "What's up? What is it?"

"Interesting that you should ask. We believe that Billie Lee is in the vicinity and wondered if you had heard from her. We expect her to try making contact with you at any time now. She may even try calling your apartment."

"I haven't heard from her. If she thinks you're onto her, she might be afraid to contact me here, at least over the phone."

"Yes, that could be true, unless she's desperate. You sound a little uptight yourself. Is everything okay?"

"Yes. It's just that I'm a little on edge these days."

"Of course. Well, look, if you hear anything, let me know. You have the number."

"Sure. I will."

Arthur hung up quickly and began to pace. *They have Donna*, he thought. *And Vic knows something.* He had to know something. Why else would he have called? Arthur wondered if he should have confided in Vic, spilled the whole story. *No,* he thought. Vic only cares about nailing Billie Lee. Donna's safety would mean nothing to him. Donna's death would be a small price to pay for getting Billie Lee.

Arthur felt as if he were caught up in an incredibly dangerous game, one over which he had absolutely no control, and it wasn't about politics any more. It was about survival—his own and, more importantly, Donna's. Feeling light-headed as he considered what lay ahead, Arthur thought he was going to pass out and reached for the couch. But after sitting down and letting his head clear, he felt a new sense of determination welling up within him. The issues were rapidly becoming black and white. He had to be sharp. He had to perform.

So what are the options? he thought. He could follow Billie Lee's instructions and hope that she would let him and Donna go, but that didn't make any sense. He couldn't ignore Vic's warning that Billie Lee wouldn't hesitate to kill him to keep things simple. Arthur was forced to conclude that Billie Lee *did* plan to kill both him and Donna as soon as she got the plutonium, which meant that he would have to be prepared to kill her first. There was no way around this logic. But how? . . . His father's Luger.

Arthur dashed into the bedroom, tore open the closet door, and grabbed the holster with the Luger from the top shelf. He then quickly filled the gun's magazine with bullets, jammed the Luger into his pants, and put on a jacket to conceal it. The pressure of the gun against his abdomen felt good. At least he would have a chance. At least he would not be completely at the mercy of Billie Lee. He might hand over the plutonium at first, but then . . . *the plutonium.*

He rushed out to the garage, unlocked the storage cabinet, and jerked the door open. Thankfully, the steel container holding the plutonium disks was still there. He then put the steel container in the back of the van and stashed the ammo belt and holster under the front seat. After a pause, he took a deep breath and began pacing; reviewing his options, plotting out what he was going to do, trying to cover every angle.

At six thirty, Arthur opened the garage door and surveyed the surrounding area. It was dark and cold outside. At first, he saw no one; then a car passed by slowly; then nothing. He slid behind the wheel of the van, and feeling some discomfort from the pressure of the Luger, he took it out of his pants and placed it carefully under the seat, next to the ammo belt and holster. He then backed out of the garage and headed toward the Notre Dame football field, watching in the mirror to see if he was being followed. *Can't afford to have any of Vic's people intruding,* he thought. *Can't let them do something stupid that will get me or Donna killed.*

After a few miles, Arthur turned sharply, without warning, into a residential neighborhood and made four right-hand turns in rapid succession, going only one or two blocks in each direction before turning again. Now sitting at a stop sign, he looked across the street, to both sides, and behind him. There were no cars. He appeared to be completely alone. Apparently, he *wasn't* being followed, he thought. Maybe Vic really didn't know about Billie Lee's message. Maybe his only concern really was Billie Lee herself.

He still had almost twenty minutes. He pulled onto Highway 31, and after a few miles, made another sudden turn, this time into Nicola's. He drove to the parking area in the back and stopped near a large dumpster. After killing the engine, he got out of the van and removed the steel container from the back. He looked around quickly, saw no one, then set the container in the dumpster and covered it with garbage. He looked around again, saw no one again, then got back into the van and sped away.

Taking big risks now, he thought. *Big risks.* But so what? What choice did he have?

A short time later, Arthur sat waiting in the mostly vacant student parking lot near the football stadium. He glanced at his watch. Four minutes early. He blew warm air into his hands. He felt nervous and alone and didn't even know what kind of vehicle he was supposed to be looking for. The only solace he *could* find came from reaching down and feeling the Luger under his seat.

As Arthur continued to wait, another van, a blue Dodge, turned into the parking lot and approached him slowly. With his eyes riveted on the creeping vehicle, Arthur clenched the steering wheel with both hands, expecting at any time to hear bullets crashing through the windshield, ripping through his chest, tearing through the seat behind him. He started to reach for the Luger but decided to wait. He had to remain calm, had to put himself at risk for Donna's sake.

As the blue van edged forward, Arthur couldn't see anyone in it, not even the driver. It then stopped about twenty feet away. The driver's door opened and Billie Lee got out, wearing a bulky jacket, her blonde hair flowing behind her. Arthur rolled down his window. Billie Lee walked over and stopped next to Arthur's door.

"So where is it?" she asked lightly, sounding much as she had on previous occasions.

"Where's Donna?" Arthur asked.

"In the back." Billie Lee gestured at the blue van. "Now, let's have it. *Please*." A menacing inflection had crept into her voice.

"I need to see Donna first."

"Get out of the van," Billie Lee ordered. She reached into her jacket, pulled out a forty-five revolver, and pointed at Arthur's head. "Now."

Arthur eased his door open, stepped out, and turned to face her. "I didn't bring the plutonium with me," he said. "I have to see Donna first."

"You're playing games. I don't have time for that. Lean up against the side of the van and spread your legs."

"Why?"

"Do what you're told!"

She patted Arthur down briskly but found nothing. "I didn't think you would be armed, but I had to make sure. Now, open up this van."

Arthur stepped to the back of the van, unlocked and opened the rear door, then waved his hand to emphasize that the pluto-nium was not there.

"Where is it?" she demanded, pressing her lips together tightly. "I'm not going to stand here all night."

"I have to see Donna first. And just so you know where I'm coming from, if anything happens to her, I don't care what hap-pens to me. If anything happens to her, I won't have anything to lose."

"Okay, okay." Billie Lee's voice was soft again. "I can un-derstand that. You can look, but she stays where she is until I get the disks."

Billie Lee and Arthur walked to the back of the blue van. She swung open one of the rear doors to reveal Donna bound and gagged on the floor. As Donna raised her head and made eye contact with Arthur, Billie Lee slammed the door shut. But Arthur had managed to see enough— enough to know that Donna was alive, enough to know that she appeared to be okay.

"Now, where is it?" demanded Billie Lee. Her revolver was again pointed at Arthur's head.

"I'll take you to it."

"Fine. Get into the van."

"No. We drive separately. I don't plan on sticking around once you have the plutonium."

"Have it your way. Just remember, I've got the gun *and* Donna. This would be the wrong time to try to be a hero."

"Right."

Ten minutes later, Arthur came to a stop in the parking lot behind Nicola's and rolled down his window. Billie Lee pulled up behind him and jumped out of her van. "Why have you stopped here?" she asked pointedly.

"Because the plutonium is nearby. But I'm not going to tell you exactly where it is until you release Donna." Arthur slowly raised his left hand. In it, he held the Luger, cocked and now pointed at Billie Lee's head. "Take your gun out slowly and drop it on the ground. And I mean slowly. Any sudden movement and I squeeze off a round. No problem."

Somewhat to Arthur's surprise, Billie Lee complied, holding the handle of her revolver gingerly in her fingertips and letting it drop to the pavement.

"Okay, good. Now, let's get Donna."

Arthur opened his door and got out carefully, keeping the Luger fixed steadily on Billie Lee's head.

"I'm taking out my keys," Billie Lee said, slowly putting her hand into her pants pocket and fishing out a ring with several keys on it.

Together, Arthur and Billie Lee proceeded to the back of the blue van. Billie Lee unlocked the door and stepped away. "Don't go anywhere," Arthur ordered as he yanked the door open and jumped in, anxious to get to Donna, to hold her, to make sure she was all right.

But as he landed, a voice behind him growled, "Hold it right there." Arthur turned his head slowly and saw a swarthy middle-aged man holding a revolver on him. "Drop the gun! I'm not playing around with you."

Arthur dropped the Luger.

"Now tell me where the plutonium is, or you and your girl-friend there are going to be found dead in this parking lot before you know what hit you."

"I'll have to show you," Arthur replied, turning back to the open door. "It's over there." Arthur stepped down from the van and past Billie Lee, who smiled at him and waved the revolver that she had retrieved at him. As Arthur set off in the direction of the dumpster, the middle-aged man followed closely behind him. Arthur could hear the man breathing and imagined he felt his hot breath on the back of his neck.

Just then, two pinging shots rang out in quick succession. Billie Lee spun around and dropped heavily. The middle-aged man also fell to the ground, obviously hit as well. Without think-ing any further, Arthur, dove to the pavement himself and re-mained motionless as he listened to the sound of approaching footsteps.

"Get up," demanded a familiar voice. "We have to get out of here."

Arthur scrambled to his feet. "Vic! What happened?"

Instead of answering, Vic hurried over to the open blue van, and with surprising agility, climbed in and cut Donna free. As she crawled out, two other figures flung the bodies of Billie Lee and the middle-aged man into the back without saying anything and slammed the door shut.

"No time to talk now," Vic snapped. "Both of you, come with me." Vic led Donna and Arthur to a parked car, a nonde-script Ford with black sidewalls. "Get in," he ordered.

Arthur took the front seat while Donna climbed into the back. "Where are we going?" asked Arthur.

"Chicago. Now be quiet for a while. I have to make sure we're not being followed."

Twenty minutes later, as they cruised smoothly down the toll road, Vic broke the silence. "You're damned lucky to be alive. I don't think you know just how damned lucky you are."

"What do you mean?" Arthur asked.

"I mean, the odds against you being here right now were overwhelming, overwhelming."

"You think Billie Lee and that other guy were going to kill us?"

"Of course. As soon as you showed them where the plutonium was."

"The plutonium! We forgot to get that."

"The plutonium was picked up well before you returned to Nicola's. Please, try to remember who you're dealing with."

"How did you know I dropped it off there? I didn't think I was being followed."

"But you were, electronically. We put a tracking device on your van last week."

"I guess I should be grateful. You saved my life."

"I wouldn't go that far. Your real debt of gratitude is to someone else."

"Because I cooperated and helped you get Billie Lee?"

"Not exactly. In the first place, we wanted Billie Lee alive. *You* would normally have been the expendable one. And in the second place, you didn't exactly cooperate."

"But our agreement was—"

"Look, when some pipsqueak jackass decides to play God with nuclear weapons and take on the U.S. government, he usually ends up with a bullet in his head, whether he cooperates or not. And let me assure you, there were a number of people on this case who wanted to see exactly that happen to you. But we were overruled."

"By whom?"

"I don't know exactly. An old friend of your father's, someone up the chain of command. Somebody with enough pull to keep you from being taken out or doing time. So when I say you're damned lucky, I mean you're *damned* lucky."

"What's going to happen now?"

"We're going to fix your record, exaggerate how much you helped us, then relocate you to Baltimore."

"Why Baltimore?"

"Well, for one thing, you can't work at the Radiation Lab any more. That point was nonnegotiable."

"What about Donna?" Arthur turned to look at Donna in the back seat.

"We're assuming she wants to go with you, but it's her call."

Arthur looked back at Donna again. She nodded her head.

"This is all happening so . . . fast."

"The details are being taken care of as we speak. Once we reach O'Hare, you'll catch a plane to Baltimore. An agent will meet you there and take you to your new home. You'll begin your new job at Johns Hopkins next week, by the way, at the research facility. But please keep in mind, you're going to be watched for the rest of your life. And going anywhere near a particle accelerator will definitely not be an option. And if you try to escape from your new life for even a minute, it will be the last thing you do."

"What should we tell our families?"

"This whole thing can be described as a simple job change that you made in order to live closer to your families. Apparently, that was a factor in someone's thinking when deciding where to relocate you. So you should probably stick with that story."

Following about ten miles of silence, Arthur said, "Can I ask you a question?"

"Why not? I'd hate to think I left any bases uncovered."

"What are your thoughts about the war? Do you think we were so wrong to want to help end it?"

"Just naïve," Vic replied without emotion. "Extremely naïve."

After several more minutes of silence, Vic said, "Now let me ask *you* a question. Suppose you were married, to someone other than Donna, say, and you found out that your wife had cheated on you. What would you do?"

"Walk out. Get a divorce," Arthur replied, glancing back at Donna to see her reaction. She had none.

"That's a young man's answer. That's what most young men would do. But an older man might consider the marriage he had and decide whether it was worth trying to save."

Arthur shrugged.

"Just for the sake of argument, let's say you were busy on the job much of the time. And let's say your wife got lonely and had an affair. Of course, that's terrible. And she has to shoulder most of the blame. But if you think about it, we're all flawed, we're all human. An older man would take that into consideration before ending the marriage.

"It's like that with the war. Of course, the politicians running this country have made a serious mistake. Of course, there's been a lot of unnecessary pain and suffering as a result. And some young people have reacted by insisting they want to dissociate themselves from this country completely. But long term, is that a solution. Long term, is a relationship with this country worth trying to save, despite a political blunder like Vietnam? You were ready to walk out the door. Then again, you're a young man."

At the airport, Vic dropped Arthur and Donna off at their terminal. "Here are your tickets," he said as Arthur started to climb out. "And here's something else." He reached under his seat for the Luger and handed it to Arthur. "It was your father's. You should have it."

"Thanks. Connections with the past can be important."